Tin Crickets

JOSEPH WISE

ISBN: 9781973372677

Dreadful Press

For Braxton, Amélie, and Aurora.

CHAPTERS

ONE

Another tram rattles away from the platform shaking dust from the metal rafters. Big swaths of it yawn under the lamps. It doesn't matter how many trams come through here, there's always plenty of dust to be knocked loose when they do.

I'm sitting on a bench a dozen yards from the screen check booth, and I'm shaking too. My pal Gibbsy isn't here yet. I keep turning to look for him under the archways hoping to Christ he'll show. All I can do is wait for him and watch and straighten my glasses.

Even at this hour, steady swarms of dingy folks scuttle through Dutcher Station, but it won't be long before this place is empty. Most of the ragged peddlers are gone already, but somewhere near the rails, a man is shouting, trying to sell matchbooks. "Light a pipe, light a stove, light a candle for the dead." His voice sounds like burnt paper. No one is listening to him, and I can't tell one person from the next. Only a few seem to have faces at all. A boy a couple of years younger than me trying to drop a yo-yo. A guy with burn scars. A woman dragging a little kid by the hand as he slides on his knees bawling, having some kind of fit. Part of me wants to grab the lady by the hand and drag her around, so she knows how it feels. I'm like a coil spring.

I'm trying to look less anxious than I feel. Sitting here alone reminds me of being in grade school and making my own way home every day. Once or twice I'd miss my train. Just this little kid scared to pieces about what to do next. Even then, I knew better than to ask the Blackbands for help. They're not here to help. Not back then and definitely not now.

These lower H Bands watch the station from their booth. Eyes swinging, looking for some excuse to start a fuss. A couple of them have been watching me. I've been here twenty minutes, and they don't like folks to linger. They're always like that, the Bands. Sunken red eyes and plenty of scruff, teetering here at the end of their shifts, thinking they might get a chance to use their batons on a delinquent like me. Charming bastards.

It isn't past curfew yet, so they won't do anything right now, but hell, if they knew I was fixing to shoot a Reel tonight, it wouldn't matter. They'd put a few dents in my jaw, right here with everybody watching, and then they'd take me someplace to draw some real blood. I can't leave, though. Not until Gibbsy gets here with the gear.

He isn't the kind of guy to be late. He doesn't have the sand to go through with a shoot tonight. After what those pricks did to him at school today, I can understand. But I keep thinking of that numb glimmer he had in his eyes when he came back to class. Like he was worse than dead. When I saw that, I knew we'd have to come out tonight and ring the havoc bell good and loud. For his sake. Gibbsy needs this a hell of a lot more than I do. I don't think I could stand seeing that look on his face again. Not Gibbsy.

The C tram clamps-to but only a few people hit the turnstiles. One of the Bands is staring at me again. Two fingers on the mace can at his belt. He's not moving, but he's thinking about it.

I look away like I'm not worried. This place is getting quiet. The matchbook man is still shouting, but there's nobody left to shout at. I figure I should move to a different bench, so I get up, and I wander. The man's voice doesn't get any quieter the further away from the rails I get. Echoing against the old brick that was made forever ago in the sunlight with straw and mud and sweat, turned to murk and mold now, waiting to crumble.

I'm about to sit again when I see a pale orb bob into the station from under the archways. It feels like I've been holding my breath this whole time and I'm just now letting the air out. He's here. Gibbsy is.

I dodge toward him through the pillars. More people are gathered at the exits than at the platform but Gibbsy's easy to track with that bleached white hair drooping forward to his chin, dyed that color weeks ago because that's how I used to wear my hair. It'll be two weeks or less before he shaves it all off like mine is now, but for now, I don't have to search all over the place looking for him.

He hasn't seen me yet. He tilts and slumps, and I

wonder if he's feeling any better. He looks like a lost little kid trying not to look at all the strangers, so I sneak up behind him and lean close to his ear. "Well, of all things. It's Charlie Gibbs!"

He doesn't even flinch. "Hey, Tommy. Sorry..."

"Yeah, I was worried. About you. You alright?" I lean against a pillar. "You ready?"

The backpack is tucked under his arm, as if he could hide the damn thing. He's hiding his face, too, behind all that hair. I don't blame him. We don't need anyone stopping to ask about the way he looks.

"I'm kinda sick still," he says. I'm not surprised. He probably wants to go home, but I need him to come with me.

"Just let's walk a ways. Come on." He nods.

We start to leave through the back of the station, but I tap Gibbsy on the shoulder. I feel much better now, but there's something I've got to do. "Those bastards over there been tilting at me all night."

I walk back past the bench and lift my palms at the Blackbands. "What? What? Fifteen to curfew, right? You fellas wanna play cards while we wait? Bocce?"

It's a stupid thing to say, and they don't react much. Maybe because they can't hear me too well or maybe because they don't care. They know what time it is. They just shift their blunt jaws and cough into their fists and hover at the mace cans.

Gibbsy comes and tugs at my shirt trying to get me to be quiet. He hates when I do this, and he's right—we should just leave, quiet as can be. It's way too risky being here with the camera and the gear in his backpack and his face swollen like it is.

I don't dare ask why he was so late.

*

The first Riot Reel I ever took Gibbsy to see was the McCorhan beating. The man they lit on fire. I'd been trying to talk Gibbsy into seeing it for a week before he agreed to go. We skipped school that day, which was a lot harder to do back when we were just sophomores, but we did it anyway.

Us and six or seven others stood against the walls of that rust-laced old breaker vault up on HW, staring at Alvey's slapdash canvas screen. Nobody in the room made a sound, not even when the Reel ended. The last of the film skittered around the spool, flicking against the projector as the screen turned manic white.

Alvey turned off the projector, and we waited in total silence. Everybody thought about what they'd seen, about the burning vagrant. Somewhere a few decks above us, the air movers thrummed, and that was the only sound in the room.

That footage had been shot five days earlier and developed in a rush, but not as many people saw it as should have. Those days, it was tough to find anybody with the guts to watch a Riot Reel. Most folks were too scared of being pinched by the Blackband patrols, not being where they were supposed to be. Others just didn't want to see the City's grit. As if you could miss it.

Standing behind me, Gibbsy had gone pale. I remember his hand covering his mouth.

"You gonna lose it?"

He said, "I'll be okay." It was about the tenth time he'd said it that day. "I'll be okay."

Gibbsy knew as well as anybody how hard the City could be on derelicts. You ask me, it's a sure sign things aren't running the way they should be. Only a few million of us left, and they still don't care if some starve. But still, it was a shock to see.

We went back to school after that. We took the back ways, through the deadhalls and the empty screencheck stations so we wouldn't run into any patrols skulking around.

We returned to Chalcenor High just as everybody was shuffling toward the auditorium for the City Bulletin. We'd gone from one projector to another, this one playing the City's bland footage for a crowd of hundreds on a smoother screen. Kennedy's tinfoil voice droned over the speakers. Friends-and-citizens this. Cooperate-and-thrive that. How lucky we are to have such a fine refuge down here. A refuge from the poisoned air. But I could tell Gibbsy wasn't thinking about Kennedy. He was thinking about the man in that rim hall.

After school, I asked what he thought about it, since he hadn't said much. He said he wasn't too surprised to know something like that had happened, but seeing it made his stomach sick.

I told him that's what the Riot Reels are for, showing you what you already know so you can stop lying to yourself about it. "Those guys who shoot the Reels would get skinned alive if the City caught them with the film, but they do it anyway because the City's got us lying to ourselves about everything, every day."

But something else was bothering him, so I asked him what it was, and he said, "How are you supposed to know it really happened, though? Things like that could be faked." It was a fair question, one that gets asked a lot when people first see the Reels, and I figured *he'd* be asking it eventually too.

So I said, "Gibbsy, I was the guy holding the camera."

He didn't have anything to say to that. He just grew pale again.

But that was a couple of years ago. These days Gibbsy wouldn't blink if he saw a man burned alive. Even if he saw it in person.

That's part of the problem. I'm just hoping we won't find that kind of trouble tonight.

*

The halls in H grow narrower and uglier the further we get from Mackey Center and Dutcher Station. We leave through a ten-foot tiled archway, into a stairwell with ringing metal steps, and spill into a six by eight rectangular hall lined with casings painted the same color as the concrete. A few more levels down and we can't even walk side by side anymore. It's like the City wants to keep you from wandering. Like they don't want you to step out from under their eyes.

By the time we leave H, Gibbsy's hives are all but gone but his left eye is still swollen, and that bruise of his is holding its ground like a champ. Looking at him reminds me to be angry, but it's a mixed bag as to why I'm doing this. Or maybe it's not. Maybe it's just something that needs to be done whether or not he had a bad day. Here under the ice, most of us have to eat fish because it's cheap and simple. But a guy like Gibbsy who's allergic to it can't survive cheap, and it isn't his fault. The City should take care of him—should take care of all of us because we're all we have left. A few million of us trapped down here. They shouldn't be lax with the regulations like they always are, the assholes.

There should be *riots* in the halls of Fallback. Every day. The City lies to us and poisons us. Kennedy is always saying we're standing our ground. "The human race has a foothold here in the Antarctic ice." But if you ask me, we shouldn't be standing our ground, we should be moving forward, and if we're not doing that, we're dying.

There should be goddamn riots. I guess I should be going after the Truancy officers too, but everybody hates those pricks already and the fact is, nobody talks about the Industrials. Nobody knows what goes on down there unless they work for the City and those bastards don't dare say word one about it. I'll take whatever chance I can get to slide under those City doors and crank some footage. Somebody has to do it.

*

"Where are we, Gibbs?"

With all of these buzzing lights and tile and steam pipes, we could be anywhere in the Kennel. It's easy to get turned around.

"'Bout 5:15, 127 double-k," says Gibbsy.

"Makes sense."

Poplar's place isn't far, but with the detours, we've had to take it's a tedious walk. We could have been here half an hour ago if we'd been able to get onto one of the K trams. That's what notches me. As many tram lines as there are in this place, you'd think a guy would never have to walk more than a couple hundred yards to get from one place to another. Used to be you could hop on or off the trains without being hassled as long as you were in-sector. But in the last couple of years, you can't even hit the platform without going through screencheck. How very convenient. Top drawer, fellas.

And there's Kennedy always trying to tell us "friends and citizens" that we should be grateful for structure. For *safety*. Safety means you can't go anywhere on the trams and you can't talk to anybody in the phone booths without the Bands listening, and you can't even just take a walk through the hall without someone asking where you're really supposed to be.

It always makes me wonder which is worse, on the surface or down here. Hell, if only I could breathe underwater.

*

The floor panels here are just loose grating, shifting underfoot, with low yellow maintenance lights back behind the pipes. The grates were painted black at some point, but the paint has been worn away here and there in odd chrome streaks. Everything echoes.

We're moving fast to make up lost time. Gibbsy is in a better mood now. He's doing okay.

I tell him about me skipping pneumatics class today and sneaking down to Ventley High to talk to Poplar. "Got stopped by a teacher but I talked my way out of trouble. Hella close."

"You talk yourself out of a lot of things," says Gibbsy.

He's seen me do it a few times. People are people, which is why I wasn't worried back at Dutcher Station, either. Gibbsy always gives me hell when I do things like that. He thinks I'm showboating, but I'm really not afraid to chat-up the Blackbands during street hours. They're just the same as us, in the same bottled-hell as everybody. They *are* pricks, but it doesn't matter. They need to know they're ridiculous just like anybody, and sometimes they cut you some slack for being honest.

I won't be talking to any more Blackbands tonight, and Gibbsy knows that. Never after curfew and never when we've got the gear with us. Kids like us, pulling a shoot like this, there'd be no leeway for it. We'd be put away, locked in Mocap way up on E, never to be heard from again.

"So, what did Poplar say?" asks Gibbsy. "Is she coming with us?"

"To be decided. She put up a godawful fight about it so yeah, I still have some convincing to do. If she doesn't, it's pretty bad news, though."

Gibbsy reminds me about the last time Poplar came with us—how she couldn't stop talking about how silly we sounded and how pointless it all was—but she was laughing the whole time, so I don't think she meant it like that.

"She just loathes me sometimes," I tell him. "That's

all. But Pop's one of the good ones, Gibbsy, even if she does love this City the way it is. Got a good mind, you know? But good god…she hasn't even been painting these days anymore. That bothers me. She's been traipsing around with those guys, Alma Davis and them. Dale Pike. You know Dale."

"Yeah."

"Fascist bastard just *loves* Kennedy. Poplar starts talking like him, and we lose her, you know? She should be traipsing with us, not him. Them. Hell's sakes Gibbsy, all I have to say is it bothers me she's stopped painting."

"Maybe you should bring flowers." Gibbsy can be a smartass sometimes. Not always but sometimes.

"Even if this *was* a date, she wouldn't want flowers, Gibbs. I just don't want her to think we're using her for her keys because that's not what it is. Reggie's pals could take care of us as far as keys go, but I'm already paying them too much for what they're giving us."

As soon as I say that, Gibbsy goes quiet. I hadn't said anything about Reggie coming along until now. Maybe that makes me an asshole, I don't know.

I don't feel much like making Gibbsy feel better about it, so I just follow him through the next bunch of zigzags, past a few backdoors to engineer shops and glass blowers. We shutter ourselves into a rattling old freight elevator and sink down to KP where the lights flicker even more than they do in the upper Ks.

Christ. Another night of this. But this is what we do instead of homework.

*

Off the elevator, we hear footsteps, and Gibbsy panics. It's nothing you would notice unless you knew him. He brushes his hair back and holds his shoulders up.

"What time is it?" he says, but then he looks at his own watch and sees that it's after eight-thirty already. We should be finding a place to hide.

We look old enough, the Blackbands might not think we're lopes at all, but I doubt it. They would ask for ID no matter what. Even if we had fake IDs, they'd ask for our shift schedules and wonder why we're in this corridor as opposed to that corridor. It wouldn't take them long to find the camera and figure out we're shooting Riot Reels, so it's much better if we just stay out of sight.

We press into an alcove and whoever's walking past keeps walking. We wait. We wait until we can't hear the footsteps anymore. Then it's onward ho, and I start to recognize where I am.

"You can have these." Gibbsy holds out a thin pair of tattered gloves. "Found 'em."

"Hot dog, my man." They fit pretty well too.

Me and Gibbsy, we have this joke. Down in the lower K's you don't put your hand on the stair rails. You can't trust the walls. They never bother to buff the metal, is what it seems like, and if you run your hand along the surface of anything, pretty soon you'll get a burr. Down here you don't even trust the walls; you don't even trust the stairs. Not without gloves.

"Reggie's pals," says Gibbsy. "They're Barkers?"

"Yeah."

"Think they'll do anything? Like those guys we ran into…"

"Naw, Reggie knows 'em. I don't know how well he knows 'em, but it has to count for something."

I tell him not to worry, which is a patchy thing to do because I'm a bit worried myself and there's no getting rid of it.

"Tommy, I wouldn't be mad if we just went home. I'm not saying I want to go home, just if *we* didn't do the shoot tonight, it's okay. I'm not mad about the hives or what those guys did."

"You're a good boy, Gibbsy. But that's not the point."

*

Poplar lives in K just like Gibbsy. Godforsaken Kennel. I don't know how many times I've tried to get her into Chalcenor. She's as smart as Gibbsy. She could take the PIPs like he did and get a scholarship too, but she just won't even try. She'd rather spend her life in the Kennel and never get a fresh breath.

She answers the door wearing something she's embarrassed to be seen in, so she goes to change. "I told you I'm staying home," she shouts from the hall.

"I'm a bad listener."

Me and Gibbsy eyeball the empty shelves in her living room. He follows me all around the room. I love the guy, but that's one of the things about him that makes me laugh—how he can't just stand still or pace around by himself. He always has to step exactly where I step.

A tube by the door shows today's Bulletin with the sound off. One of the City scientists, talking about the wreck of the Dulcet 11 again. Pop just doesn't care. She was probably sitting here staring at that without the sound all night, making up her own version of the report in a funny voice, perfectly enter*tained* by it for hours on end. You'd think she'd be upset about the Dulcet 11 sinking. About all those people dead. But even after what happened to her mom she still jacks around with things like that. She's the most interesting person I know.

I turn the sound up when Kennedy cuts in, just long

enough to hear him say, "…every life is precious, every soul is vital…," before I shut the tube off altogether. I really don't want to hear it. As many Drowners as they've lost, you'd think they'd stop drafting folks onto those goddamn death subs until they found a safer way to fetch salvage. Every soul is expendable.

I shout to Poplar, "It's not the prom," and then I prance back there to make sure she heard me.

"It's not the ever-loving prom, Pop."

"Tommy it's never *going* to be the ever-loving prom."

She has already changed into a good enough set of street clothes. Shorts and a sweater, nothing fancy. Her room has one shelf, and it's the most tilted shelf I've ever seen. A few books cling to whatever friction they can find on the sloping wood. These are the good books that the City doesn't let you keep if they find them.

"Seven by seven," she says. "I'm staying here where it's quiet. You can take the keys." But I sit on her bed and stare at her until she feels compelled to add, "Why should I tag along, Tommy?"

"People don't even notice the taste of salt in the water," I tell her. "We gotta ring the havoc bell whenever we can."

"You're trying to make me feel guilty," she says. I avoid giving her any kind of reaction. "But I know how it will go," she says. "You'll be excited all night about filming whatever you're going to film, and when you get there, you'll find out you were totally wrong, and nobody was trying to be evil, after all. It was just a mistake. Havoc bell. Some guy wasn't paying attention, and that's all it was. Then you'll spend the *rest* of the night mad at everyone because you don't like being wrong."

"That's not the point," I tell her. "Far from it."

"What *is* the point?"

"The point is the City keeps letting it slip, Pop. Letting it happen and letting it happen and they never try to do anything about it because why should they?"

That's when she starts to laugh at me. She always does that. Just when I'm as mad as hell, that's when she loses it.

"There's nothing funny about it," I try to remind

her, but it only makes her giggle. "You wanna keep living in a place like this, Pop? Show your papers everywhere you go? Where's the City's papers, twinkle toes? We have to show them who we are and where we're supposed to be all the time, but the goddamn City won't let us know a goddamn thing about who it is or where it's supposed to be. I didn't even tell you what happened to Gibbsy at lunch after he got the hives. He's not okay, Pop. He's not doing so good at all, if you wanna know the truth."

Pop pulls a straight face, first I've seen from her all day, and she says, "What happened?"

So I tell her. "He tried to leave the cafeteria. I'm sitting there with him talking to him. One minute he's eating a bowl of oats, then he starts to choke and turn red, and the hives start bubbling up on his face. He looks at me, thinks about what's happening, and then he gets up and tries to leave. Tries to go to the nurse for a shot. He gets through the cafeteria doors, and a couple of Truancy bastards knock him to the ground. They think he's trying to ditch. One hits him in the face with a strap, so that's why the bruises. The other guy maces him. His whole face goes red. He couldn't keep his eyes open.

Everybody in the cafeteria is just sitting there, and we can hear him screaming. I knew better than to go out there."

Poplar looks at me, and I don't know what kind of look it is. She doesn't say anything.

"The worst part was later. The nurse took care of him, sure, but his face was all red and puffy when he came to physics. And there was this look in his eyes. I asked him how he was, and he just stared at me like a doll. Like his eyes were just sewn there, into his face. Like glass beads. Pop, I'm not kidding. If we don't show him he's still got some say in his life, he'll slip away. He'll turn to steam. We've got to do this tonight."

She's not laughing anymore, but she's not surprised, either. Nothing surprises her, and she's always polite. "Alright I'll go," she says. "But only for the entertainment. You sure can kick up a fuss."

"It's a serious thing," I tell her. "A goddamn *dangerous* one."

"It's another late night is what it is. Grab me some shoes, Tommy. But the second it stops being fun is the second I come back home and go to bed, okay fella? I love Gibbsy, but the world is the way the world is, and your havoc bell won't stop that."

I wave at her and give a bow before rummaging through her closet. "Blue? Black?"

"I don't care. Blue."

The blue sneakers are smudged with grease. "Dirty as hell…"

"Perfect, toss 'em over," she says.

I tell her "Nice gams, kid," and she winks at me.

"It's not the prom, Tommy."

*

Poplar's dad works the steam pipes in the Kennel and when he's not doing that he distills on the sly. He's gone a lot, and her mom was lost on a Drowner, the Thalius 17, which is a sad enough story. Honestly, though, none of us has a happy story to tell, so I don't get into it much. The point is her dad has keys to places we need to be and tonight no one's home to notice his spare set is missing.

"I don't think these'll get us where we're going." She kneels to the lockbox and starts wheeling the combination.

I tell her, "I know." But they'll get us far enough, and after that, we're riding on trust.

"CURFEW," Reel 3 of 5, 16mm, 24fps

The first frames of the Riot Reel are damaged. We see warped images. Shapes. A wide shot of McCorhan Market from the back of the square. The crowd sounds like static. A minute passes, the clock strikes eight and a few hundred dangling lights dim all at once, nothing but glimmers against the black ceiling like stars used to look in the real night sky. Shop windows and neon signs shine in the dark, and the tin crickets began to chirp from the ductwork.

The crowd thins. Two men come into the square wearing hazard suits. We know they are Blackbands because of the batons on their belts. They have kerosene and all of the good citizens back away to let them pass.

The Blackbands check the market looking through shop windows, looking behind the kiosks and carts, everything lit different colors by the neons. The Bands are too far from the camera to notice that they are being filmed. The cameraman stays back, hidden and always close to cover.

The Bands ask citizens to leave, the few folks who

hadn't gone already. When the square is clear, they slip into a rim hall with their kerosene tanks. The camera follows after them.

They move from one trash cage to the next burning the day's garbage like the City joes sometimes do when there's a rat problem, spraying lit kerosene through the bars and letting the overheads suck the smoke away while they do it. The flames sound like static.

Cage to cage, they burn everything and never noticed the camera.

A quarter of the way through the rim hall they are startled by a vagrant looking for scraps in the garbage. The old man only has one eye and a bad leg. His beard is matted with some old sort of grime, and his face is smudged.

He holds up his hands and argues with the Blackbands. They are stepping closer to him with every wave of his sooty hand. He tries to edge past and run but one of the Bands trips him, and he falls to the floor. They beat him with their batons until he stops moving altogether.

The Blackbands in their hazard suits chat over the old

man for a while. Then they spray him with kerosene and burn him. His body is lost in the flames. The camera lens blears from the extra light, and the reel ends there.

TWO

We're supposed to meet Reggie Stamp in the Antrum Markets where there are plenty of people out at this hour and not enough Blackbands to care if any of them are underage.

The three of us dissolve into the cackling masses, Poplar humming to herself the whole while. Everybody's here because there's nothing else to do in the Kennel. They're buying this and that, coming off of shifts, browsing from one place to the next. Their clothes are just as ragged as the ceiling beams, and their faces are just as crooked and sooty as the awnings. Their eyes are just as blank as the shop windows all around, completely oblivious to the twitching neon signs that hang over every little stall, every cluster, and every balcony, buzzing and buzzing in our deaf ears.

The funny thing is, the things you buy here, you can buy the same stuff from the City warehouses on ration coupons. I think people just like dealing with other people and they don't know that it's all a lie. Every market in this place trades up through the ration chain anyway, so it doesn't matter where you get flour. This shop, that shop, the City warehouses. Doesn't matter. It's all the same flour or rice, and it all costs exactly the same amount of money, and it's all sub-par, half-dust, and probably toxic.

We go completely unnoticed. You can *always* find a few schoolers in Antrum after curfew, and the Blackbands stopped trying to do anything about it a long time ago because it's easier to catch them going to and from and less trouble to just let them shop.

We're not a quarter of the way into the place, and already Poplar is drifting toward a dark corner where a couple of grubby scarecrows are setting up a puppet theater. As much as she likes the shows, we can't be stopping for the marionettes right now, and I twirl her by the shoulder and tell her to keep moving.

In the middle of the square, I trip over a crippled man. He's sitting on the ground playing a ukulele for spare change. It only has two strings, and they're both loose. The neck is painted blue with swirling flecks of light like the real sky might look if you were half dreaming, and along the side of it he has scratched "Zanzibar was a lie."

I tell him, "Sorry," and he nods.

Most of his face is wrapped in old bandages. They're falling apart, and I can see some of his scars. His ear is almost gone. It's not too hard to guess this poor old bastard has seen the inside of a burnbox at some point or other. Those metal floors, those metal walls, never knowing when the heat will come or how hot it'll be when it does. Looking at him I have to wonder what's worse. This or to be lit afire with a flame gun.

What he must have done to deserve it, I don't know. But I'd bet he never hurt anybody in his whole life. I'd bet all he did was steal a loaf of bread or try to ride the trams without a token.

Anyway, that's a Reel for another day. It's time to move on. The tin crickets are chirping from the rafters, and the good children of Fallback will soon be drifting off to sleep. But not us. We still have a lot to do tonight.

*

"There he is," says Gibbsy.

Reggie is in a line buying dim sum, and I can't blame him. The market hotcarts are better than any top-drawer diner in Fallback, if you ask me, and I figured Reggie'd be there because he can never get enough of the stuff. He's leaning against the cart wearing a slashed yellow track-team shirt that he stole a few months back, and his hair is up in a short mohawk.

I point at him and jab Poplar in the ribs. "To think he used to wear coveralls."

I've known Reggie since we were kids. His parents make as much scratch as mine do, and we grew up on the same block. We've always been friends, even when he fell in with the Kyle Finnagan bunch over in B-South.

Things have changed these last couple of years, and not just his sense of style. I guess he's got more to prove, the older he gets. We still listen to the same kill-your-mama Stick Jazz, but he's usually at Guffsters or Loungedeath. Me, I keep to the younger crowds at Lillian M's. But one thing that hasn't changed is Reggie doesn't miss a chance to come with me on shoots.

He's balancing his bowl of rice balls now, paying in coins with his free hand, and he notices me waving as he counts-out.

The two guys on either side of him are his Barker pals. One of them looks normal enough, the shorter one. This guy's in a full-on suit with a vest and everything, but at least he's wearing the sleeves rolled up, so he doesn't really look out of place here.

The other guy would look out of place no matter where he was. He's even taller than me, and it doesn't help that he's wearing a red banded top-hat. A red Barkers' rag in his back pocket. And to tip it over, he's wearing war paint: two red stripes under his left eye. I've never seen anything quite so stylish or classy.

Reggie introduces us to, "Sticks and Rake," which I'm half-past sure aren't really their names.

Rake, the little guy, he goes to shake our hands practically pulling Gibbsy off of his feet with the first drop. And Sticks, over there, he gets this big smile, and I can see the dark stains around his gums from chalk opium. Jesus. The last thing I want to worry about is a hazed-out Barker coming down from a buzz, so we'd best settle our business and part ways sooner than later.

I tell Reggie to get his food and sauce-up so we can leave, and I grab Poplar by the wrist so she won't wander back to the puppet show.

Sticks and Rake don't say much. They follow us out of the market, and already I'm thinking of ways to ditch them once we get what we need. I adore the Barkers as much as I adore this fabulous city of ours, but they come in handy sometimes, I have to admit. They're always trying to sell us things like information, key molds, whatever. They practically *beg* us, every time I see a goddamn Barker. I cherish those moments.

*

Gibbsy would never say anything about it but if he had his way none of us would ever say word one to a Barker. We've had some run-ins, and there's no love lost between them and us.

Last time it got pretty sour, even with me batting my eyelashes the whole time. It was a few months ago I think. Me and Gibbsy, we were shooting in the Llewelyn Markets at about four in the morning. We tagged the City logo onto a couple of shops that were supposed to be privately owned joints but that we found out a few weeks before were run by the Blackbands so as to nip some of the blackmarket deals that always happen in places like Llewelyn or Antrum or even Donovan Square. You ask me, a good blackmarket is a sign that people still have sense enough to live their lives and that's a wonderful thing. Of course, the City thinks otherwise.

We got about ten minutes of film that night, but that

was all we needed. As soon as Gibbsy started packing up the gear, we heard someone clapping from the alleyway. We knew right away that we were in some kind of twist. At first, I thought the Bands had been staking the place out, but no--it was a couple of Barkers. Turns out, they'd found out the same thing we'd found out, and they'd come to blow-up those shops in true Barker style.

They started giving us hell about tilting their planks and demanded our footage as compensation. Or else they'd cue the Bands. Our film ended up spliced in with other footage they took later of the storefronts exploding.

Me and Gibbsy, we spent a month worrying the City would trace all of it back to us since we never had a chance to cut the marks. They would have pinned us for the bombs, too, so I'm glad it didn't come to that.

The worst thing about the Barkers though is that they call themselves anarchists when in fact they're pretty damn well organized. They pretend to be changing things, but they're just out to keep them the same, just like the City. Normally that would be enough of a reason for me to have nothing to do with them but tonight we need their help, and that's all there is to it.

I just hope these guys don't run the kind of game we're used to seeing.

*

It turns out these Barkers don't even have the stuff with them, which makes me nervous all over.

"Say that again? I thought we were just dealing with *you*."

"Tag along is all," says Sticks. "It's close enough."

I look at Reggie, and he shrugs. His lips are still red and raw from the chili sauce. My hands start sweating in these gloves, so I pull them off and wipe them on my pants and wipe my forehead with my sleeve.

Gibbsy tugs at my shirt and I tell him to just keep an ear to the ducts. Poplar is humming.

The Barkers take us past the KP water pumps and into a pipe corridor with only a few scattered doors and the occasional death-trap of a staircase. Places ripe for ambush.

My nerves are stretched all up and down the hall, listening for the turning of knobs or the soft steps of a jittery mob. All they'd have to do is corner us, and we wouldn't be able to do anything about it. They'd take our cash and the gear, which isn't cheap. But if these Barkers are in on any kind of heist, they're not acting the part. Even Sticks seems a bit too polite by most Barker standards. It's off-putting. I guess I'd prefer it if he were an asshole.

"See that," he says, elbowing me and tipping his tall hat. "That block through there. I used to live down there. God, ten years ago. Power goes out twice a day and the drains back up. Hell. But you go down that hall not too far, and there's this playground for the kids. Buncha swings and see-saws and a merry-go-round. Ten years ago."

Me, I'm looking down that hall, thinking about that playground, and I can't imagine any kids ever use it. I guess the merry-go-round is stuck with rust. The swing chains are broken to bits. I elbow Poplar and point in that direction. Not too many things make me sadder than looking at a City playground.

I ask where we're going and Sticks waves at me like I'm not to worry. "The Machinist," he says. It's not a handle I've ever heard before, but I'm not exactly up on Barker social news these days. "Needs to know a few things first. That's all. You got the money?"

Yeah, I've got the money, but I'm not giving any of it to him until we're holding the blueprints and the pegs and whatever else we need.

He leads us through a couple of unmarked doors. Wherever we're going, it's really secluded. Now and then we pass clumsy graffiti from some defunct gang. The paint is chipping, and the words are unreadable. Some of the lights in the narrow, domed corridor are broken and will never be sought out for repair.

We stop outside a metal shutter which Rake starts to lift from the bottom. The track sticks so Reggie helps him until it's open. I flinch at the shrieking of metal, half-sure some crew will come pouring out into the hall holding clubs and grudges. But none does.

We're about to step through the doorway when Sticks grabs me by the shoulder. "Something you should know," he says. "Be careful in there, is all. The Machinist, he doesn't like folks staring at him, see what I mean? And believe me, he'll chew your throat to the bone if you make him mad."

That's the Barkers for you. Always making sure you know how dangerous they are.

For a machine shop, this place is sparse as hell and very dark. The Machinist's gear is spread all over the table. Tools, chemicals, things like that. But the rest of the room is empty. Some wire casings. Fragments of words finger-carved into the dust years ago. Vague shadows.

The Machinist is standing in the back, in the darkest corner of the place, backlit orange by a humming forgeplate. I can't see his face, and we don't get any closer.

For awhile no one says anything. Everyone's watching the Machinist, and he's watching everyone else. I'm guessing Poplar's getting bored with all of this.

The Machinist says, "Which one is Reggie?" His voice is full of little holes. He's been breathing chemicals for too long, and the chords are rotting away. "Almost everything you need is there on the table."

Reggie inches forward and lifts a wrinkled envelope by the corner like he's afraid it's laced with poison. He pulls out a few filament-read keypegs, a set of floor schematics and what looks like a list of pad codes. I've never had to use FRs before, but it doesn't really surprise me that Processing would be so tight on security. The City's always trying to keep honest eyes out of their filthy basements.

"That will get you from place to place," says the Machinist. He stretches his back. There's something odd about his arms, too, and I'm wondering why he's staying in the shadows. I met a guy once who'd been caught in a steel press--just the hydraulics, not the press itself--and he had a crooked slant to his whole frame. The Machinist reminds me of him, and I'm guessing the poor dreg's been mangled somehow, the way he moves, the way his skin doesn't seem right. "But you can't get to Processing from any public hall. You know that?"

Reggie looks to me for the explanation. "We can get through Geothermal and Water Treatment on our own."

"Very good. And from there…the Hatcheries?"

"Yeah," I say. "So I'm told."

"The Hatcheries," says the Machinist.

He sits at a little bench and trundles some sort of machine, like a small pneumatic drill. For a while, he's grinding away at a pegblank, and when he's finished, he blasts it with cold air from a tube feed. "The Hatcheries," he says. "This is for that door." He says it like we should already know. Like he doesn't need to say it at all. Like we're old friends. There's something creepy about that. Barkers are always trying to spook you, but this guy's got it down to an art. "Better than any rich or goodly armor."

Rake juggles the freshly minted peg, and he brings it to Reggie.

"That would be…door WT31, on the map," says the

Machinist. "And that same peg opens the graveyard gate if you should find yourselves no longer among the living. Unfasten the door by means of this secret key, without which no other god can open it."

"Downright poetic," I say as I pluck the peg from Reggie for a look-see. "Coins on the eyes, and all that? We'll be fine."

Christ. I don't know much about filament-reads, but he would have to be one deft hand to counterfeit something like this so quickly.

"Speaking of coins," says the Machinist. "How about that money, Tommy?"

I've got it wrapped in paper. Sticks takes it and counts it. All the while, I'm wondering how the Machinist knew my name. We were never introduced.

*

As we leave the shop, Poplar pulls me to a slant and whispers, "Did he creep you out?" She's close to laughing.

"He was a real charmer. Blue ribbon and all."

"Did you notice how all of his tools were perfectly set on the table and everything was polished and clean and wonderful? You see someone who's really good at something, and it's because they love to do it is why. I don't care if he's a Barker. He loves his little shop."

"Blue ribbon."

To be honest, I hadn't noticed how neatly the tools were arranged in the shop, and I don't think it matters. What I did notice was the large, wheeled trunk in the corner. Big enough to hold all of his stuff. I don't say anything to Poplar about it now because there's no point, but I'd bet the Machinist never stays a day in the same place twice. His "little shop" doesn't even exist.

*

Sticks and Rake lead us back to Antrum where the sound of the crowd calms me down again. But just as I'm leaning into the cozy fray, I feel a hand on my collar, and I stop where I'm standing. The short guy, Rake, pulls me back into the shadows, reaching into his coat.

I'm ready to fight him off if I have to. There are just two of them and four of us and Reggie's no pansy.

"Hold on," says Rake. I think it's the first time I've heard him speak. "It's alright, just stop a second."

He lets go of me, and I back away to the wall, ready to bolt.

"You got any more cash?" he says.

"I got three friends and twenty pounds on you."

"No, it's... look, if you've got an extra ten I can give you a Jigger. It's loaded and everything. You might need it."

I tell him, "We don't need a Jigger."

"I mean just in *case*. I think you should take it," he says. "You'd be damn snuffed not to. Honest."

All this fast talk's got the others looking our way. Sticks too. He comes striding over. "Ten? Naw, twenty-five for a gun like that. I got kids, and you got kids to feed too. They can have it for twenty-five."

"We don't *need* a Jigger, citizens. We don't need it."

Sticks gets close to me and looks out from under his brim. I'm close enough to see that it isn't paint on his cheek. Those two red stripes have been tattooed there. Permanent like. I can smell the chalk opium on his breath, like a cloud of oil.

"Rake here's so bent on giving it to you, maybe you should pay us twenty-five for the trouble of keeping it."

"Ask the Machinist for a cut if you want money, I don't have any left."

Sticks breathes at me and backs away. "I'm just giving you hell." He forces a smile. "Good luck down there." And he saunters to the wall.

"Look," says Rake. "I'll just *give* the gun to you. Forget paying for it, just do me a favor and take it."

Barkers don't just give you something without having a reason, so the fact that he wants us to have the gun so badly is a pretty good reason for me not to want it. When Reggie reaches for the damn thing, I slap his hand away.

"I'm not taking that, and neither is he. Whatever else happens that'll make it worse. Just go torture some dogs and let us do what we do."

"Look, there's gonna come a time," says Rake, "where you'll think back and know all this time you were just stripping the bolt. Grow up a little and take it, huh. Be smart. It'll make me feel a hell of a lot better if you do."

"No thanks," I tell him, "we get by just fine on vandalism and trespassing, and I'm not gonna let my pals get mixed up with guns."

He has nothing to say to that. Sockdolager. The argument's done. We sift into the crowd.

As soon as we're out of the noise, Gibbsy asks me why they'd even think we needed a gun. He sounds more worried than I think he should be.

"I don't know," I tell him. "You know the Barkers."

That thing about torturing dogs is true. I always try to point that out whenever a Barker's giving me hell. I saw this Riot Reel the Barkers circ'd once, with a dog they taught to smoke a cigarette. I know the City tobacco is laced, and I know people are ignorant and need their eyes opened sometimes, but that dog didn't ask for any of it. It was a prick film to shoot, and it's not the kind of thing we would ever do.

"ARDELL STATION - SUGAR WATER," Reel 2 of 2, 16mm, 24fps

The frame shakes, blocked now and then by frantic hands and rustling sleeves. The scratch of canvas as the camera is shoved fast into a backpack with the film still rolling. Finally, it settles. A flap moves out of the way revealing Ardell Station, mid-day and busy.

By now the Blackbands have already seized the man's wagon with all of the colorful jars. The camera draws closer to catch their voices on the soundtrack. The Bands are telling him he isn't allowed to sell the jars here. He says it was just sugar water and they say he can't sell food without it passing City inspections.

He argues the fact. He talks about the market hot carts. Then they tell him to drink down one of the jars, and he does so and says there isn't anything wrong with it.

The Blackbands say they will impound the wagon anyway and they tell the man to leave. So he begins to leave.

Half a second later a quick figure rushes out from somewhere near the camera. A boy. Fast even at fourteen. He crosses to where the man was walking and takes the empty jar from him.

Above the camera, we hear a voice, "Reggie! Shit." But this is just a whisper for the camera to hear.

The boy throws the jar. It spins in a tight arc and breaks against one of the Blackband's shoulders. The boy jumps onto the tracks and runs into the tunnel. The Blackbands can't catch him, and return to the platform and never notice or hear the cameraman who has not moved from his hiding place.

Another whisper. "Christ, Reggie," and the frame goes dark.

THREE

We're down on KS now, keeping to the fringes, halfway to the Industrials. Somewhere ahead, a steam pipe has cracked, and the corridor is filled with thick humid air. My glasses are fogged up and useless, but I can see fine without them.

Everybody's been quiet for the last little while. Finally, Reggie points to Gibbsy's face and says, "All that from crushed oats?"

Gibbsy says, "Yeah. Well, not the oats. Whatever else was in there, as soon as I ate it I knew something was wrong."

"You should have seen the *hives*," I tell him.

"I mean didn't they give you a shot?" says Reggie. Already I think I know what he's getting at.

Gibbsy nods. "It stops, like, my throat from swelling and all that but the hives don't go away right away. When I first started having allergies…"

"It makes you bruise too?"

Gibbsy stops talking, probably because he doesn't want to tell Reggie about what Truancy did. Reg makes things worse when we tell him things like that, but he won't stop pestering us until we do tell him, so I get it over with.

"The bruises are from Dutch and Tiegs." Reggie knows them well enough to sniff at hearing the names. He's had a few chats with Truancy over the years. "Thought Gibbsy was trying to cut. Maced him, beat him, dragged him away. Assholes. You'd know that, Reg, if you hadn't ditched half the day yourself. Hell, Truancy should have been after you, not Gibbsy here."

"So why the hell'd you let *Dutch and Tiegs* get at you like that. You didn't even swing?"

"No. They're Truancy, they…"

"The hell not? That's the whole problem, people not swinging back. You're no riot punk, not even standing up to Dutchy and his grunts, running away when you should be standing your ground and all that. Some prize melon you got there, Gibbs. That's all I'm gonna say."

I tell him to leave Gibbsy alone, and he does. Gibbsy stays quiet. That's the thing about Gibbsy. There's nuance in the way he does things. Nothing I could explain to Reggie.

"We should be going after Truancy," says Reggie. "Right?"

I tell him no, Processing's the bigger problem here. "Processing's what we need to film." And Reggie gets it.

"The oats, that's all prepackaged, isn't it?" he says. "The stuff they give you. Kitchen couldn't have messed it up or anything? Happened for sure in Processing?"

"Yeah," says Gibbsy. "Someone down there hates me I guess. 'Hold on there, Charlie Gibbs, no need to be pretty for the *ladies* today.'"

We go quiet again and spend half an hour moving through deadhalls. Not a soul to be seen or heard and in some cases no lights either. Just the hiss of the steam, the buzz of a flashlight, the four of us shuffling or scuffling or stomping along. We pass machines nobody's ever used before. All this Crackjaw technology we borrowed and never understood. Things like that make me worry. Like the City has never really been under anyone's control, not even its own.

The public corridors end just ahead, and Geothermal is across the spoke. Before we empty into the bigger tunnel, we listen for footsteps, wait, and when we're sure we're alone, we hurry across to a small metal door in the shadows. Poplar thumbs the key, twists the lock, and we get the hell out of sight.

We're now on City property.

*

Geothermal is a like a second home to us. I'm surprised we haven't worn the metal into a rut. Poplar's dad doesn't have full access officially, but his keys can get us through most doors in GT, and he has "acquired" a few others over the years that'll get us into some parts of WT. Used to be I only had respect for him because of the moonshine since it means another throat the City doesn't have a boot on yet, but after I found out about his keys, it was a matter of worship. The promised land had been found.

City divisions don't use the same radial grid as the rest of Fallback, and we've been lost in here before. Poplar has the usual layouts stamped in her brain, but already we're looking over Reggie's map. Once we get into WT, it'll be hell's-loose unfamiliar.

"So. How long will this all take, Tommy?" GT is empty this time of night, but Poplar whispers just in case. No sense being stupid if you don't have to be.

"Twenty minutes for the tag and the shoot, once we get there." How long it'll take to get there and back, I have no idea.

Gibbsy holds up a hand, and we all stop because that means another Blackband. They're rare enough here because of the locks, but we still have to be careful. Sometimes they do happen by, walking in their circles, never really going anywhere, strutting through their usual turf.

I press into the dark behind a steam pipe and look past it. I can see this one, an older guy, gun holstered, baton in one fist, head down. He's facing away from us, doing his rounds.

Reggie steps out into the middle of the hall, real quiet, as if *daring* the old guy to turn around and see him. It doesn't matter. The Blackband doesn't turn around, and before long he's gone again down another corridor.

"You don't have to do that," I say to Reggie.

He says, "Helluva sunny day," and he says something tough about wanting to see what the old guy would have done but it's all dust, and I tell him so.

"You would've dove out of the way if you thought he was going to turn. I'm not saying you're a trembler, I'm saying you're not that stupid. We know you hate the Bands, so no reason to show off."

Reggie gives me crazy eyes and a fake laugh.

I elbow Poplar and point. "You see what hardships I have to endure?"

"Yeah, it's tough not to *yawn* sometimes," she says. "Hardships, huh? What about me? Do you fellas really like having me around?"

"No."

"Good," she says, and she pretends to lean on Gibbsy like she always does. "Then I won't feel bad if you all get arrested."

*

We traipse from shadow to shadow for a long while. Another few Blackbands pass, and we move to the next quiet place. This is what we do. Shadow to shadow, just so we can turn on a few lights.

There is no one in Fallback better at what we do than we are. The Barkers can't move without knocking a hole in a wall. Most riot punks get rap sheets pretty fast and give up or disappear. Not us. We know what we're doing and how to get from place to place and we never get caught.

Mostly it's about patience. You've got to test your route and know where and when the Blackbands are going to be stationed. You have to know when shifts end for the joes. You've got to know where the maintenance corridors are, and you've got to use them as much as you can because they'll be empty. Sure, it means crawling under a pipe or over a cluster of wires sometimes, but it's better than being out in the open. Waiting at doors, listening ahead, walking slow and quiet. As a rule of thumb, once you've been noticed, you've been caught.

We know a few worst-case tricks, though. We know how to bust a steam-tap in a pinch, so we can get away without anybody daring to follow through the scalding halls. We know how to pop a grate and hide under the floor. We know about the maintenance hatches and how to short-out a corridor long enough to duck through unseen in the dark.

Our best tricks came from Gibbsy. He's the one who first thought to bring a pocketful of cinch-ties, so we could block the doors. Like a Slipknot for instance. A Slipknot is where you trap whoever's chasing you in a detour. First, you sprint through one door and out another. From the outside, you cinch the second door shut and wait until the guy on the other side tries to open it. As soon as you hear that knob turn, you run back to the first door before the other guy can get there and you cinch it shut too. Now the guy is trapped. He can't open either door until he breaks the twine and by then you're gone.

Gibbsy has a whole list of things like that. The Jump Rope, the Tailchaser, the Dead Man. My favorite is the Dog Collar, which is where you tie a chime to a valve differential and when the Blackbands follow the sound of it, you slink away in some other direction. That one keeps us out of a lot of trouble.

The thing you have to remember, though, is that no matter what you do, the Bands won't be fooled long. Get out fast before they start using their spec radios because once that happens, they'll close in on you fast and no tomfoolery in the world will do you any good.

This is always a risky prospect. But I don't mind. It's worth it. Folks need to know what kind of life they're really living. They need to know what this world of ours has come to. They need to taste the salt in the water, and they need to know how thirsty they really are.

If the City won't regulate itself, we have to regulate it.

*

Reggie keeps kicking Gibbsy's shoe, and it's starting to wear on my saintly patience. The last time we all went on a shoot together, Reggie was fooling around and pushed Gibbs down a couple of steps. He sprained his ankle, but even then he didn't so much as holler at Reggie for it. He just limped along and kept his head down.

He's ignoring Reggie now, too, kick after kick, but I'm fed up, and I shove Reggie into the wall and tell him to stop being a prick.

He says, "I'm trying to get somewhere," which is just the kind of thing Reggie always says when he's tormenting someone. Sometimes I have to keep him away from Gibbsy when he's like this.

For now, I'm walking between the two of them, and it works well enough. We stay to the edges. GD runs all night and all day but only at the core. The rest of it vacates after ten. WT's the same. We hear steamboys now and then, echoing from someplace where there is work to be done, but it's funny: we can tell when it's just some joe, and we can tell when it's a Blackband, because of all the protocol.

Pretty soon we're at the back of WT, where the Barkers' map shows a D-type conduit. We follow that to the Sector 31 junction airlock, which is unsealed, and past that is a very slick looking door.

Reggie tilts the map and squints.

"Is that the one the Machinist was talking about?" I ask.

"That's it," he says, swaggering forth, peg in hand.

But I don't let him get far. "Give me that, son, I have a speech prepared."

I take the peg from Reggie, and I stand in front of the door, facing my pals with my head cocked back like Kennedy. "Friends and citizens, tonight we find ourselves in the City's Processing division. On the other side of this fine door is where they cut all the fish into tiny bits. And beyond that, they mill the oats and the trough wheat and that godawful rice, so as to fill our shriveled bellies. Lesser men and women have tried and failed to get beyond this door. But, friends and citizens, we have the key. Let us go forth and bring about a fine riot."

I dance a full Salaam jig, in the name of victory, waving my hand like I have a hat. Then I slide the peg into the slot and bow low as the needles trace the grooves. Poplar is dancing too.

*

Not half a second after the door opens the lights all drop. Utter black, up and down the corridor. Everywhere. Not even the redbells flash.

You don't see blackouts too often in the Industrials.

They used to happen a lot in places like the Kennel but not here.

This one lasts over a minute. As soon as the power comes back, we keep moving, and Reggie reads the map as we go.

We need to drop a few decks from here, but the lifts are at the far end of the wing, and it's a good long while before we get there. We pass a few big doors that Reggie says don't matter. We spend an hour in a tangle of passageways, him swearing the whole time that he knows where to go. I tell him to give the map to Gibbsy, but he says, "*I'll* read the son-of-a-bitch map."

*

Hall after hall, none of us have said a word. Now all of a sudden Reggie's whispering to Poplar about something he and Beth Stevens were fighting over last night, something that doesn't matter.

I say, "Shut it off, darlings," and Reggie gives me one of his open-palmed shrugs.

"There isn't anybody here," says Poplar. But she's

wrong. Someone is coming.

We duck into a wiring conduit and wait, watching through the casings. The floor here is welded steel-grate with routing posts underneath. It's loud as a bell if you step too hard and whoever's coming, they're not too close, but they're moving fast.

Poplar wanders over to read a few random gauges ten feet away, and I have to drag her back to where we're all crouching, just to be safe. We edge back into the cluster just in time to see who is coming and seeing them scares the hell out of me.

Three Hectors round the angle at a jog. Christ, they're not the kind of people you ever want to be hiding from. Blackbands are one thing. But Hectors are another thing altogether--they don't even *have* rules. They're trigger happy, and they just don't care. City security above all things, even its own people.

What really scares me is the artillery. They've got S8s, Lebanov's and one of them is carrying a big mountable Plug-20.

As they pass, I can hear them chatting through their filters. "Gotta be Mycroft," says the lead. "Drill or something."

The guy at the tail says, "If it ain't...well, I don't want to consider if it ain't."

Whatever they say next, they're too far away to hear.

*

We wait. They go through the next door. We wait some more.

"Why would they need all that?" says Gibbsy.

I don't know. I've never seen anything like it in the Industrials.

"Goddamn City's always gotta have a bigger gun," says Reggie.

I can tell Gibbsy is in doubt about this whole mess already. Of course, he won't say he's in doubt, no matter how worried he gets--he'll just keep following me and twist the valve--but I can tell.

"The reason it's risky is the reason it's worth doing," I tell him, and he knows I mean it.

It doesn't matter if it ends up in a swanky restaurant or the grimy markets. Everything that comes in from the sea or grows in Hydroponics eventually goes through the same place. More than a million people down here and *everything* we eat or drink has to visit Processing.

"See what I mean Pop." She only shrugs. "One day you'll be just as notched about the City as I am. Just keep your eyes open, and it'll happen." Another shrug is all I get.

*

For most shoots, we scout the place first so we know what to avoid. We didn't have enough time, this job, so now we're on unfamiliar turf staring at this little map.

We know a little about the Hatcheries from Robin Tulsa. His uncle works here and says there won't be many joes or Blackbands. He never said anything about Hectors, the old drunk.

I'm trying to think of a reason for them to be here,

the Hectors. All I can guess is that it's because of the Hatcheries. Because of those huge moon pools with nothing but steel mesh between us and the sea. If anything tries to come down here from the surface, I guess it would use the Hatcheries to get into Fallback, and if there's one thing the City hates more than its own citizens, it's whatever lives up there.

It doesn't really matter. A few Hectors being here is no reason to stop what we're doing. We'll have to keep to the edges, but we were planning to do that anyway, and we'll take extra care, under the circumstances.

I may be an asshole sometimes, but I'm not a maniac.

*

Elevators are always a bad idea. You can't scout the other end of the shaft, and you never know when the doors will open, and you'll find someone standing on the other side. We avoid them as much as we can, even if it means walking out of the way to a staircase or a friendly ladder hatch, but you can't always skirt the lifts.

The only way to get from where we are right now to

where we are supposed to be is to use a cargo elevator. We get in, shut the gate, and cross our fingers. When it opens, we wait at the gate, ready to spring out running if necessary. But this time we find ourselves in front of an unmanned tug run, thank Christ, and we're safe for now.

Past that is a long, narrow, streamlined corridor that bends fifty yards from where we're standing. "The Hatcheries," says Reggie with a flourish. He has one hell of a demented smile. What a ham.

I tell the others to hold still while I trot ahead. Something is bothering me already, and it isn't the Hectors. I don't know what it is yet, but it's there, scratching at my skull.

After the bend, the hall blossoms into a nice wide vault and I go back for the others. We skirt a deck of catwalks and stop in the shadows. "Pull out the gear," I tell Gibbsy and we start rummaging through his pack. It's best not to waste film, but you should at least have it ready as soon as you're near where you want to be. No telling what you might catch on the eights. Sixteens. Whatever. "Wake, wake, sweet Cassandra."

Gibbsy usually runs the camera because he's shorter than me. Plus, he's the best camera jockey in Fallback. No question. He's got a real talent for it.

We pass a couple of huge wire slips, and he films those. He films the hatchways, even the lights. We're not tagging yet since there's nothing worth tagging, but we're sure setting the scene.

By and by we make our way to the rail, and we see something that shouldn't be here. I flinch at the sight of it. We should stop what we're doing and go back the way we came. And we should do it now.

Five stories below, water ripples in a dozen moon pools. But these aren't what you'd expect to see in the Hatcheries. They're too narrow, and in one of them, a huge metal hull presses heavily against the water, moored there with its dark windows looking over the docks. Jesus, it's a hand-to-god Drowner.

Gibbsy touches my sleeve and says what it is that's been bothering me. "It doesn't smell like fish," he says. And he's right. This isn't the Hatcheries at all.

"UMBRELLAS AND SWINGS," Reel 1 of 1, 16mm, 24fps

A steady shot. A small playground near Rabbish Court, after curfew. At the left edge of the frame stand a few empty cans, lining the windowsill where the camera has been propped and hidden.

The playground is pristine and looks out of place beside the rotting steel and concrete of the square. The whole scene is vacant until a woman enters from the right edge of the frame carrying an umbrella. The kind they sometimes sell in curio shops. The kind that wouldn't last long if it ever saw real rain.

The woman takes small steps, like she'd been injured long ago. She doesn't seem too old. She has a bag over her shoulder, and she digs through it to find a few cans of polish and wax and some rags. She starts polishing the metal slide, making it shine. She polishes the merry-go-round rails and oils the swing chains and files away burrs.

She finishes, packs her things and leaves.

The Reel then cuts to footage of that same park, taken a couple of months later. The camera moves from place to place, from the swings to the monkey bars, showing the tarnish that has since begun to creep into them.

The final shot focuses on the wall of the playground where a few words have been spray-painted. Graffiti, like an epitaph. "Someone is missing."

FOUR

We're in a hell of a spot now. Those son of a bitch Barkers put us in the wrong part of the city, and we *paid* them to do it. I'm notched about it, and I pin Reggie to the rail.

"The hell *are* we? It was your pals who gave us directions and this *ain't* where we're supposed to be. So, where the hell are we, Reg?"

He shows me the map and points to where we are. "It says Processing division. It says Hatcheries."

But the map is lying.

I should have known better than to take what the Barkers gave us, and I should have thought this through.

They don't like us. Our Riot Reels are a thousand-and-twelve times better than their petty snuff, and they know it. They know what we think of them, me and everyone who's got a real sense of this place. Leave it to the Barkers to send a bunch of kids someplace *no* one should ever go. Drowners, for Christ's sake, and water open to the sea. No wonder those Hectors were stomping through the halls. I start to wonder if the Barkers meant to get us killed, but Mocap is bad enough.

After a while of fussing over the map, Reggie throws his hands in the air. He won't talk to me anymore. I need to think about this. We need to leave, but where we go next, I have no idea. I tell Reggie to give me the map and get the hell away from me. "Gibbsy, help me figure this out."

We start looking through the floor plans, trying to make sense of it. Everything's mislabeled. Hell-and-gone. But sometimes you can guess what a room is used for just by its shape. Maybe we can figure out where Processing *really* is and not make such a mess of this shoot.

"Think about all the machinery they have to use," says Gibbsy. "They'd need silos too. Maybe those are close."

The more we look through the map, the more I doubt it.

All the while, Reggie's getting restless. He never can stand still for long, and now he's talking to Poplar about who knows what.

"Hey Tommy," says Pop, "we're going to look at the Drowner. Now or never."

"No, you're not." It's a bad idea. "One of them Hectors sees you and thinks you're messing with the Drowner hatch…they will shoot you dead."

She says, "We're not going down there. Just a little closer." I can already tell she won't be swayed, but this isn't a game, for hell's sake.

"Don't make me get a leash."

She's not smiling. She curtsies and the two of them tiptoe away. I'm just hoping they're smart enough not to get too close to the water.

I've got other things to worry about anyway. Gibbsy has no idea where Processing is from here, and neither do I. We've got a few likely spots, but we can't be wandering blindly through the Industrials all night. Eight hours from now our parents are going to be wondering where we are.

"Let's just try…Jesus, here I guess." I'm pointing at a long narrow vault a few decks up and five-hundred yards away. Perfect for a conveyor line, I'm thinking. Gibbsy agrees. "But if that isn't it," I tell him, "we should find that Machinist and do some damage."

Gibbsy nods but something else catches my eye. Poplar and Reggie are coming back fast.

They're both pale. The closer they get the louder they get. I can practically hear the echo of soles on steel.

"Fellas, fellas," says Reggie. He's pointing to the Drowner. "Look at the name on that thing. THAT…is the Dulcet 11."

I'm about to say, "So what? Let's get out of here,"

but then I remember where I've heard that name before.

*

Four flights down, the Drowner dock is shaping up to be a broad and incredibly tall room.   I run out onto the ground floor, stooping, rattling the grates but in a quiet way. The floor is rich with zap boxes and pump housings so I can stay out of sight for the most part. My pals are just now getting to the bottom of the stairs, and I whistle for them to hurry and catch up. Gibbsy is filming again.

The Barkers couldn't have known about this. No one is supposed to know about this. They were trying to be assholes, but they handed us a prize instead. This is a hell of a find.

I get the paint out of Gibbsy's pack and mark the date and time, big black letters, on the deck. Next to that, I write "Still above water?" I stay out of frame so Gibbsy can film it all without me getting picked out of the grain.

I never show myself on camera. Different riot punks have different opinions about that. Take Reggie, for example, he always likes to get his hand in-frame, like a tease, like he's saying, "Try and figure out who I am." I've known guys who put on hoods and stand in front of the eights, talking in fake voices. Earlier today we wrapped Gibbsy's face in bandages so that we could film the hives without showing much else. And Pop, last time she came with us, she talked the whole time. That giggle of hers, or a bit of song. There's nothing wrong with any of that. But I know how clever the City can be. I leave no trace of Tommy Molotov. Not on camera. Not with Cassandra.

Our gal Cassandra--we call her that because of the girl from Troy on account of how nobody ever believes the truth even when they're staring right at it. She's like an old pal, and Gibbsy's a pro with her in his hands. Polished brass and black leather fittings. Wood handles. Burning everything she sees into the film, exactly as it is.

*

The Dulcet 11 is one huge boat. The big brass name-plate is as tall as I am. It's crusted with salt now, and the paint's not what it used to be. Otherwise, there's no mistaking it. Here it is. It looks just like it did in the

Bulletin from when they christened it. Christ, they made us watch that thing twice, which is always pure hell.

While Gibbsy gets all the angles, I wander off. There aren't any more Drowners here, just empty moon pools. I look down into one. Light shimmers blue in the water, tapers down and goes dark. I don't know if there's a hatch down there or if the pools are open to the sea, but I can't stop thinking about the ocean. Out there, swimming in waters just like this and not far from Fallback, are beasts that did not exist fifty years ago.

That's why it's so easy to believe, I guess. About the Drowners. I mean, if you ask me you'd have to be insane to go out scouting on one of those things. And for what? Precious resources? Maybe, but we've got all we need down here, and it's not worth the risk. No reason to go back to the surface for anything except to have a look around and see what an impossible world we left behind. It's not our world anymore. *This* is our world. *Fallback* is our world. Up there? That's the Crackjaw's world now.

So yeah, when the City tells us another Drowner went missing, we believe it. When the City tells us "another hundred friends and citizens were lost in a valiant effort to gain a foothold on our once and future home" …we believe it. But not anymore. Not after this. Not after everyone sees the Dulcet 11 still here in one piece.

We've caught the City in one hell of a lie. The newsfeeds said it went down, what, a couple of weeks ago? Lost and gone, they said. And then on the Bulletin, *Kennedy* himself said it was lost and gone, its mission failed, its lives wasted for no earthly gain. This wasn't some Blackband speaking out of place or overstepping his authority. This was Kennedy, lying to us. And so now *our* boot is on the *City's* throat.

*

Something touches my hip, and I flinch so hard I almost fall into the water.

Poplar tucks her hair behind her ears and sways. "Just wanted you to see that," she says, pointing up.

"See what?"

At first, I don't know what she's talking about. Then

I find it. The overheads are glinting off the water and way up there on the ceiling, five or six levels, a shifty reflection dances against the metal.

"Kind of like having a sky," she says.

"I wouldn't know."

She starts to twirl away, but I pinch her sleeve.

"Is that all you can say, Pop? The sky? What about the fact that this Drowner here means maybe your mom didn't die. And maybe the people who 'died' on the Dulcet 11 didn't really die. What about that?"

She just smiles and pulls away, same as ever. Even back when she first found out about her mom, whenever anybody tried to make her feel better, all she would ever say was, "People die," and she'd walk away. Never cared.

So, I remind her, "You're not here to paint, Pop, you don't have the time."

*

Gibbsy is finished with the Drowner. He films a bit

of the room and stacks the gear in his backpack again. Sleep well, Cassandra. He stands behind me saying, "What now?" and I walk around looking at some of the control terminals while he follows close behind.

"We gotta go back and get this circ'd," I tell him. "What's Reggie doing?"

He's standing on the far side of the decks, a little too much out-in-the-open for my tastes, but Reggie is Reggie. The room narrows back there and becomes a big arched tunnel, long and well lit, ending at the biggest door I've ever seen. Thirty feet high I'd guess. Rails run along the floor toward it, and I'm thinking they must have a freight tug back there someplace for loading and unloading the Drowners.

"Checking things out," says Gibbsy. But already, Reggie is coming back.

"Got a key for *that* thing?" I say, pointing at the big cargo door.

"No."

"I know you don't. The key for that's probably the

size of a hotcart." I'm just messing around, and I pretend to slap him.

"Shut up Tommy."

"By the way," I tell him, "there's no way your Barker pals are taking any credit for this. They blew the tap this time."

"And look what it got us," says Reggie.

"I'm not saying that. I'm saying look what it could have got us. I should go naming names, for them putting us down here. They blew the tap and could have got us killed, and we're lucky this place is empty because we walked in blind and all."

Reggie stops arguing. He never does mince words for long. Well, not with me anyway. He knows he can't wriggle out of anything with me. "Let's go cut the marks," I say.

We walk along the decks toward the staircase again. It's quiet here. The airmovers are humming like always and under that is the soft shuffle of our feet. But that's it. No other sounds. No echoes.

"Why *is* this place empty," says Gibbsy. He's got that nervous voice again.

It's a good question. There's no one here. Sure, it was hard to get at it, but you'd think something like the Dulcet 11 would be watched all day and no blinking.

"Who cares?" says Reggie. "Let's just go home and let the City off the hook." He stops walking, so I know he's serious.

"What?"

"That thing?" he says pointing at the Drowner. "Coulda crashed like they said. Could be the City just dragged it back, after, with some other Drowner. That's what they'd say."

"Shut up Reggie. *Nobody* will believe them if they do. And what else are we supposed to do about it?"

"That big door…" he says.

"The one you don't have a key for?"

"Don't need a key," he says. "It's not even shut."

Hell. "Then let's go."

*

Reggie's right about the City. They could lie their way out of this one just like they've lied their way out of other messes. That's not to say a Reel like this wouldn't do some damage to Kennedy's image...but it wouldn't be as heavy a blow as it ought to be. It wouldn't bring people out of their seats like it should.

It's got me thinking about the Reel I shot with Martin Bastian after the bulkheads broke in Fl.

The flood itself had been big enough news on the feeds that week, most folks knew the broad details. Probably because it would be too hard to hide a catastrophe as big as that. They even had one of their regular experts on the Bulletin with Kennedy. Some doctor, if I remember. He kept saying, "That sector was due for maintenance and had been evacuated. There were no casualties of any kind."

If you ask me, ax marks on the window and those scratches on the ceiling meant the place hadn't been entirely empty when the rivets burst, and the floodchecks tripped. Somebody had been in there with the water filling the place and from the looks of it, that someone didn't have much luck getting out.

But Alvey, he didn't want to show the Reel because he said it didn't prove anything. We talked him into it. If nothing else, it would get people thinking. And sometimes that's all we can do, is get people wondering, get them thinking about one lie at a time and hope they all add up to something people will notice.

*

We can't really hide anywhere in the cargo tunnel, so we wait at the mouth while Gibbsy looks for a way to short the lights. It doesn't take long. Things go dim with just a few base lamps glowing at the fringes, and we run the length of it, careful not to trip on the rails.

The doors are heavy, thick steel. I can't budge them, but it's cracked enough that we can slip through. It's tight, but we all make it.

The breakers reset just as we get through and now

I'm looking at a room full of cages.

"What did they bring *back* in those?" says Gibbsy.

That's what we're all wondering, but I don't have a guess. The cages are about eight feet tall, twenty long, with slats to fit on the freight tugs. Metal walls with round air holes scattered across. They're empty now but not clean. The first one I look into is smeared with mud tracks and what looks like blood.

"Get some film of this," I tell Gibbsy. "Get up close. Those are fingerprints in the blood. Fingerprints. They weren't hauling ore, I know that much. They weren't bringing back soil either."

He snags every angle, and we move across the room to where Poplar is standing. Big stacks of cargo, covered with dirty canvas. Nothing unusual. Supplies and whatnot.

A bundle of white cloth lies separate from everything else, a bit out of place. Too clean. Poplar pulls the cloth away, and the four of us find ourselves staring at a ship's plaque.

Troubadour 7. I can tell by looking at it that it's never been used.

"So they just rename the same Drowners and send 'em out again?" says Reggie. "Think any of 'em ever really wrecked?"

"I don't know. Maybe some. Maybe they only ever had one to send in the first place." I'm wondering what Poplar thinks about all of this. She's not saying anything, but she's pale as all get-out, and I'd bet high chips she's notched at seeing this. "See what I mean, Pop? See what this place does to folks like your mom? If the Drowner she was on didn't really wreck, where is she?"

Poplar doesn't say anything at all.

"The news feeds, the Bullets, the City. They're all liars."

I tag the floor. "Rebirth?" Gibbsy films that too.

*

Poplar drags me by the belt to the side of the room. She hasn't said much yet, but I can tell she's upset. She's pale, under these lights.

"This is gonna bust a few valves," I tell her. "Holy, holy. Are you finding any beauty in this?"

"No."

"You see what I mean about the City, though. This is what they do."

She stops me. "Tommy, it's up to you, but I don't think you should show the reels to anybody..."

It comes out of nowhere, her saying that, and even as she trails off, I'm not sure how to respond. Here she is with proof positive that Fallback wronged her own *mother* and lied about it, and Poplar's saying we should bury the footage. Her logic is flawless. I'm starting to think I shouldn't have brought her along.

"What do you want me to do, paint a trompe l'oeil on one of these crates?"

"You remember that little girl with the parakeet?" she says. "In the little cage?"

"Yeah. Poor kid but what of it?"

She's talking about this girl we saw in Donovan Square a few months ago. She was maybe five years old. She was walking through the crowd holding a cage with a bird she must have just bought in Marius, and she tripped. The cage hit the ground, and the bird flew out into the rafters and down along one of the main halls, out of sight. Her parents were telling her to stop crying, telling her that the bird was going to find its family somewhere in Fallback and would be very happy once it did. But the truth is, the bird didn't last long. This place ain't too easy on the living.

Poplar says, "What if that girl's parents told her, 'Your bird is never coming back and is going to die of thirst in a few days'?"

"It would have been the truth."

She shakes her head. "It wouldn't have done anybody any good. A lot of fuss for nothing."

Fair enough. But this isn't a lost bird we're filming here.

*

The Drowner cargo must have been unloaded out there and brought through here, but I'm a tad curious as to where it all went next.

A couple of smaller freight doors glare at us from the back of the room. FR readers, just like everything else in here. I'm yanking on one of the handles, about to ask Reggie if he has a peg for it, when it swings toward me.

"This one isn't locked either."

The tug rails swerve into the next room, a broad sort of warehouse with crates stacked high. Dead-end track spurs branch out with a turntable in the middle of it all.

I'm not sure what to make of the warehouse. It's clean and big, and there's nothing much to say about it, except that it has a strange, eerie glass observation booth two levels up. The booth is empty, but the light is on, and from what I can see, the door at the back of it is open.

What I ought to do is climb up there and pocket some cargo records. The problem is, there's no way up. The booth's only door leads back into some other hall that I can't even imagine how to reach.

"What else?" says Gibbsy, wondering what to film.

"Nothing left in here," I tell him. The spurs all end at cargo lifts. "I'm not taking a chance on another lift. Not here."

"So…"

I point at the booth until they're all looking. "So let's go around, back to the stairs. Maybe a way in from there."

"We're still *shooting*?" says Poplar.

"As long as there's more to shoot, girly."

And there has to be. For all the bloody cages and the open pools, this place is way too empty. Those big doors, they shouldn't have just opened like they did.

So we move fast, out of the warehouse, into the freight hall and onto the docks again. Reggie looks scared.

"Hey, Reg, what's got you trembling?"

Something has put a clamp on his tongue. He's

looking over my shoulder.

When I turn to look, my tongue's in a clamp too. The Hectors are here.

"Stay low. Go around through there." I don't know if my pals can even hear me, but I don't dare talk any louder.

The Hectors still have their backs to us as they walk the decks. They might not be the same fellows we saw earlier, but I don't know, and it doesn't matter. Only two of them now.

My pals seem to know what I'm trying to say even if they can't hear me. We all crouch behind the nearest pump housing and hold our breaths.

The Hectors spin on their heels and pace closer. They're talking, but I can't make out any of the words. I'm listening to the footsteps instead, trying to figure out where they're planning to go next so we can skirt around and stay out of sight.

The trouble is, Reggie's getting itchy to bolt. I can tell by the way his leg shivers. Any second now, he's going to run for the stairs, and the Hectors will know exactly where to find the rest of us. He's done things like that before, Reggie. If anybody gets too close, he doesn't just wait. He can't ever sit still.

I grab him by the ankle, and he kicks at my hand. I know what he's thinking. He's thinking, "Let the hell go of me Tommy, I'm outta here." But I'm not going to let him do that. I grab his ankle again, and I hold it tight this time, and I mouth the words "Don't be a prick."

The Hectors are close now. I hear a little of what they're saying.

"Naw, they checked 25 half an hour ago. It's locked tight. That's not where we need to be."

"Dawson ain't chimin' back. You don't know any more than I do. Hell's breaking loose. This ain't no drill."

Hell's breaking loose. I'm wondering if that has anything to do with us, like we triggered some bells, but I really don't know.

They're turning now, toward the stairs, and we're pinned. I try to push Reggie around to the other side of the housing, so we can all slide over and hide better. We don't have much shade here, that's for sure, but by some damn lucky angle the Hectors walk past and don't even notice us.

Five minutes later, we remember to breathe.

*

"Did we trip the alarms?" says Gibbsy.

"Maybe."

"The hell we did," says Reggie. "There's no alarm." He's right, but he has no way of knowing and neither do any of us. If we did trip an alarm, it's a silent one. I can see a few redbells here and there, but none of them are flashing at the moment. None at all.

"We just got lucky," says Poplar. "Count your blessings, boys."

"It's not luck. It's years of experience and discipline."

She laughs at me. "If they'd turned their heads just a bit more to the left…"

Maybe, but the fact is they didn't turn their heads to the left. We've been in enough situations like this to get a feel for what's going to happen and how to keep out of its way. Twenty Riot Reels in the locker and luck rarely had a hand in any of them.

"So back the way we came?" she says and Gibbsy nods.

"Hold on, friends and citizens. We're going to snag some waybills first. Besides, *they* went the way we came. We'd run right into those bastards, up that lift, if not before then."

"I don't know," says Gibbsy. It's that same tone he always uses when he's too afraid to up and tells me I'm wrong about something.

"They went up those stairs. We saw them go up those stairs."

Gibbsy points at the far end of the room. "It sounded like they only went up a couple of, uh, flights, though."

"I saw one of 'em, hand-on-rail, up where we came in. That's where they went, Gibbs."

I let my pals mull things over for a minute while I climb on top of the pump housing so as to get a better look at the docks. Then I see it. A small door at the back of the room on this side. It's at the top of a narrow flight of steps, and it seems to me, eyeballing the lay of the land, it leads to that booth we saw from the warehouse. And that's exactly where I want to be.

"That there's what I'm looking for," I tell them. "Onward and upward. Look at the map Gibbsy."

I climb down, and the two of us trace it over. "See, that's the good ol' dockmaster's perch. And when we're done, this hall here, it'll double back. We can go through there, grab some paper, cut through this junction and before you know it we're on our way to Water Treatment."

Gibbsy says, "I don't know," again, but I'm tired of standing still. The longer we're in one place, the worse it is to be there.

"Stay low and quick."

*

The first thing we ever do whenever we open a door is listen. And the first thing we hear when we open *this* door is music. Something tinny and full of echo. A bad phonograph in a distant room, filling the shabby white hall.

"Hey, Tommy don't." Gibbsy is gripping my shirt. "Someone's down there."

"Maybe."

Poplar taps the wall. "If I may quote from the infamous Tommy Molotov, 'We never go anywhere unless we're the only ones there. That's rule one.'"

"Yeah, yeah. We'll do a Flyby."

Gibbsy tries not to react, but I can hear it there in his lungs, a heavy breath struggling to come out. We've never actually had to do a Flyby before…which is to say, we've thought about it plenty of times and decided it was a bad idea.

A Flyby is when one of us runs past a nest of unfriendlies to lead them away from where the rest of the crew is going to be. You keep your steps nice and quiet at first, and when you get close enough, you smack your feet or stomp or make a bunch of noise so they'll hear you. Just run past as fast as you can, turn a corner and go quiet again, so they lose track of you. Meanwhile, your crew slides past, and you meet up with them.

"It won't work," says Gibbsy. "They have guns."

"Reggie here's not afraid of guns."

Reggie looks at me, but it takes a second or two for him to get what I mean. "Sure," he says. "I'll do it. None of you pricks can do it. I'll do it."

"Reggie here eats a side of bullets with every meal. Reggie here brushes his teeth with gunpowder."

I smack him across the cheek, so he'll know I care. The truth is, I'd do it myself, but I want to get into that room when it's clear. I want to rummage through the files and snag whatever tells the tale. Reggie is faster anyway.

"It might not work," says Gibbsy. "If there's a couple of guys in there one might stay behind while the other goes chasing."

But I tell him it'll be fine. It's all we can do.

*

The hall is long and narrow, littered with a few alcoves. Plaster walls and those dusty textured ceiling tiles. Dented tin sconces here and there.

The booth isn't far. Another corridor crosses this one not twenty feet past the door, so anybody who hears Reggie will have to be awfully fast if they want to gun him down before he's out of the way. If that's a Blackband nest, no problem. If it's full of Hectors...he'll just have to hope for the best.

He really is fast. Reggie sounds like a pneumatic tube, the way he shoots down the hall, clothes rattling in the wake.

A few yards from the door he starts clapping his hands and singing, and I'm watching the light from the booth, looking for startled shadows. But Reggie doesn't reach that next hall. He draws level with the room, glances, and slides to a stop.

"Run, run," says Gibbsy but Reggie just stands there

in front of the door.

He holds up his hands and waves at us. That could only really mean one thing.

"I guess there's no one in there," says Gibbsy.

"Guess so. Let's check it out."

The phonograph sits on the edge of a small desk playing something by Schuller and Johnson. The record is scratchy, faded and sounds like the tale-end of a dream. The last thing you hear before you wake up.

I stand at the back of the room, looking through the glass at the warehouse turntable where we had been standing not seventeen minutes ago. I tilt at the board, and the control panel hums against my hands, just the faintest tickle.

"Why'd they leave the record on?" says Gibbsy. "Think they might be coming back?"

"Could be."

Poplar leans her head on my shoulder and starts talking about how much she loves this song and that we should dance.

"Save it for Harvest," I tell her, which makes her laugh.

Come to think of it, that's where we always hear this song. At the Harvest Dance, as if there's any such thing as a *season* in this place. The lyrics are about some sappy guy who's too shy to ask this girl he likes to go to a dance with him. I can't imagine what sort of world I'd have to live in to think stuff like that's important but here in Fallback, people want you to think that's what life's still about.

*

I was hoping to find some drawers or lockboxes or something, but this is just a control room for the cargo lifts and the turntable. Not a cabinet to be found, just a bunch of switches and levers and a PA mic for hollering at whoever might be working the tugs.

At first, I think it was pointless to come in here, but then I see the labels they've got on those lift switches.

"Gibbsy, get some film of this."

Quarantine, Cellular Transmutation, Pathology, and Hazardous Materials. It's not hard to imagine what those mean but honest to god, the place we're in right now looks nothing at all like a hospital.

And where the hell *is* everybody?

*

"This probably doesn't go back to the junction," says Gibbsy. "I don't think so, anyway."

No, he's certain of it; he just doesn't want to say it out loud. The hall that we're in angles away from where we actually want to be, no doubt about it. Gibbsy tends to be polite even when he's mad.

We'll have to double back and go through the Drowner docks and back up the same elevator we used to get here in the first place. Past those Hectors again, wherever they are.

"This is a bad place to be," says Gibbsy.

He's right. We should leave the booth and get moving. Anytime you stay in a place that only has one exit, it's like you're begging for the noose.

I'm staring at Poplar as we stand here in the hall. Something tugs at her. Something sad and vague and full of steam. There has never been anybody more beautiful in all the world.

"Quit frowning," I tell her.

"Where to?" she says, and I point back toward the docks.

"Every now and then, I'm wrong about something."

It makes her smile. It makes her punch my chin, just hard enough that I feel it.

Low and quiet, we creep back toward that little door, toward the docks. My hand is half an inch from the knob when I hear boots on the stairs, and I know what's about to happen.

"Turn around, go back, go back."

But the door opens before we can spin, and the Hectors flinch when they see us. They glance at each other through their crimson goggles for less than a second, and then they pull their guns.

We can't run. Sometimes there's just no way to be careful enough.

"The Christ is this?"

None of us makes a sound. None of us moves.

"APOTHECARY," Reel 4 of 7, 8mm, 16fps

The City pharmacy near Antrum has been shuttered. Citizens line up near the window, holding their little slips of paper, coughing, sponging away sweat from fevers, glancing toward home as they wait for some explanation.

Soon we see a crew of Blackbands, asking the crowd to disperse. One of them places a notice on the shutter. A few of the citizens argue with the Bands, but they know better than to seriously interfere.

When the crowd has gone, the camera moves close to the notice, close enough that we can read the small type. "This location will remain closed for maintenance."

The cameraman reaches out with a pen and scribbles, "...but only if you can pass screencheck."

. The camera then leads us around to the walk-up counter, close enough to see the faint residue of blood and bullet holes.

FIVE

"Sit on the floor."

The nearest Hector holds the tip of his S8 against my skull, and the other guy is pointing his at Reggie.

"Sit on the floor," he says again.

We sit. All of us, even Reggie. It's all we can do. We can't bolt now, not with them this close and nothing behind us but a long narrow hall. Not even Reggie could get to the corner before the bullets would catch up with him and he knows it.

Gibbsy is shivering. He's in a *panic*, probably because he still has all the gear on his back.

I should have known this would happen, that they

would never leave this place empty for as long as we've been here. I'm so goddamn mad at the Barkers right now, for sending us here and not telling us where we would be going.

For awhile the Hectors don't say anything else. They kick our pockets checking for weapons. They take Gibbsy's pack, they feel the weight and Cassandra's edges through the canvas, and they set it next to the stairs. They whisper about it, but they don't open it yet.

"The hell's in the pack?" says the old Hector. His name patch says Lt. Feisner, and I'm guessing he's in charge since the other guy is following his lead.

I point at the pack with my toe, and I say, "Just a bunch of cans is all. Found 'em in a trash bin, thought we might be able to sell 'em as scrap."

"How old are you?" says Feisner.

"Seventeen. I know it's past curfew, but we're just trying to scavenge some money is all. Things at home are getting worse, and we got kinda lost. All these doors were just open, and…"

When I say that, Feisner jerks his chin to look square at me. "You know something about all this?" He puts the S8 closer to my left ear. "How long you been down here?" he says. "When'd you get into the docks?"

"Just taking scrap, that's all."

The other guy, Cpl. Dunning, he kicks at the backpack again. He opens it, looks inside, and closes it again without saying anything about it. They don't care what story we give.

The lieutenant says, "Doesn't matter. You're Captain Grovesner's problem now. Like he needs another. Come on, get up and walk."

Christ. He's taking us to the Blackbands, and we're never coming back.

*

One thing they tell you in high school is how "now is the time to plan for your future." As if there's a livable future waiting for any of us. Someday we'll be grown-ups with children of our own living down here with the dripping pipes and the rattling grates and the constant slithering hiss of steam and stale air, and we'll be starving and so will they.

You'd have to be damn mad at the City in the first place to do what we do. You'd have to be willing to be caught. Life in Fallback is no life at all. You're either invisible and numb, or notched and antsy. We want this to be a better place and if it isn't going to be a better place, why does it matter if we're locked away for the rest of our lives? Would that be any worse?

*

Feisner is behind us fiddling with a spec radio while we cross the docks. We climb two flights and ease into an arched corridor on the far side of it.

"Dawson for hell's sake." All he gets is static from the other end.

Dunning says, "That ain't where we need to be..." But he doesn't even finish because it's obvious that Feisner isn't paying attention to him.

For awhile Feisner just keeps chewing on that radio, trying to get a response from different folks. Nobody ever responds, and he's starting to get loud, the more frustrated he gets.

For Hectors, both of these guys are as nervous as hell, and it reminds me that they're just people like the rest of us. Just doing a job.

I try to chat with Dunning like he's an old pal. "That an S8? What's that beast sound like when it goes off? I hear they're not that loud. You ever shoot someone with that?"

He ignores me and talks to Feisner instead. "What channel is Parker on?"

"He's on this channel. Losing it here."

I keep messing around, "Does it kick a lot? Like, you ever have it bruise your face or anything?"

Dunning looks over his shoulder for half a second and says, "No, these are really smooth. You'd never know." Then he goes back to ignoring me and talking to Feisner about the radio.

*

I'm still glad I didn't take that gun from Rake when I had the chance. Me and guns, we don't see eye to eye.

The Barkers carry Percivals sometimes. Not because they're effective but because they're loud as a quake and they want people to know a shot's been fired if a shot's been fired. Jiggers, if they really mean business.

Whatever I've got to do with myself, I'll never need a gun. I just need to say what needs to be said and that's it. If I get kicked in the teeth for it, it's not because I failed. It's because I didn't fail. Nobody ever got kicked in the teeth for going unnoticed.

*

We wind through enough twists and turns that I lose track of the place. The Hectors know where they're going, and they don't stop. The strange thing is, none of the doors are actually locked. They don't need to be, this far into whatever division this is, but every time Dunning touches a handle, he pauses, FR peg at the ready, and he seems a sight upset by the fact that the door swings free without him needing to use it.

At one point we pass through a long room, cut in half by a thick slab of smudgy glass with a keypad and a door in the middle of the divider. The space on the other side of the glass looks to me like some kind of holding cell, with benches along the back wall. I'm thinking, well, this is where they're going to put us. Into that smudgy cell with those rusty benches. But they don't. Feisner just taps on the glass with the tip of his S8 and says, "See, that ain't right."

He tries his radio again. We keep moving, through another unlocked door and into a lit metal span and all I can think about is how far we are from WT now, and how far from home. We're in real trouble.

*

Maybe Mocap isn't the worst place for me. What else am I going to do with myself? Study law, like my old man? The City's idea of "law" is a joke.

At least I tried. What really tickles my chin is that they'll torch the footage. The footage is what's important. That, and my pals.

Anyway, they'll burn us until we're not sane anymore, so it doesn't matter.

*

We rest in a dingy floodcheck junction with six other hatchways leading in all directions. Metal grating covers the floors and ceilings, behind which run a few big steam and wire conduits. The Hectors stand in front of the sector 28 hatch, hands trembling, staring at the wheel.

Feisner thumbs his radio. "Dawson, come back. We're outside C-Tran, ready to seal-off 28. Dawson…"

Static.

"Some kind of disruption," he says. "Spec tubes are jammed. Got to be Blankface again, no question." This guy is really on edge. "Nothing from Mycroft, nothing from Llewelyn. I'm telling you." He keeps saying it over and over.

Corporal Dunning stays quiet. He seems more annoyed by the lieutenant than anything else. "No," he says, "you don't know for sure. Let's just go to the bunks."

He reminds me of a teacher I had last year, Sevier. The kind of guy who would be a lot happier if he never had to be around other people.

Feisner knocks against the hatch and waits. He tries the radio again and waits. "It's all wrong. Those dregs should be in screencheck. God almighty."

Dunning tries to calm him down. "He *said* not to go into C-Tran until we heard him say it's okay. We can't open that hatch. We gotta get these kids to Grovesner and then we can come back here."

They keep arguing about it while the four of us lean against the walls. They say a lot of things that don't make sense to me. Hector jargon. All I know for sure is that something terrible is happening here. I'm wondering if it's the Barkers. Maybe they put us into the mix as some kind of distraction while they pull a bigger job. But it's not like the Barkers. They're just not that sophisticated. I don't think they could cause as much trouble as whatever it is that has put these Hectors in the oil.

All the while my pals are quiet and wide-eyed.

Gibbsy looks a little sad, which isn't any surprise, and Pop looks as blank as ever. Reggie is tapping one of the other hatchways, looking like he's ready to bolt again, but I can see he's too afraid to try the wheel. It'd make enough sound, even these ripplers would hear it over the quarrel.

Dunning points at us. "We should've taken them up to the bunks first."

Feisner shakes his head. He says, "Could be that's no safer. Could be right *here's* no safer. They've gotta follow us and *close*, or no way to know what'll happen. And we've gotta find Dawson. We're opening this hatch. Take it as an order if you want."

*

I'm trying to look calm, but I'm a wreck, wondering what I'm going to do about all of this. I've had some close calls before. Nothing like the trouble we're in now, but close. The Bands almost nabbed Reggie and me just a few months ago. Some undercovers showed up at a Reel screening. We were lucky, and we got out, but some of our pals didn't.

I don't think we'll have the same luck tonight.

*

Feisner spins the hatch wheel. Gears hiss, sucking the metal disc inward and to the side.

The screencheck cage is empty and open, and so is the booth. The smell of lilacs swirls into the junction. That's the thing I hate about screencheck: the perfume in the air. It's like they want you to forget you're under a microscope, waiting in that cage while the Bands stare at you through their thick glass. All on account of keeping the Bands from having to smell too much of the rabble, I guess.

This screencheck is like any other, but it's on the small side, and the fact that it's empty and open makes me nervous. I've never seen an empty screencheck.

"Sit over there," says Feisner. He's pointing to a couple of metal chairs. "You kids'll be alright, I promise you that, but just sit over there."

He and Dunning go sneaking toward the guard booth calling, "Dawson? Dawson." They open the booth's door, stoop, and lean to the side like they're looking at the floor under the desk. Whatever they see, it makes them both stagger away from the door again. The mesh on Feisner's mouth filter starts beating like a drum. He must be breathing damn fast. "The hell..."

"What, oh god, what..." says Dunning.

They stand there awhile, practically shivering.

Poplar leans into me. "Tommy," she says. That's all. Just my name.

None of us knows what to say, and the Hectors aren't moving much either. Just staring and clenching their fists. But it doesn't stay quiet long.

Somewhere past screencheck, along that twisting hall, someone is singing. It sounds like gibberish, like something operatic, but I don't think it's Italian or any other real language. It just sounds wrong, somehow. Rotten. And whoever it is, he's getting closer. We can't see anyone from here, but we can tell he's walking in this direction, slowly, unevenly, like he's swaying.

"Stay in that cage," says Feisner. He watches until I nod.

The Hectors edge to the back of the room and peer into the hall.

"You with Quarantine?" shouts Feisner.

The singing grows louder and doesn't pause for an answer. "Clavitorio esta esta dole trompe."

Feisner and Dunning ready their S8s and step into the hall. We can't see them anymore.

Feisner says something to the singing man again, but he just sings louder and louder. They shout at him, and he just gets louder. "Maestra caliph loom, caliph loom!"

Then they start shooting.

A million little chirps flock out from the S8s so fast I can't tell one shot from the last ten. The singing man must have a gun too, something louder and slower, and the reports beat against my eardrums as he returns fire. Now and then a bullet traipses through the room we're in, and I can hear the buzzing wake as it punctures the wall. Dust starts to sift out from the hall. Plaster falls in big sheets and shatters on the tile. The singing becomes screaming, and the man runs away from screencheck, firing as he goes. A clatter of footsteps fades.

White clouds of plaster billow into the room, and I can almost hear the dust in the air because there is no other sound.

We watch the hall, breathing plaster for a long goddamn time. The dust starts to settle, and we can see blood, sprayed faintly over the wall. We should leave. We should get away from the Hectors before they come back to the cage. I don't even know if they're both still alive, but someone is moving in that hall. Dragging over the tile toward screencheck. I don't know what to make of any of this.

"Gibbsy. Reg. Pop. Come on."

We all move to the back of the cage, and I spin the wheel on the hatchway. The hiss is so loud, I jerk my hand away as it opens. I'm ready to rally for friendly turf, but something awful occurs to me.

"Wait, I have to get the bag."

I can see Gibbsy's pack from here. Dunning dropped it near the booth, before the gunfight, and it's fifteen feet away, is all. It wouldn't take long.

"No, Tommy," says Pop. She grabs my sleeve.

"What? Christ, Pop. Film's in there."

"Leave it there," says Pop. "Tommy, those guys might be dead, and someone's coming, so let's just go home and forget it. Please."

But we need the bag. The camera, the reels.

"They're not dead, they just…chased somebody off. It's fine, Pop. It's fine."

It would be easy enough to run over there, grab the bag, and leave. We stand, quiet for a second or two, everybody thinking about the same thing.

"The pegs." My stomach turns. "We can't get out of here without those."

"*None* of these doors are locked."

"None of these, but the door at WT was locked. Remember?" It's a fact. We'd be trapped there if we left now. I've got to get the bag. The dragging sound is closer. We need the pegs, and the sooner I dash for it, the better.

"I'll be quick," I tell Poplar. "Stay. Just stay there."

I shove the cage gate. Crossing the tile floor, I can see further into the hall. Just the first bit of it. It's dark, and a few of the overheads spark from being hit by the gunfire. The floor is thick with plaster and blood. Blood is splotched over the walls too. I'm not about to stick my head out for a better view.

I reach for the bag, stand up, and I start to turn when my eyes catch sight of the guard booth floor.

The corpse of a Blackband is crammed under the desk, crumpled like a marionette in the corner, dead and broken. He looks like a child, lying there. Everything about him that might have made him an asshole or a moron or a feeb—it's gone now, and all that's left is a man who knew what rain smelled like, once upon a time. His blood is starting to film-over and dry at the edges. So that's what Feisner and Dunning had seen. That's what knocked all the wind out of them.

For whatever reason, seeing that body reminds me to be angry again.

*

I start to pull Cassandra out of the bag. I need to get this on the eights, the whole bloody scene. My pals are all waving for me to hurry up, but this has got to be filmed, this mangled man, these pools of blood, and whatever's left of the Hectors in the hall. I can't walk away from something like that. There's a whole city of people out there who would never know of the horrible things happening tonight, here in a part of Fallback no one ever sees. It's just not something the City would put on the feeds. But Cassandra will tell them what she has seen, and then they'll have to believe.

I haven't cranked more than a few frames when I notice someone standing next to me. I reel back, almost hitting the wall. It's Dunning. His arm is bleeding, and the sleeve is torn. His neck is bleeding too, with a red line all the way around like he's been strangled. At first, I think he's going to shoot me, but he just shoves me out of the way.

"You okay?"

"Out of the room," he says. "I'm sealing 28."

He steps into the guard booth without even a glance at the camera. He clears the control panel and wipes it with his gloved hand.

"What happened?'

"Nothing. The lieutenant, he'll take care of it."

"No, what *happened*? That doesn't explain anything."

"It doesn't need to," he says, and he's not even getting upset, which is weird considering I'm practically yelling at the guy. It strikes me, maybe I should take a better look at that hall, but the second my feet turn in that direction Dunning says, "Don't go over there. That's none of your business. Just get in the cage. I'm sealing this place."

He points at the control board and with the tip of his gun taps the floodcheck switch. "You don't wanna be locked in here."

"Wait, what about him?"

But Dunning pulls the lever anyway, and the redbells start to flash. "Go, go, go," he says, jogging out of the booth. He practically shoves me into the cage, and I shove Gibbsy and Poplar out through the hatch in front of me, into the junction, with Corporal Dunning and his S8 right behind us.

The hatch shuts, nearly pinching Dunning in half. But he makes it through, and another redbell starts to flash overhead.

"Christ. You coulda hit the floodchecks from out here."

Poplar's hand is on my shoulder like she's afraid the Hector is going to hit me for mouthing off. But he doesn't. He just says, "Yeah. Well, just sit down a minute. Sit down and wait. And gimme that pack 'till Grovesner comes to see about the bells, wherever the hell he is."

I put Cassandra back to sleep, and Dunning takes the bag and slings it over his shoulder. It doesn't matter. All I can think is, what's so important that he would have to seal off a whole sector for it? My mind keeps shifting back to the Barkers and the fact that they put us here for their own goddamn reasons and not ours.

I feel like I'm going to pass out. But at least we're still alive.

*

Corporal Dunning sits with his head on his knees, tapping the muzzle of his S8 against the junction grating, watching us all from the opposite side of the room. He has taken off his filter and goggles, which dangle by the straps from his free hand. From what I can see of his face, he's a pretty young guy. Only a year or two older than us, and I start wondering if we went to school at the same time. His skin is as pale as a stone, and his eyes are glass, staring through us and out through the metal walls, out of the City and through the ice and through the festering air.

Gibbsy asks what happened. He's dazed too.

"I don't know," I tell him. We're whispering as best we can. "Someone…I don't know what happened."

"Why'd they start *shoot*ing," says Gibbsy and I tell him again that I have no idea and to stop asking.

We sit there for half an hour. We're breathing normally now. We're glad we weren't in that hall with the singing man, and we're glad we're not on the other side of that hatch.

No one has said much, except Poplar who keeps pacing across the junction with no regard for how edgy Dunning is. Every time she gets too close to him the S8 comes up and hovers until she paces away again. And Pop, she keeps asking how everyone is doing, or talking about the way the steam pipes hum.

"Maybe," she says, "…a few cartwheels would pass the time."

I tell her to sit with me, and I pat the grating.

"If I keep doing what you tell me to do I'll end up with a reputation."

I'm still trying to cope with seeing that Blackband. I've seen dead men before but never that much blood. I don't think I'd have gotten used to it even if I had.

Now and then Reggie whispers in my ear, telling me we should rush at Dunning while he's not paying attention, beat the hell out of him, and take the pack. But I'm not about to do that, and neither is he. Dunning is a Hector, for Christ's sake. None of us wants to be shot.

That aside I think everyone has calmed down some, and that's a good thing. I'm sure my pals are worried about whatever's coming next, and I'm sure Dunning is anxious in his own way. But at least nobody's shooting at us. In that respect, I guess we're at peace.

Sitting here looking at him, I can't shake the notion that I've seen Dunning somewhere before. Maybe he grew up in H just like me.

"You okay soldier?"

He lifts his eyes, just a sliver. "Huh?"

"You okay?"

"Did you call me 'soldier?'"

"Sorry, I can be a bastard sometimes. But I mean it, are you okay?"

"Yeah, I'm okay," he says.

I glance at Poplar, and sure enough, she's watching me. One eye wider than the other. I ask the Hector, "Do you wanna know why we're really here?" He shrugs. "We came down here to film the *Pro*cessing plants. See that guy, that's Gibbsy. You can't tell anymore, but he's had hives all day because his lunch, just this bowl of rice, had fish in it somehow and he's allergic."

Dunning acts like he's not even listening. He doesn't even look at me.

"Gibbsy there, they give him this special diet, see. He has to have a form filled out every month from the doctor. But a couple of times now his 'special diet' hasn't been so special, and the first time it put him in the hospital. We came down here to film Processing and to show how it's not sanitary even though the City keeps saying it *is*."

"Processing?" says Dunning.

"Yeah, that's the whole problem. We meant to go there but stumbled in here like a bunch of strays." I should tell him about the Barkers, but I'm not sure it's a good idea yet, to tell a Hector we were even involved with those clowns.

"Stumbled," he says. "You know something about this place?"

"No, that's what I'm saying. We don't even know why we're here…but it sounds like somebody else is here too."

Dunning takes two long scoffing breaths and shakes the tip of his gun in the air. "You don't know, do you? Well...sounds to me like you know more about this than I do. How'd you trip the locks? You do something to 'em? Or the spec tubes?"

"What?"

"Never mind," he says. His voice twitches, careful, dusty, the last splinters of an old bench. Listening to this guy, my chest feels like a broken bell. He's needled, and I can't say I'd blame him, but he's saying a lot of things that don't make sense to me as if I should know what they mean.

"Look, trigger, we didn't do anything but trip on our own shoelaces. Whatever's going on, there's somebody else *here*. We just wandered into it is all."

"There's nobody else here," he says.

"I mean, we saw that dead Band. Whoever killed that guy, that's who you should be talking to, not us. If you ask me, they set us up as tin crickets. A bunch of dummies making a lot of noise is all."

"There's nobody here but the four of you. Don't go telling me somebody else is here unless you can tell me why and where and what the hell's in C-Tran. Nah. You don't know."

"Nobody here? We heard that guy in the hall. We didn't imagine that. You're talking about shorted locks and then all the sudden you're saying we're the only ones here that shouldn't be?"

For a minute Dunning just stares at me, then his eyes drift to the side, and a tired smirk does its best and fails. "They were already here," he says.

"What, locked up?" I ask him. "What's C-Tran, a prison ward or something? You're goddamn right, I don't know. I don't know anything. I'm just a dumb kid, right? I don't know what's going on and, Christ, nobody's telling me anything, so what does it matter?"

I half expect the guy to stand up, walk over here, and hit me for being obnoxious. Hell, I'd hit me if I were him. But he doesn't hit me. He just shakes his head.

"That's how it is," he says. "They point and don't say a word and when you jump you do it with your eyes shut. Hell of a City. Okay. You're just a stupid bunch of schoolers is all. But this isn't any kind of night to be wandering into the middle of things."

"I know. Believe me. But…into the middle of what?"

"Yeah, well. They haven't told us yet," he says. "And

what I do know, I just can't tell it to you. The Herds are guiding the sheep, so you've got that going for you. But my guess is you'll talk to Mycroft before the night's done. If he wants to tell you anything, he'll tell you. And if I were you," he says, pointing his gun at my face without looking at me, "I'd make sure I had a little less personality when I met him. Mycroft's not the kind of guy you want noticing you, if you know what I mean."

I ask Dunning if he ever went to Chalcenor High School. He says he doesn't remember.

*

These last bunch of weeks, ever since Lewiston talked about it in class, I've been thinking about Hydroponics a lot. About the arbors. I've never seen them, but I can picture them. Huge rooms, filled with trees. Huge rooms filled with crops.

I heard someone say that if you're in those arbors, you'll see birds flying around. Not those ragged pets, either, but wild birds. Sparrows and blue jays and such. Someone thought to raise songbirds, here a thousand feet under, and let them have the run of the treetops. What use that is I don't know. It's not like they can chase down the tin crickets for a meal. But from what I hear, those birds are doing just fine. It goes to show, there's real genius at work in this city. Things we didn't intend.

But it doesn't matter what you intend. It doesn't even really matter what you actually do. What matters is what you refuse to do. The problem with Fallback isn't that it's short on genius, it's that even brilliant men can fail at this.

You have to know what your job means. You have to know what'll happen when you do it. And when the City tells you to do something that might make a kid like Gibbsy sick, or get a few Hectors killed in a hall, you have to be brilliant enough to tell the City "no," even if it means getting kicked in the teeth.

If you ask me, there's no excuse for failing at that. Not for them and not for us. And if you ask me, those birds know they're in a cage.

*

I don't know how long it's been. Maybe forty-five minutes, now. The footsteps come marching toward the junction. In here, with the echoes and thick steel, it's almost impossible to tell which hatch these boots are behind until a dull click sounds and one of them opens.

A dozen Blackbands crash into the junction, guns in hand. They seem godawful surprised to see us. Dunning stands and tells the main guy, the squad leader, where he found us and to take us to Grovesner. "Oh. And your boy in 28 is dead."

"Shit. You sure?"

"Yeah," says Dunning, unfazed.

"That was, uh…"

"Dawson," says Dunning. "Dawson."

"Right."

Dunning doesn't say much about us, but it doesn't matter. The Bands tell us to spread out. "Lie on the floor, hands back." We do as we're told.

Dunning stands against the wall and says, "Where's

the boss got his nest at?"

"Triage," says the SQ, pointing to the open hatch. "Not far."

"Things okay there? The locks in 32? I hate to ask but Mycroft's not telling us anything, and I don't even know what these good old boys in C-Tran want."

"Neither do I," says the SQ. "You're asking the wrong fella. Admin locks are okay, sure. Fine for now. But we can't raise anybody in 28, so we don't *know* what's what."

"Same here. Hell."

"Can't raise anybody *anywhere* on these," says the SQ. "We been using the switchboard." He lifts a spec radio. "Grovesner?" More of that delirious static. No response. "See what I mean? It's been like that for, god…are you bleeding?"

"Yeah."

"The Doctor, he's in there with Mycroft. He'll sew that up nice'n clean if you'll come along and let him do it."

But Dunning slaps the guy's arm away. "I'm not going anywhere near Mycroft."

"What?"

Dunning puts his goggles on and says, "I've gotta check with Richie's crew in Quarantine. I just wanted to hand off these kids off to somebody is all. This is fine, it'll stop bleeding, but if you see the Colonel tell him we need more guys if he can spare 'em."

"Hell, you can take a few of mine," says the SQ. "Theo, Steph…"

"Nuh uh," says Dunning. "Not your guys. You don't wanna be a part of this, and we don't want city flats along for what we've gotta do. Just get word to the Colonel."

The SQ shifts his weight. I've heard there's not much love lost between the Bands and the Hectors, but this guy holds his tongue. "Fine with me," he says. "Just…watch for the Herds tonight, okay?"

Dunning nods, gives Gibbsy's pack to the SQ, and leaves.

"THE FUNERAL," Reel 1 of 1, 8mm, 16fps

Nine men wearing dark suits pass into Donovan Square each dangling a chain of incense. They chant some old chant and stand on the bandstand behind the ropes where the tables have been moved away.

Four other men in dark suits follow through the same colonnade, carrying a very small casket made from an old chifforobe.

A marching band joins them from the opposite side of the square playing a brass tune. They play for ten minutes before the PA scratches away their music.

Marion Ventley herself comes to stand on the central balcony, having been interrupted during some meeting of the City Council. She tells the people to go home. The Blackbands issue out toward the bandstands both left and right and begin to usher the men and the players away.

The pallbearers leave Donovan Square first. The others follow except for one. He meanders toward the corridor, doubles back and shouts, "This is the funeral procession for General Carson Archibald! He was the finest German Sheppard ever to walk on four paws. Follow along and pay your respects."

The man hurries away after the casket. Marion Ventley has by then left the rail, but the Blackbands stand in rows in the square.

If anyone in the crowd dares laugh about what has just happened, it is a muffled, sleeve-covered laugh and doesn't last long.

SIX

The Blackbands march us past empty offices and jittery light bulbs. They don't talk to us, and we don't talk to them. Blackbands never talk to you when they're taking you someplace. They just take you there, and someone else comes and talks to you after you've had a while to think about things. One thing I notice--the FR locks are working just fine in this sector, whatever sector it is. Or division. I really don't know where we are. But the locks are definitely working here.

The Bands leave us in a mess hall, and they bar the doors. This is no prison cafeteria. It's just a regular mess hall, for regular folks, and the Blackbands have taken it over for some reason. I'm still plenty worried. But after

C-Tran I'm not as damn worried as I should be.

The back of the room is divided by a long lunch counter and a shallow kitchen. We've been waiting here long enough, all four of us have gotten our cuffed hands down around our legs and in front again, so we don't have to walk around like cripples. Now we're sitting at the counter on stools.

Through the mirror behind the soda fountains, Poplar is staring at me.

"Bet you wish you were at home right now watching Kennedy talk about how great life is."

She shrugs.

"Well, we can thank Reggie and his pals for such a fine evening." I pretend to give a regal bow. She dips, atop her stool, as if to curtsy. I say, "You don't think so?"

"I don't know, Tommy."

"What else could this be about?"

"I don't know," she says. "It's best not to guess unless you want to be wrong most of the time."

"Not most of the time."

"Like today when you broke into my school," she says. She laughs. "When you ran into Mr. Hadley, you thought he was sneaking out because he 'hates the City.'"

"Middle of a Bullet…"

"He was going out for a smoke, that's all. Everybody knows, and nobody cares. He's a good guy."

"He let me go because he was afraid of getting caught."

Poplar shakes her head which means I should stop talking now. Whenever you've got a gorgeous girl like her, toying with a chittering fool like me, the best thing is to stop talking. She stands up, kisses my forehead, and says, "What's a girl gotta do around here to get a bite to eat?"

For a second or two, I forget where I am. I'm just thinking about that kiss. I know this is no time to joke around, but the next thing I do is vault the counter and find a pan and pretend to cook something. "What'll it be Mac? Come on and order already."

Poplar's the only one who *does* order. "I'll have a pancake," she says.

A pancake. That's the Kennel for you. Everyone ordering *a* pancake. One.

"How 'bout a short-stack, toots. Comin' right up."

Reggie tells me to shut up. I ignore him.

"What about you, long face, you wanna roast beef sandwich? Eh? I make the best in ten counties. Fella uppa Syracuse says no, he makes the best roast beef, but you know how he cooks the friggin stuff? Boils it! Roast beef and here's this guy boilin' the whole roast like he never heard of an oven."

I don't think I'll get a laugh out of Gibbsy but at least Poplar's playing along. "Can't boil a roast," she says in an old accent from some movie.

"Had a guy come up for a sandwich every Tuesday from Allentown, that's how good they are. Aw, hell, we're out of roast beef. Short stack?"

Gibbsy laughs. I find a service bell, and I ring it, the

way they do when a dish is ready. "Shovel it down while the steam's still on it."

Poplar smiles at me and winks. "Ring the bell again Mac, it's a beautiful sound." I've never seen that sort of smile on her before, and I just hope I see it again some time.

After a few seconds, I realize I'm staring, and I start to panic, and I say, "You have to admit it, Pop, even though we're probably going to die you'd rather be here with me than out with Dale Pike."

And she looks away and says, "I'm not arguing."

*

Back in those early days, when I first started bugging Gibbsy to come along on shoots with me, he kept finding reasons not to. I told him we'd start easy, let him get a feel for the eights. But he always had family things to do or too much homework or whatever. He'd seen enough Reels by then to know what was what

Then one day out of nowhere he said he had an idea for a Riot Reel. I said, "Good. You gonna help film it?"

And he said yes, he would.

He told me about that playground in Rabbish Court. He'd passed the place once or twice on his way home and seen the woman there. The one who carried the umbrella for some goddamn reason and kept sprucing-up the place. He said it was nice to see somebody making this a better world to live in instead of just ignoring the rust.

I couldn't argue, but at the time I told Gibbsy he was missing the point. I told him I wondered what the Blackbands would do if they found that woman there cleaning the place like she did, after curfew when it wasn't even her job in the first place. I figured they'd ask for her papers and they'd take her away someplace dark.

We shot the Reel anyway. Gibbsy hid the camera by one of the storefronts, and we hid ourselves up on one of those catwalks. Not bad footage, really.

But a few weeks later the batty old gal turned up missing. Gibbsy actually found her umbrella under the swings, broken in half from being stepped on.

He thought it was my fault. Gibbsy wouldn't talk to me for awhile. I kept trying to tell him I had nothing to do with that. That I didn't tip off the Bands. It was just her time to be caught, I told him. It was just a coincidence. Finally, I think he believed me.

I think Gibbsy still has that umbrella somewhere. By now the rust has probably reclaimed the playground. It tends to do that.

*

We're sitting on the floor again not saying anything. Just staring at the cafeteria ceiling. Dust is clumped thick atop the light fixtures. The tiles up there are water damaged. Mildewed.

After a while, a couple of Blackbands hold the doors and in comes the captain himself. He's wearing exactly the same uniform as the other Blackbands, but he *walks* like a captain, and that's all I need to know. His patch says "Grovesner."

Grovesner drags a chair from one of the tables and sits in front of us. He's an average looking guy. He's not too tall, and he's slim, but he looks like the kind of guy that if he hits you, it'll hurt. "How'd a buncha schoolers get into the docks?" he says.

I'm already notched-up, and the fact that he's asking *that* question makes me even more notched-up. I ask him, "How'd a guy like you get to be in charge of public *safety* when he doesn't care a guy or two were murdered an hour ago?"

Grovesner doesn't flinch. He leans close. "The Hectors," he says, glancing at his men. "Did you talk to them? What were they doing in C-Tran?" He keeps his voice low and looks back a few more times at his men. They're still at the door but leaning forward like they're trying to hear.

"They didn't say why. Your guys talked to Dunning. How come *you* don't know why? Why you asking us?"

"Did they say anything at all?" asks Grovesner. "Anything you maybe didn't understand. Anything you could tell me about what the Hectors were doing?"

I think about it and decide a smart-ass answer isn't necessary. "They just couldn't get anybody on the radio is all."

Grovesner shrugs. This is no news to him. He's got a

poker face, that's for sure. I've known guys like him, holding cards you didn't even know were in the deck, staring at you, waiting for you to say too much so they can turn what you know into whatever they want, lay down the hand and take the money.

"We'll talk about the S-O-B Hectors later," he says. "So, how did a bunch of riot punk schoolers like you get into the Docks? And do you know what will happen to you now that you did?"

His tone scares me. Like he's trying to imply a lot more than he's saying. But I don't care. I tell him everything. No excuses. I tell him about Gibbsy's hives and how this City doesn't care a wink about the people who actually make it a city. I tell him about Processing, and that if the City doesn't regulate itself, someone else has to, and how there should be riots in the corridors of Fallback. I tell him about the Barkers, about Sticks and Rake. I tell him I don't care about spending time in Mocap because someone else like me will find out what I found out and there'd be no stopping it from spreading to every ear in the city. I even tell him my name, just my first name, so we can talk like civilized people.

Grovesner doesn't flinch. He just sits there listening.

"Alright," he says. "That…matches up with what we already know, so I'm going to believe it. Except you're not going to Mocap. We can't even let you leave this room."

He walks away, and they shut the doors again.

*

My parents are too young to remember much of anything before the Spanish Flu. My dad remembers being in hiding somewhere in Louisiana when he heard about what was going on in Zanzibar and Dar es Salaam. My mother doesn't even remember that. They both remember coming here, though.

My dad told me once about being on the ship, headed for Fallback, with so many people on board he could barely move. Some people couldn't even go below deck when the cold air hit. There just wasn't room, and they had to wait up there in the icy wind. A lot of people died, I guess, on the edge of the crowd. My dad saw somebody frozen to the ship's rail. A boy, not much older than he was.

*

Gibbsy has gone pale and mute. He doesn't say anything. Reggie, he's just the opposite. He's red as a shell and sweating under the eyes, muttering. I can tell they're both thinking the same thing, though, that they wish they'd seen this coming and stayed home and gone back to school in the morning, invisible like everybody else. I don't care.

Grovesner comes back every ten minutes or so with another question. "Which one of you painted the tag?" or "Which *junction* did you come through?" or "What was his real name? The Barker who gave you the map. The Machinist." That's it, just the one question and we answer it as best we can, and he leaves. Probably to watch our footage again. It's enough to make a guy bust some valves.

He asks how we knew about the Drowner dock and I lay into him. "We *didn't* know. *You* told us it sank. It was a hell of a surprise to see it after hearing everyone on board died in some kind of implosion. So, where are *they*?"

He says, "I told you..."

"Yes, you did. The City did. The feeds. The feeds and the City and Kennedy himself and there's no difference between those things and you as a person, because you as a person let *those* things exist. You can't blame it on anyone else."

"I can't," he says. Not a question.

"How many *bruises* have you left on joes who never left a bruise on *you*? Isn't civil *dis*obedience much better than *un*civil obedience? Don't answer like a Blackband, just answer like a regular guy..."

He says, "Civil disobedience," and stares at me. "Doesn't that mean you have to stop being a burden?"

"I'm not a burden."

"You breathe city air," he says. "That isn't free. You have light and heat. Those aren't free either, but you keep using them up, same as everybody else."

I've heard this argument before. Teachers, Blackbands, even my parents. Everyone who ever felt apologetic for having a *job*, they always say how nothing's free in Fallback. I get that. But I didn't ask to be born in Fallback. I didn't ask to be part of this city. And if I try to leave, they won't let me. If Fallback is more like a prison, I only have one question. What was our crime? Being born?

"And you burden *me*," says Grovesner, standing to leave again. "Because of you, I'm going to have to shoot four children tonight, and that's something a man never wants to do. But I'll do it. I grew up a long time ago."

*

Reggie and I once saw a couple of Blackbands beat a fifteen-year-old kid half to hell, behind the Antrum gage clusters. All on account of him being a flit. The kid kept reaching up, not to fight back or anything, but to try and grab hold of something so that he could turn over and let them hit the other side of him for a change.

We tracked that kid down the next day and asked if we could get some film of his bruises and cuts. He said yes, and he joked, "but I sure wish you had that camera with you last night."

"We did," I told him. "Got the whole thing." It was true. We'd been out filming graffiti in Antrum, and so we kept rolling when the beating started.

The kid looked up at me and said, "Why didn't you *do* something?" I was surprised to hear him say it.

Do something. Like what? Go fight the Blackbands off of him? No, we *were* doing something. That *Riot* Reel hit harder than we could ever hit with our fists.

*

The next time Grovesner comes into the room, he brings another Blackband with him, and this other guy has a notepad. He's following close, which from the looks of it is making Grovesner nervous.

Grovesner says, "Try to remember everything the Hectors said. Just spout it out, anything you can think of. Every word. Even if it doesn't mean anything."

I don't know what else to say, other than how they kept trying to call Dawson. I just keep saying that and I throw in smart-ass things too, like about Dunning telling the Lieutenant he had pretty shoes. The other Blackband writes it all down anyway. It's not that I don't want to help, it's just I don't know why they're asking.

At first, I'm the only one talking but Gibbsy kicks-in with a few things too, and something he says makes Grovesner take a hard breath.

"They said 'Blankface?'"

"Something about all the radio static being Blankface's fault. That's all they said."

"The hell it is," says Grovesner.

He tries to look at the list, but the Blackband jerks it away from him and goes out of the room with it.

"Come here," he says, pointing at me. "You're the one making all the noise, so come here. I want to talk to you."

Jesus. When a Blackband wants to talk to you alone,

he usually doesn't say much. But what can I do? I go with him, around to the pantry. I keep one eye on his pistol, but it doesn't matter. If he wants to use it, he'll use it whether I'm watching or not.

"Something serious has happened here tonight. The Hectors won't say at all what it is. They don't talk to us. They don't think we're worth the air in their lungs. Us being city police."

"Yeah. I can tell."

"I know I said I would shoot you," he says, "but they don't really want me to do that. The Director wants a few words with you about all of this, so we're supposed to take you to him."

"Not much more we can say that we haven't said," I tell him. He nods.

"Do your friends listen to you, Tommy? If you knew you could…get out of here and make a run for it, they'd follow you, wouldn't they?"

"Yeah, they'd follow. All I have to do is whistle."

"Good," says Grovesner. "Good, Tommy. Well, I'm going out now, and when I come back, I want you to rush the door. Make a break."

I'm wondering how stupid he thinks I am. "You just want an excuse to shoot us."

"Yes," he says. "You won't get far. That's the point, and there's nothing I can do about that."

"If you want to shoot us, just shoot us." I'm on the verge of shaking so bad I'd lose my balance.

"I can't just *shoot* you," he says. "Mycroft would want to know why I didn't send you along to him like he asked. You've got to make a break for it. Put on a show for the boys in the hall there. You don't want to end up in Mycroft's hands, and this is the only way to avoid being put there."

"Being shot to death."

"It would be worse if you weren't," he says. "I'll come back in a few minutes."

*

I tell my pals about Grovesner's "suggestion" and they stare at me for awhile, in different ways.

"Wants to see if we've got the sand," says Reggie. "Hell, let's show 'em. Take a few under with us."

"With our hands?" I say.

It's just what I expect from Reggie. If he didn't have cuffs on and if these guys didn't have guns, I bet he'd be a little more diplomatic. That's just the way he is. He acts tough when he knows somebody will talk him out of it, but if anybody thinks he's got good odds in a scuffle, he all of a sudden doesn't want the scuffle.

I ask Gibbsy what he thinks, and he just says, "I don't know."

"What about you Pop?"

She sways her head, side to side, and says, "Sounds like a lot of effort for not much payoff."

Pop has a good point. We never leave a mark, that's the thing about us riot punks. It's what separates us from the Barkers. Barkers always leave a mark. They always break something. We never do, except a little paint, and the paint rubs off. That Drowner was left just like we found it. Everything we film is still fine and dandy afterward. We just shed some light on things and leave them be, and we let them die of natural causes.

"If they want things to get rough, they aren't getting any help from us. Anything rough happens it's their fault, not ours."

Reggie still doesn't agree with me. "Worse is coming."

"The Hectors aren't going to do anything either, Reg. It'll be more questions, then Mocap. Let 'em put us in Mocap if they want to be pricks."

But to be honest, I'm still thinking about the tone of Grovesner's voice when he said we would be better off shot. I'm prone to believe him. Dunning didn't have anything good to say about Mycroft either.

*

It's been longer than usual. Maybe twenty minutes. The lights flicker. We hear voices arguing in the hall.

Poplar leans close and puts her head against the wall next to me. She's shaking. She looks up at me and almost says something but stops herself for whatever reason and goes back to putting her head against the wall.

"My arm is a lot softer," I tell her, and she tilts toward my shoulder. "If you want me to think tonight was a bad idea, you're not doing a very good job of it."

She doesn't laugh. "Just…try not to get too mad about anything," she says.

When the Blackbands return we stand. I'm watching Reggie, but it's just like I thought: he doesn't rush the door. He stands still like the rest of us.

Grovesner has his hand on his gun, but he can see that we don't want to make it easy for him to use it. He says nothing and leads the way to wherever we're going next. And we follow.

The corridors are empty. Pipes hiss overhead. The airmovers whir. We pass a little room where one of the Blackbands is working a switchboard, talking to somebody on the phone. Grovesner stops there and says,

"Tell Mycroft we'll be along shortly. We don't want to get shot, do we, Tommy?"

The switchboard bloke quotes him exactly, even using my name like some sarcastic asshole. Grovesner lifts Gibbsy's pack from an old light table and shoves the reels back into it.

Part of me is wondering whether or not they ruined the film. Another part of me thinks we'll never find out. We walk, and nobody speaks.

The Blackbands stop outside a wide set of frosted glass doors. "Triage," it says. A couple of the Bands knock, and they all stand to the side like they're worried the door will blow.

Three tough-looking Hectors step out pointing S8s at the whole lot of us. They take a long look at our faces before they back off and lower the guns.

One of them calls back, "Affirmed," and a tall guy in a gray business suit comes marching out like he's ready to take a swing at someone. He's seventy or eighty but tough as a rivet. He doesn't even look at Grovesner, like he wants him to feel ignored. This must be Mycroft, then. You sure don't expect a suit and tie to be running around with all these Hectors.

"Who's got the bag?"

Grovesner hands it over. "Here they are and here it all is. Are we done?"

"You? You're done," says Mycroft.

*

Triage is filled with glass-front cells, at least two dozen little rooms, each with a metal chair with straps, pneumatic surgical posts, tanks of oxygen and carbon-dioxide. Everything is clean and sterile, but it makes my skin crawl anyway. All those sharp tools.

I'm more worried about Gibbsy. He tends to be fairly calm, even in tense situations, but right now he's sweating, and I keep thinking his knees will buckle.

"You okay?" I don't get an answer.

We file into what I'm going to call the Hectors' "command room." It must have been an admitting office once, but they've got a bunch of gear in here that doesn't belong. A couple of spec towers sputter on the table, not working any better than the other radios we've seen tonight. In the corner, a tech sits on the floor with a portable switchboard that has been patched into the office lines, with eight or nine telephones scattered around it. Every now and then one of the Hectors dials a couple of numbers and talks to somebody too fast and low for me to hear the words.

Mycroft tosses Gibbsy's bag into a drawer.

"You saw Lieutenant Feisner?" he says.

"Yeah."

"C-Tran," he says. He turns to the guy behind him, a crooked Hector with a ruinous slouch. "C-Tran," Mycroft says again. "This is Colonel Virgil. He's in charge here. You were in C-Tran."

"Yeah," I say. "Something...I don't know."

"We know," he says. He turns to the Colonel. "Don't we?" Then back to me. "We know."

"Feisner. And Dunning."

"Dunning." Christ, I hate the way he's talking to me. Like he's trying to get me to fill in the blanks or something, without saying what he means.

Mycroft stares at me. I let him stare. Maybe he's no Blackband. Maybe he's no Hector, but I get the feeling he's worse. Like he has no interest in stomping on my throat--he just wants to tear it out.

"We told Grovesner everything we know…so what do you want to know? Who we go to school with? Do you want us to take you to where we got those pegs and the map? What?"

Mycroft straightens his tie. "Like you said, you already told Grovesner. Are you hungry? These are peppermint."

He opens a small envelope under my chin. It's filled with black lozenges that don't smell anything like peppermint. They smell like oil. I know chalk opium when I see it. "I'm not going to eat those, they'll put me in a goddamn coma."

Mycroft tilts his head and says to the Hectors, "Let me see his teeth."

A couple of them pin my arms and a third puts me in a headlock. He pries my lips open, and Mycroft squints at my mouth for a couple of seconds before letting me speak.

I tell him, "I'm no chalkie. I don't even smoke, for god's sake." The way these guys are holding me, my shoulder is wrenched. But they don't let go.

"How about one of these?" says Mycroft. He digs another little envelope out of his pocket. I can't see what's in it. "Open his mouth," he says.

The guy who has me in the headlock uses his free hand to squeeze at the hinges of my jaw. His hand is like a clamp and as much as I want to keep my mouth shut, I can't. Whatever Mycroft is holding, he pushes it past my teeth, and the Hector covers my mouth so I can't spit it out.

At first, all I can taste is the chalkiness, and I think I'm going to pass out. But then the flavor of it reaches my tongue, and I know it's just peppermint this time. The Hectors drop me to the floor.

Mycroft, the deranged son of a bitch, is smiling at me and patting my shoulder. "Why struggle? Those taste much better, don't they?"

*

Mycroft's men cram the four of us into one little glass observation room at the mouth of a dead-end spur hall, just off the admitting office. Five cells just like it line the hall on either side, every inch flooded with clean light.

I'm looking at some of the heavier medical equipment thinking I could break the glass with something, but I doubt it. Plus, we would have no place to go even if I could bust through. The only exit from this hall is back the way we came, past all those Hectors.

"Gibbsy, you got any ideas?"

He looks at the cell and shrugs. "I don't think it'll break," he says, knocking on the glass. His fist stops mid-knock, and his face gets close to the surface.

"What are you looking at?" I ask, but then I see it too.

A man sits in the cell across from ours, unconscious in the surgical chair. The instruments have been removed from that room. So have the table and the chart-recorder and the IV drip. Compared to our cell his is empty. Just him and the chair. And the blood that is trickling from his mouth.

"Happened to him?" says Reggie.

I can't tell, exactly. The blood is dripping very slowly, and some of it is old and dry and has stained his shirt-collar black. I would think he was a corpse, but he is definitely breathing.

"Hectors beat him to hell," says Reggie. "Jaw's all swollen up."

He's right. They must have hit him hard plenty of times with a heavy pipe, to make something like that happen. His arm is broken too.

*

A doctor comes to watch us through the glass briefly and leaves again. His badge says, "Dr. Rothschild." He's not terribly old, and he's wearing a close-fitting white eight-button surgical coat with a mask over his mouth. He looks familiar to me.

We can't hear anything through the glass, but the doctor eventually comes back, this time to look at the unconscious man in the other cell. Except he isn't unconscious anymore.

When Rothschild walks away the man stands up out of the chair and comes to the glass and looks back at the four of us. His eyes are bloodshot. His lips are torn up and ragged. The way he's looking at us, it's like he wants to come over here and rip the jaws from our skulls.

For ten minutes he stands there. We glance up now and then, and he's still watching. Finally, he lifts one bloodied hand and smears a few words over the glass in grime and blood.

"Zanzibar was a lie."

I can't look at that man anymore, so I ignore him

even though he's still staring at us.

Reggie is sitting on the floor, motionless, while I wedge myself into the chair with Poplar. Gibbsy paces, shuffling near the wall and Reggie slips out a foot to trip him. Gibbsy almost falls, and I almost smack Reggie, but instead, I say, "You're a prick."

Gibbsy stops pacing.

*

One of the Hectors comes to the door, opens it, and points to me.

"Come see Mycroft," he says.

"All of us? Why me?"

He doesn't answer. I file out alone and follow him out of the hall.

Mycroft sits in a little side-office, and they put me across the desk from him. Two Hectors stay in the room and two more outside the door, like the Bands do for interrogation. Mycroft is in here unwrapping a big sandwich which makes me wonder how late it is and how long it's been since I ate anything. I'm starving. But he only takes one bite of the damn thing as the Hectors drag me through the door and when he sees I'm here, he wraps it up again and shoves the whole thing off the desk into the trash.

"You don't have to stop eating," I tell him, but he doesn't say anything about it.

Mycroft has a bunch of gadgets on the desk, too. A microscope, a surgeon's satchel. He turns the knob of a burner until the flames pulse, hissing and cackling. All the while he stares at me.

"Okay, what else do you want to know?"

"When did you first hear the Machinist's voice?" he says.

"Just met him tonight."

"I don't care when you met him," he says. He's got that smirk again. Laughing at me while he turns the burner up and down, the blue flame swelling until the tip is white, and dying again to almost nothing. A soft powdery orb.

"Then why'd you ask? I told you, I just met the guy tonight. You know more about him than I do. And if you don't, you can go ask him yourself what you want to know."

"I'm not asking about him," he says. "I'm asking about you."

"I'm nothing special."

He turns the burner up so high the flame starts to sputter, and he leaves the valve open while he stares. He leaves it that way long enough, the gas burns out, and the burner goes dark. He tells one of the Hectors to get another canister, and we wait.

This guy's attitude is bothering me as much as anybody's ever has. The way he just looks at me and doesn't explain anything. He's just another City patsy set-up to make sure they hold all the keys.

"Are you worried I'll tell folks what you're doing here?"

"You don't know what I'm doing here," he says.

"You're just scared you can't keep a handle on it," I tell him. "Folks will come tearing through this place. The people, they'll rip the City to shreds and let the water in even if it means they drown doing it. You can't keep us out of our own lives like this and think it will last."

"I don't care if it doesn't," he says. "Nobody likes Fallback anyway, right Tommy? There will be other cities when this one is gone. Other people after you've drowned. Do what you want. I'll do what I want. Sometimes those things don't get along, but that's nothing to worry about."

The Hector comes back with a new fuel can. Mycroft relights the burner and turns it low and leaves it alone. Then he jumps to his feet.

For an old guy, he's fast. I haven't even flinched yet and already he has a scalpel in his hand. Half a second later the blade sighs through the back of my hand, cutting it so deep blood spurts half a foot into the air.

I hardly realize what has happened until I see my hand, and by then I'm practically falling backward out of my chair. One of the Hectors catches me. I wrap the cut in my shirttail, wet warmth seeping through the cloth.

Already Mycroft has stowed the blade and is swabbing some of the blood from the desk, putting it onto a glass slide, putting the slide under the microscope. A wave of the hand so smooth it's like he's dealing cards for the sharks.

"The hell. Why'd you have to do that? You really that scared of what we'll do?"

Mycroft adjusts the slide and looks through the microscope's eyepiece. "Don't worry too much. Your body, it will make more blood."

"I'm not sick. You coulda asked. Christ. It's not like we don't all have to do that every couple of months anyway."

None of the Hectors give any reaction to the scene or the blood, which means they see this sort of thing all the time. It wouldn't surprise me, in a place like this. A maniac like this, running City business.

"Do your eyes ever twitch?" he says.

"I don't know."

He stands straight, looking for all the world like he is deep in thought. Meanwhile, I'm over here bleeding half to death. Crazy old prick.

"I could take your eye," he says. "I just need one to get a good look at the nerves."

"My eye?"

He starts to round the desk, taking the scalpel again with a brush of the hand, like dust to a feather. I'm halfway to my feet, but the Hectors grip my shoulders and push me down into the chair again.

Mycroft holds the scalpel in front of my eyes and tilts it back and forth like a metronome. My glasses are still on, but any second now, this bastard's going to take them off and stick that blade into that left socket and cut away the lid. That's all I can think about as I watch the glimmering metal swing from side to side just a few inches in front of my nose.

But he doesn't cut me this time. Mycroft backs away. He sets the scalpel down. He sits.

"There are still plenty of people in the world," he says. "Then again, I'm an optimist." He has no trace of a smile on his lips anymore. His face is blank and lost, which somehow scares me even more than the smile did.

"Put him back with his friends," says Mycroft. "Tell Rothschild. Let's see what kind of monster he can make of them."

*

"*That* son of a bitch is out of his mind."

Poplar is rewrapping my hand with some gauze from a shelf under the chair. "Did you mouth-off to him?"

"That's no reason to slice my hand to the ever-loving *bone*, Pop."

"Didn't say it was."

Reggie is behind me, standing close to the glass, tapping his forehead against it in rhythm. He's said a couple of times now he'll bust all the fingers on the next guy to open this door, but I doubt he'll do anything of the sort.

"You see this Gibbsy?"

"Why'd he do that?"

"He thought I was sick I guess. Ffffuck."

Poplar tells me to stop bawling, and she ties the gauze and kisses my hand in the most delicate way.

*

Static rustles out from an intercom speaker near the ceiling. Someone's trying to say something to us, but the voice is chopped to bits, like whoever it is can't figure out how to work the mic on the other end. Finally, something solidifies.

"Young friends? I'm Dr. Rothschild, you've seen me through the glass. I'll be coming into the chamber in a moment, but please stand against the back wall until I've shut the door again. If you don't, I'll have to gas the room first, and it is very unpleasant."

We do what he says and line-up.

Here comes the doctor with a steel cart. A couple of Hectors follow close behind, and they hold the door, but only the doctor comes into the cell. The Hectors just wait out there with the door open and their guns ready. They turn now and then to look at the mangled man across the way.

"I have to inject this into your shoulders so please roll your sleeves up or pull the collar down. Whichever." The words are crisp despite his cotton mask.

I know where I've seen him before. I know that voice, too. He's been on the City Bulletin's a few times, talking about this or that. One of Kennedy's "Scientific Experts."

"I know you," I tell him.

He glances at me. "Yes, well I suppose you do."

The doctor pulls a cloth away from the cart. A row of syringes is queued-up there, filled with something vaguely red.

"What is that?" I ask.

The doctor doesn't answer. He goes about tapping air out of the syringes.

"Do you see the man in the cell behind me?" he says.

"Hard not to."

"What do you think happened to him?" says the doctor. He doesn't give us much time to answer. "He wasn't beaten. In fact, no one has laid a hand on him, if that's what you were thinking."

I tell him, "That's what we *are* thinking."

"This is a vaccine," he says. "Sometimes the subject responds favorably and is moved to more sophisticated surroundings, in another ward. But if the subject responds unfavorably, I'm afraid he is to be destroyed. The man in the other cell responded unfavorably."

Christ. And now he's going to put the same stuff into our veins. I don't know what to say. My throat is closing.

Reggie has his wits though. He tells the guy, "None of us is getting jabbed without you getting hurt."

"I could gas the room," says the doctor. "You're much better off without that."

Reggie is practically shaking. He says, "I don't care

what you do, that needle's not going in my arm."

He means it, and I'm with him on all counts. We're all a bit dazed by what the doctor is telling us, sure, but that doesn't mean we're tame. Not by any stretch. We're one-hundred percent adrenaline right now and Reggie's absolutely right. Those needles aren't going into our arms. I can't even look at the man in the other cell.

The doctor turns to the Hectors. "Please, go and ready the valve for this cell, would you? The canister is already mixed. But...wait a moment before you turn the knob, of course. I'll be along shortly."

One of the Hectors nods and goes toward the command room. The doctor looks at the other Hector. "You too," he says. "Please. I'll be alright; I want to reason with them. They're frightened, is all, and the guns are making it worse." So off *he* goes, too, and all I can think is, now we're really in trouble.

I don't know if I trust Dr. Rothschild. He's being too polite. Why didn't he just tell us the syringes are filled with something harmless, like a tranq? It reminds me of

Grovesner and his "invitation" to get shot. It's like Rothschild wants to make us fight so he'll have some excuse to do something worse to us. I don't know.

When the Hectors are both out of sight, the doctor shuts the door, pulls down his mask and picks up one of the syringes, hovering the needle over his open mouth. He drops the plunger, empties the syringe, and swallows the liquid before any of us can wonder why.

"Just water," he says. "Dyed water, nothing else."

"Water? What…"

"You shoot Riot Reels?" says the doctor. "You were filming tonight, is that correct? In the docks?"

For half a minute I don't even realize that he has *asked* a question. Then it just sort of bubbles up from the murk, the whole baffling *Now,* and I'm alert again. "Yeah. The Drowner. Everything."

"Not everything," says the doctor. "But it's a good start. If I can get the camera for you and if I can get you away from Mycroft, would you be willing to film a bit more?"

I'm too startled by it all to give much of an answer. This son of a bitch, who has been in I don't know how many Bulletins, is all of a sudden offering to help with a Reel. It can't be on the straight and plumb. It just can't be. I feel like I'm swimming in oil. Like there's nothing solid in all the world.

"He's very angry," says the doctor. "Mycroft is. At whoever caused the whole mess with the locks. But if you ask me, he's the one who caused it. This was bound to happen."

"What was?" I'm trembling like a cable. "What was bound to happen?"

The doctor looks toward the hall and empties his other syringes. "Earlier this evening…well, last evening, I suppose, since it's well past midnight now…the security doors in Sectors 28 through 31 *failed*. We don't know how it happened because it's not supposed to be possible. But they did fail, and a lot of doors were opened. Doors that should *never* be opened."

The doctor points across the way, to the other cell.

"Look at him. There are worse things than that, in Fallback, and I need you to film some of them for me."

Everyone's looking at me now, even Poplar.

A very big part of me wants to say no. I can't trust a guy like this. Maybe Mocap would be better than playing pawn. The problem is, they'll never take us to Mocap. We'll never get out of this place. "Christ, man, you're going to have to tell us what's going on first. Okay?"

"There's not enough time right now," he says. And he's right. Here comes Mycroft.

The doctor slips something to me. An FR peg. "That will get you out of Triage. Out of this cell. I'm going to gas the cell across the way in a moment so that the Hectors can dispose of that poor man. Except I'm not going to mix the proper chemicals and it won't work. He'll come to, and he'll attack me, and I want you to slip away in the confusion if you can. Find Dr. Casten, Sector 26 Pathology. He's one of our chemists. I'll meet you there if I can, but if I can't, he's a friend."

Dr. Rothschild covers the syringes casually, wheels

the cart around, and leaves the room. I can't hear what he says to Mycroft, but Mycroft seems to believe every word of it.

*

Poplar sighs and leans toward me. "Tommy," she says, but she doesn't say any more than that. Her eyes are shaking in their sockets, back and forth.

I've seen her like this before but not often. She's angry. On the cusp of rage. The last time this happened, it was some guy being an asshole to Lilith, and Poplar practically skinned the bastard alive with just a handful of words. Made him shrink back and forget what to say next. He didn't even try to save face. He just walked away.

She doesn't get like this very often at all.

*

In the opposite cell, thin red billows swirl down from the vents. The tattered man over there doesn't really notice. He's been looking at us, the whole while, not moving at all. Soon he is nothing more than a silhouette in the thick red cloud. Half a minute later, he falls to the ground. Five minutes after that, the air starts to clear. The fans reverse, and the red gas vanishes into the vents again.

Dr. Rothschild jogs to the door with a Hector close behind. He doesn't open the cell yet but stands there explaining something to the Hector for a while. I guess he has to time things just right. Part of me thinks this is just another set-up. They just want to see us barrel out of *our* cell so they can open fire. It's no surprise. City guns are always itching to sound. Itching for an excuse.

Rothschild opens that cell's door and taps his foot on the tile. He's very, very careful. He glances at us, just a flick. The man on the floor doesn't move. After another fit of tapping, the doctor looks at the Hector and smiles and starts to go into the room. That's when the man on the floor stands up and quick as a spring, he reaches for the door.

Dr. Rothschild is ready for it and he bolts. He sprints toward the back of the hall, where it dead ends past the last few cells. The Hector stands there dumbfounded as the twisted man bursts out of the room, lurching, awkward but fast. He careens into our cell door, smudging it with dried flecks of blood, before backhanding the Hector.

It's one hell of a blow. The Hector spins in place and blood spurts over the glass. His cheek has been cut by the edge of his goggles, and he might have even broken his neck. He goes down and doesn't get up. The twisted man stands over him saying something we can't hear. He turns to follow Dr. Rothschild.

Five more Hectors rush past us, the Colonel among them. They're not shooting…probably because they don't want to hit the doctor. I don't know. And behind them, striding his even stride, is Mycroft. He eyes the fallen Hector and keeps walking.

Now is the time. I know it is but I seize-up, wondering how many Hectors were in that office when we came through. If anyone stayed behind, we wouldn't be able to get past them, and they'll know what Dr. Rothschild did. But if we wait too much longer, the Hectors who *did* jump into the fray will finish with the twisted man, and we'll miss our chance. No. Now is the time and there sure isn't much of it.

I twist the peg and open the door, and we whisper out into the hall.

Behind us, Hectors struggle with the twisted man and never once do they glance in our direction. Mycroft is shouting at them. "Pin his arms. Don't touch the blood."

My pals follow close behind me trying to be just as quiet as I am. The office isn't empty. The tech is still here manning the switchboard, shouting into it about the dust-up, and when he sees us, he looks for his gun.

I get to it first and slide the S8 away from him. It clatters to the floor behind me.

Before the tech can shout, Reggie grabs him by the collar and tries to drag him to the ground, but the guy is a hell of a lot bigger than Reggie. The two struggle, slipping on the tile, before they both go down.

"It's one of these," says Gibbsy.

We start opening drawers against that wall, looking

for the backpack. I don't remember which one Mycroft used, but it doesn't take long before we find it. Gibbsy slings the pack over his shoulders. Poor sweet Cassandra, shivering in the canvas.

Reggie and the tech are still struggling, and I'm starting to notice the glorious amount of noise they're making. The guy is screaming at us as Reggie gasps and pries at his grip. I kick the man's ribs and his whole body springs back in a twitchy spasm.

Reggie squirms free. Before I know it, he stomps at the tech's face. The guy starts to bleed. Reggie keeps stomping and blood leaks over the floor. I have to pull Reggie off of the guy. He's still stomping even as I drag him through the doorway.

"Goddamnit Reggie. Stop." Goddamnit.

The tech is writhing on the floor. Reggie almost killed the guy, and I still can't believe he did it.

But it doesn't matter anymore. The tussle at the end of the hall has stopped, and Mycroft slides into the office, blinking at us. I suppose it's time to run.

*

As soon as the Hectors are well enough out of sight, Gibbsy wrestles with the floor plans, trying to find a maintenance corridor or something we can use to get out of sight. The thick paper flaps and threatens collapse as he traces along the page with his finger, but we can't stop running yet. "Left up there," he says. "Through those doors," he says.

After that, we turn right along a pump access and left again as soon as it opens up, tubes lining the walls and the hiss of water all around. We can hear Mycroft's voice shouting to the Hectors somewhere behind us, following us even though we're never in their line of sight. It bothers me that we can always hear those boots no matter what we do to lose them. Whatever turns we've taken, they take too. Whatever rooms we've passed through, so do they.

The only consolation is, we're young and fast and not carrying much gear. Careful about the hinges, we inch through a narrow door and into what looks like a storeroom filled with shelves and boxed inventory.

Medical supplies, I'm guessing. It's a long and crowded room, and pretty soon the door is well out of sight. But that doesn't mean we have much time. We can practically *feel* the Hectors crowding at the door, the way you can feel the trains coming before the tracks even start to sing.

"Hatch, hatch, right there," says Gibbsy.

I slide to a halt near this big breaker cabinet. The maintenance hatch is only about two by two, held with a screw latch.

"Knife, Reggie?"

He doesn't answer me, but it doesn't matter. Poplar dives into Gibbsy's pack and grabs his pen-magnet for me, and I start turning the screw with the edge of it. The hatch opens, and we start to crawl into the conduit.

Away at the far end of the room, the door opens. Mycroft tells his crew to split up and keep moving. They start coming past the shelves, and they'll be here any second. I'm sweating like mad.

I can't leave the hatch open like this, so I thread the

pen magnet through the bracket and line it up with the screw as I swing the whole thing close. This is one of the tricks we've learned. I use the magnet to tighten the screw from inside. It's not easy to do, but it means if anybody out there thinks you might have used the hatch, he'll see the screw and stop thinking along those lines altogether.

Footsteps approach, smacking the tile, running toward us. They stop near the breaker cabinet, but I'm done. The hatch is shut, and the screw is turned home. We stop breathing and wait until the footsteps move away again.

Gibbsy is still looking at that map, even here in the dark.

We have enough room in here to walk, if we stoop. Gibbsy leads us back past a whole wall of wire-posts, to where the conduit bends. "There should be a ladder," he tells us, and so there is.

I'm last on the rungs, and I haven't taken more than a few steps when I hear something that rakes at my joints.

Someone is unscrewing the access hatch.

We practically fall down the ladder, we're moving so fast. The rungs drop two deck lengths onto a wide mezzanine filled with airmovers. The Hectors haven't reached the ladder yet, but it's only a matter of time.

We sprint past the airmovers, through doorways, into narrow pipe corridors, all the while too scared to look behind.

Along the way, Gibbsy untangles a cinch-tie. The next double-doors we pass, he stops, shuts them behind us, and cinches the handles.

"Maybe let's do a couple," he says, and he wraps another tie around the first one, crossing them so they'll be harder to break. He sits there staring at it. He looks around the room, slides the metal bracket out from the top of an intercom terminal and puts that through the door handles too.

I kiss his head, and we keep moving. But at least we don't have to move as fast, now.

*

Gibbsy keeps saying we need a new map and he's right. This one is labeled all wrong, which could mean trouble. All the same, my eyes are rolling because I can't imagine what we'll *do* about it. "Where we going to get a map, Gibbs?"

He just smiles, and pretty soon I understand why. "Engineer's room," he says.

That's Gibbsy for you. His dad's an engineer...but even then, you'd have to be Gibbsy to recognize an engineer's room on a map when it's labeled "Blade Reserves."

We gather around the door, and I check through the vents to make sure the room isn't occupied. It isn't, and we file-in and I sit down for what seems like the first time in a week.

Gibbsy was right. It's an engineer's room, no mistake. The walls are covered with close shelves made from scrap metal and leftover screws, and the shelves are covered with small boxes of parts, poorly labeled in faded pen. Three odd desks are scattered here and there, all of them covered with this or that. Everything in the room has at least one smear of grease on its surface, and the workbench looks like a butcher's table with gruesome streaks of oil, like old blood.

While Gibbsy looks around for a good schematic, Reggie paces near the door. He keeps grabbing his neck, saying, "No, no, no, no, no." Sometimes he gets so worked up he pounds his hand against the wall, and I have to tell him to shut it off. But he's not listening to me, and I can't blame him.

Gibbsy tries to talk to calm him down. "We'll get out of here. It can't be too far to…"

"And where were you?" says Reggie. "Huh, Gibbs? While that son of a bitch was trying to break my neck."

Gibbsy reaches out a hand and tries to shake with Reggie, but Reggie won't.

I tell Gibbsy to sit down. "Leave him alone." And he does.

Poplar is shaking her head, but I don't need to ask why. I tell them all to cool down. "Everybody just relax.

We can relax. They're not coming in here anytime soon so just catch your breath and sit down, and we'll figure out what to do next."

I lean my head back and close my eyes and think about the cool air from the vent above me.

*

It's easy to get lost in Fallback, no matter where you are. Everybody has his own version of how to get from place to place, and there's no sense taking directions. The City maps never tell the whole story either. What you think is a dead-end could really be a nest; they just don't want you to know it's there. Their maps are full of phantom halls, too, and I don't understand why. A dozen little corridors and passageways that don't even exist except on the map. It's like they don't want you to feel at home here. They don't want you to think any of it belongs to you. They want you to feel lost.

City maps aren't the only option though. A lot of folks sell blackmarket maps. The problem is, you never know if their versions are any better and if you get caught with one you might be put in a place where maps don't make any difference.

I actually tried to make my own map once, when I was a kid. Just HH and Hh. I took some graph paper from my dad's desk one day and set out to chart whatever I could. Three hours later I'd quit the whole notion. All I had were the main halls. There I was, sitting up on a catwalk looking down at all the alleys coming into and out of Blakely Square, and I just got overwhelmed and fell asleep on the metal.

On the way home, I made a point of finding a back trail from 9:15 to 10:10, between 200 and 350, just using maintenance tunnels. I mapped those at least, so it wasn't a total loss.

The truth is, the best you can do is get your hands on a good maintenance schematic. Then you'll know all you need to know about the lay of the land. They're illegal too, without the right ID, but they're a hell of a lot more useful.

*

Gibbsy rustles through a few drawers and finds a set of blueprints that cover this whole division with as much detail as we'll need.

"We can get back to the docks," he says. "If we follow this, through here."

"No, we're not going to the docks," I tell him. "Where's the Pathology ward? Does it say?"

I get a sharp look from Gibbsy, like he was hoping I'd forgotten all about what Dr. Rothschild said. Like he was hoping we could just leave with nothing to show for it but a bunch of footage that the City will just explain away and bury.

We have this moment of silence, me and him, and it almost drives me into a rage.

"Yeah," says Gibbsy. "That's…here. But it won't be very easy to get there. Through Triage. Past all those guys."

"What about up or down a few decks?" I'm wondering. "Sneak under or over the whole bunch of 'em?"

Gibbsy says no, that's not possible. "There are a few access shafts, some maintenance runs, things like that. But they're all on the same deck, the only deck that doesn't dead-end before the junction."

"Fine. We just go slow and quiet and hope they're not thinking the same thing we're thinking."

Poplar leans over our shoulders. "They're looking for us, Tommy. It's not like sneaking around some empty turbines or the warehouses at three in the morning. These guys are *looking* for us."

"Probably the first place they'd look is back where we came from. We can't go back to the docks. Look at these choke points. Right Gibbsy? Here, here, and there. That's where they'll be waiting. We can't go back to the docks."

I try to show Poplar the map, but she doesn't even look at it. She says, "You can be mad at the City again tomorrow, soldier. I'll be mad with you. You can be mad all you like from someplace safe. Tommy…"

"They're lying to us every day, Pop, and all we

need is a bit more footage to prove it. You want someplace safe? You won't get one until the people run the City and not the other way around. The City's had a clamp on us all along and if we go home right now, they always will."

"Tommy," she says, but she gives up and doesn't say anything else.

For a while, I just stare at her, and she stares back. I almost want to go over there and put my arm over her shoulder but I'm too mad, and I'm not going to do that.

Gibbsy keeps rifling through that map, page after page. He says, "Are we going to find what's-his-name?"

"Yes, we are." I don't remember his name either, come to think of it. The guy Dr. Rothschild told us to find. Not a clue in the world. But it's worth a try, anyway, and it's the only thing we *can* do right now. "All we need is a bit of luck and, Christ, I don't know."

Poplar keeps shaking her head. I should really go over there and lean against her or something, but she would just step away.

*

A couple of months ago, a bunch of us went to Thurstein's to watch the Roosters at a flashrant. All of a sudden half my pals went missing, lost in the crowd, so I started looking for everybody. I figured Poplar crept off with Alan Kotter since that was back when they were going together. I found her back in the alley, but Alan wasn't there. She was leaning her head on Gibbsy of all people. I don't know if there had been any more to it than that but all I had to do was clear my throat and they both flinched.

"You been drinking Pop?"

She didn't try to give me any excuses. That's Poplar for you. But why would a girl like her need to get drunk, if life's so grand?

Gibbsy never talked about it. It was like he wanted to pretend that whatever had happened never *had* happened, even though it was nothing. He knew I liked her, even back then, so eventually, I had to raise the issue with him. I said, "Pop's got a way about her, I know that as much as anybody. Don't worry."

The fact is, he was truly *embarrassed* by the whole phantom thing. By what he thinks I imagined, by what he thinks I assumed at the time. But if I'm over it, he should be too. That's just the way things work. Meanwhile, he rarely ever talks to her anymore. Gibbsy is more of a problem for himself than anybody else.

*

Reggie has been pacing in the middle of the room, bristling and ready to spring at the first person who trips the wire. He gets like this sometimes. Like one time in school, Reggie spilled juice on his shirt in the cafeteria, and he started yelling, and he pushed another kid over a bench. That kid had nothing to do with him spilling…he was just *there*. I know better than to say anything when Reggie's like this. We all do.

But if he takes one step toward Gibbsy I swear I'll knock him to the ground.

We're all so clamped, every one of us flinches when the PA speaker crackles at us from the corner of the room. Someone is using the address system. I'm half expecting to hear the Bulletin intro, but it's nothing like that.

"Listen closely."

It's Mycroft. In here, in the hall, probably piping his voice out to the whole sector.

"I want you to look out at the hall," he says. We all watch the door, but none of us moves. "In the hall, there will be a red panel," he says. "I know you haven't eaten tonight. Those are first aid cabinets, and they have packets of sugar water and wafers. Feel free to have a snack."

Reggie is closest to the door. He inches toward it, opens it just wide enough to get a look at the hall and shuts it again. "Bastard knows where we are," he says.

"What?"

"Red panel, right out there, like he said."

But that doesn't mean anything. "They have those everywhere, Reg. Right Gibbsy? He probably just wants us to open one because they're on a circuit and he'll know which one we opened. It's okay."

Reggie doesn't say anything else about it.

Mycroft is quiet for a while, too. When he speaks again, his voice has grown harsh and quick. "Starve, if you want. Tommy Molotov. Reginald Stamp. Charlie Gibbs. Poplar Meer." Our full names. He knows our full names. "Those are not the only things we know about you," he says. "There's nothing to explain now. You know what you've done, and I leave the rest to you."

We stare at the speaker the way you would stare at a bomb that's about to explode.

"What does he mean?" says Gibbsy. "He knows our *names,* Tommy."

"He means they'll know where to find us even if we do go home. That's what he means."

"UNLIVABLE PLACES," Reels 1-3 of 3, 16mm, 24fps

The roll-up doors outside the housing block must have been padlocked ages ago. All of the windows and all of the doors too and the padlocks are rusted. The guards no longer hold posts at the entrances. The camera pans from one lock to the next showing disuse.

A pair of gloved hands stretch into the frame holding a pick, and the pick pries away one of the weak locks from a window. It hits the floor with a blunt sound, the metal no longer capable of ringing against the concrete.

The footage cuts to a moving shot as we follow a pale flashlight through the halls of the condemned district. Most of the doors on the first level are shut. A few are open. The camera and the light peek into some of the apartments. Mattresses have been overturned. Cupboards have been ransacked. Dust stands thick on the counters and the arms of the chairs. One room holds a child's bed with the sheets and blanket still on it, but no pillow. The faucets no longer work, and the lights will not turn on with the switches.

In the room are three corpses, dry and wrinkled. Two children and a woman. They have been set out in a row on the rug, their hands crossed over their chests. Each has been shot in some way, the oldest boy through the chest with a single round.

A fourth corpse is found in the empty bathtub, a man who had slit his own throat.

The cameraman speaks, but through a pitch filter so that his voice is mutated and stretched.

"A home for the homeless," he says. "And justice for the fugitive."

SEVEN

If we're going to reach Pathology, we'll have to climb a few decks, cross over, and come back down on top of Triage at the other end. We will be close to Mycroft's office, but at least we won't be backtracking too much. It's off to the dim tunnels again among the arrogant pipes and the wires. Stairs and ladders.

After fifteen minutes the PA sounds again. They don't put speakers in the maintenance shafts, so I have to scramble out to the nearest hall before I can catch the last bit of whatever Mycroft is saying.

"…what you thought would happen? You failed before you started and now we have our doors back. Hide wherever you like and do a better job of it than you've done already."

It doesn't mean anything to me, but it certainly has the ring of bad news to it.

*

Triage is quiet. Seventeen minutes ago, the Hectors were chasing us down this very hall. They were on our goddamn heels. Now they're gone, and as much as I'd like to be glad about it, it's also making me feel a sight uneasy. Maybe they really did go to the docks to cut us off.

The door to Pathology is thick, and I'm hoping Rothschild's peg works on the lock. The needles trace and click, and the door opens. I can breathe again.

Someone has scratched a symbol into the paint next to the door, no bigger than my hand. A circle with a hook in the middle. I'm not sure what to make of it or why looking at it makes my skin crawl. A wayward thought comes scrambling up through the fray. Dunning said something about being a sheep. He said that the Herds are in charge.

"Get a shot of that on the eights," I tell Gibbsy. We find a shadowy alcove and start rummaging through the film. Gibbsy loads a new reel, cranks the handle a few times to charge the spindle, and shoots the door.

"Tommy…what did he mean?" he says. "The Herds are in charge?"

I don't have a guess yet.

Reggie is leaning against the wall, fingernails scratching along the canvas of his pockets. "Somebody we haven't met," he says.

*

Pathology is polished to a well-lit aluminum sheen. It's a sterile ward with no pipes, smooth walls, and lights that don't flicker. This hall is lined with those pneumatic pocket doors like they have in the City hospitals, with flat levers, so the nurses don't have to fuss with a knob when their hands are full.

We're not sure where to find Rothschild's buddy now that we're here. Looking at the map, this is a pretty big place, and we don't really have time to wander.

"Labs," says Gibbsy. "That's my guess, if this guy's a chemist." It sounds reasonable to me.

"What's between here and there?"

"*O-b-v-s* Gallery," he says, reading from the schematics. "Maybe that means Observation? Labs are past that, next deck down."

"No, I mean what about back-roads? This place is wide open."

Gibbsy shakes his head. "We'll have to walk in the open," he says. "At least for a little while."

That's not what I want to hear, but it isn't going to stop me, either. "Keep Cassandra's eyes wide open."

*

At one point we pass a narrow passage that Gibbsy says isn't important. But I can hear something, like one of these pneumatic doors opening and shutting, opening and shutting, and it makes me worry. I tell my pals to wait while I duck through to check it. I don't want to be lazy and get flanked by Hectors.

After a couple of dog-legs, I find a waiting room with chairs and low tables. I can see into it from the hall, through a couple of big windows. One of the lights in there is burnt out giving a broad shadow to that corner of the room. A chalkboard on the far wall shows a drawing of a hip joint, the chalk smudged around it.

The waiting room door is moving by itself, and I guess the circuitry to the lever has shorted. It keeps moving into the wall and out again, pfssst, pfssst. The room itself is empty. A long narrow hall behind the desk leads to examination chambers and restrooms. Another couple of doors here are malfunctioning too. Sliding into the wall and shut again over and over. But the place is vacant, so I get back to my friends as fast as I can trot.

*

The observation galleries are wide corridors lined on the left side by a series of glass cells, set into the wall. These are much bigger than the ones in Triage and from what I can tell they house no medical equipment whatsoever. Just a few shower nozzles in the ceiling and some drains in the floor. Each cell has two doors, one in the steel wall at the back of the cell and one in the glass wall at the front. Both are sealed with titanium FR locks, and the glass itself is incredibly thick.

The first couple of cells are empty and clean, but I can see movement from a few of them further ahead. The brief flash of mottled haunches and a ragged tail.

"Dogs."

I hurry through the gallery for a better look.

"Goddamn dogs. Where's the paintbrush?"

I can't even find words for what I'm seeing.   If I ever had any shred of respect for the City, it has now been snuffed completely.

I'm guessing they have seventeen or eighteen dogs in this gallery alone, various breeds, all huddled together and crawling over each other. Some are barking, but we can't hear it through the glass. Maybe just a hint of it. They have smudged the glass, and the floor of the cell is filthy with grime. I'm guessing the room is sprayed-down daily from those nozzles, but some of the muck just won't wash away.

Most of the dogs look weak and hungry. Some are injured, probably from fights with other dogs. Three dogs at the back of the cell appear to be dead, lying on the ground, frothing at the mouth, probably rabid.

But what bothers me the most are the three dogs nearest the glass. They don't look sick at all. They are large, healthy, and calm. They breathe in unison, and they watch us through the glass as we film. These three have a certain viciousness to them. A tilt to the shoulder blades that just isn't natural and an intelligence in the eyes that makes me uncomfortable. I get the impression they would kill the whole lot of us if they weren't locked in that room.

Everyone else seems just as disturbed by the sight as I am. Gibbsy is getting nauseous, and he's having trouble holding the camera steady. He keeps backing away and leaning against the other wall for a few seconds before filming again.

Reggie is getting annoyed. "Don't ruin the shot," he says. "Get over it and hold still. Don't puke all over the place."

Gibbsy waves him off. "I'm alright," he says, but his camera hand is shaking like a needle.

"The hell you are," I tell him. "Gimme that, Gibbs. Sit down."

"I'm okay," he says, but he really does look like he's going to puke. Reggie actually reaches out and tries to take the camera from him, but Gibbsy steps back and waves and says, "No, I'm okay. I'm okay."

Pop is looking at me like I'm an asshole, but I'm trying to *help* the guy, so I don't pay any attention to her scowls. After awhile Gibbsy starts to look better anyway.

He films everything. The sick dogs, the healthy dogs, the nose-smudges on the glass, the shower nozzles, the frothing jaws.

I paint "Man's best friend?" on the glass and Gibbsy films that too.

"Pathology," says Reggie. "The hell?"

"We've been here too long. Why's this place empty?"

Reggie shrugs. "Pricks are off looking for us maybe. Or whatever was happening in that, uh…"

"C-Tran."

"Maybe they're all over there. Don't ask me."

*

The first Riot Reel I ever made was about a buddy of mine. He went into Parson Hospital a couple of years back, sick with a fever. We didn't see him again for three months. He came out and wouldn't talk about his time there. We kept asking him if it was the Spanish Flu. They say there hasn't been a case of that in Fallback in twenty-five years, but us young folks, we always wonder about that. About why the hospitals are so thick with Blackband patrols all the time.

We convinced this buddy of mine to let us film some of his scars. Strange scars, all over his back and arms, ones I couldn't imagine a cause for. We covered his face, so he wouldn't be recognized.

But he never would talk about what happened to him in Parson Hospital. Not a word.

We know about the burnboxes, but we still have no idea what happens in the hospitals. I'm guessing it's worse.

*

The door to the lab is just ahead but the one that grabs my attention is the one that says, "Autopsy 1." I'm curious enough to try the door, but Poplar tugs my sleeve.

"We don't need to see that."

"I do." She waits against the wall, but Gibbsy and Reg follow me. We film the tables, the bloodstained floors, the canine chest cavities, and the separated organs.

"Try not to breathe," says Gibbsy and we back out into the hall again.

*

The lab is quiet. Most of the lights are out. Beakers line the workbenches, most of them empty, others not. It's a broad room with clean equipment, and a man is slouched on a stool near the back, so still, I don't notice him until I'm looking right at him.

He's old and half blind. He squints at us through mile-thick specs and brushes his hair away.

"You're the schoolers from the docks," he says. He points to the camera. Gibbsy isn't filming, but this old guy keeps edging out of frame anyway, like he's afraid we'll get his face on the eights. I don't blame him.

"We're not *from* the Docks," I tell him. "We're just...here."

"I'm Dr. Casten," he says. "Dr. Rothschild will return in a moment. Sit. Sit."

"He's still alive?"

Casten nods his old head. "And don't worry about Mycroft's men. They won't be coming here."

"What...*happened* tonight? What are we in the middle of, all the sudden?"

Casten droops into one hell of a frown. His whole *body* frowns. "In the middle of?" he says. "No. You *caused* all of this."

"So they say." But I'm getting tired of hearing it.

*

Casten won't tell us anything. He keeps saying, "Rothschild knows more about it than I do, let's wait for him." No matter what we ask. The door locks, the Hectors, Mycroft and the Herds--he says he's just as confused as we are and to wait for Rothschild.

"Well, what about those dogs?" I ask him. "What happened to them, or do you not know anything about that either?"

"The what?" he says. "Oh, here in observation? Yes. There's nothing wrong with any of that. That's how they're supposed to be."

The hell it is. "They're sick. That's *not* how they're supposed to be."

"Rothschild will explain…"

But I don't want to wait for Rothschild to explain. "Damn things look sick as hell, and some of them look like they'd rip our lungs out."

"Well…they would," says Casten, almost *giggling*, for Christ's sake. "If they got out. Even the docile ones, you never know what will trigger them. One of our chemists, uh, he tried to take one for a pet. Thinking it healthy of course. This was many years ago. He was found dead in the corridor…the dog had bitten through his femoral artery, just that one spot, just that one bite. But it was enough to bleed the poor chemist to death. The dog knew exactly where to bite."

"So, what *happened* to them?"

Dr. Casten's glasses bounce on the bridge of his nose as he nods his head. I think they'll fall off any minute. "That's how they're supposed to be," he says. "We *caused* them to be sick."

*

Rothschild stumbles in from a door at the back of the room. We all flinch when we hear the pneumatic gasp, but we relax when we see that it's him. He's sweating, but he smiles when he notices the four of us.

"Doctor," he says, patting Casten on the shoulder.

"Night of nights, wouldn't you say?"

"Night of what?"

"Young friends," says Rothschild. "I'm sorry for putting you in such a spot, but I must thank you for coming."

Even though he was the one who sprang us, I'm not really happy to see him. Maybe if I hadn't seen those dogs…I don't know. But the way I look at it there's no difference between the doctor and the City.

I point to the hall. "Is that what you were supposed to stick us with? In those needles?"

Rothschild takes a second to think about what I'm asking. "Ah, yes, the vaccine," he says. "Yes. Dr. Casten can explain…"

"No. No, he said you would explain. So who's going to explain?"

Rothschild gives Casten a glance. "Dr. Casten is the foremost scientist in Fallback, apart from Mycroft of course. Doctor, the vaccine…"

But Dr. Casten shrinks against the table, rubbing the bridge of his nose.

"Yes," says Rothschild. "You saw the dogs? Good. Did you film them? Good. I'm glad you're here. We need to get this out into the world, right?"

I'm wondering why it isn't out in the world already. "You know more than I do. Why haven't you done anything yet? Why haven't you circ'd something if you're so against it? You've been on the Bulletins for hell's sake. Why do *you* need *us*?"

"You're right," he says. "We should have done something before tonight. Think of it as a catalyst. Of yourselves as a catalyst. Will you? I'm glad you're here with your camera and the know-how to get bad news out to good people. Tonight, these halls are empty. They're not crawling with the City Guard, watching everything we do. I'll explain. Just follow me. Dr. Casten...well, I'll stand in front of the camera and explain everything. Like you said, I've been on the Bulletins. Maybe the people will believe what I have to say tonight."

*

Rothschild leads us past the labs, and Casten follows. Casten won't let us film him.

"Quite a scrape," says Rothschild. "Mycroft saved my life you know. And he thought nothing of the ruse. Don't worry about him, for now. Or the Hectors. I set a trail for them to follow. Maybe you saw the malfunctioning doors?"

Opening and closing. Opening and closing.

"I had to do that manually," he tells us. "How was it you tripped all the locks, I wonder?" He laughs. A nervous laugh.

"We didn't. We're goddamn decoys. The Barkers maybe."

But I don't think he believes me.

"Well, someone tripped them. 28 through 31 are all on the same security grid, but I can't imagine how it was done."

We take an elevator down two decks, but I don't

complain. When we reach our floor, I ask, "Who are the Herds?"

Rothschild spins toward me as a reflex, but he doesn't answer my question.

"There was this mark," I tell him, "on a door, like one of those old hooks shepherds used to use."

"What? Which door?" says Rothschild.

"When we came into Pathology I think."

For a good few seconds, the doctor doesn't say anything. He just breathes deep is all. Then he says, "I'm not sure what to make of that."

It's not what I want to hear, but I guess that's how the day has been going all along.

*

"I'm going to show you some things that you won't like seeing." Rothschild says it to the lens. His hand rests on an FR lock and waits there. "We have been studying Influenza D since before Fallback was ever built and we continue to study it to this day."

He slips the peg through. The door gasps.
"Influenza D has been commonly called the Spanish Flu,
but to call it that is grossly inaccurate. The virus that
causes Influenza D began life as a strain of influenza A,
which spread widely during the Spanish Flu pandemic. It
was artificially changed sometime during the Great
War."

"By the Crackjaws..."

"No," he says. "Not exactly. I'll explain."

We follow him into another observation gallery.
It's no different than the one we filmed upstairs...except
these cells are not filled with dogs. These cells are filled
with human beings, and Cassandra takes a glance at
every face.

"Of course, you saw the dogs already," says
Rothschild. "Dogs are not ideal for the study of Influenza
D, but it does affect them similarly to the way it affects
humans. However, to truly study the disease we do need
actual human subjects, and we have some of those too."

More than a dozen "subjects" watch us from the

first cell and just like the dogs they are in various states of pain and sickness. Some standing, some lying on the floor, some bleeding from the eyes and nose. Tattered clothes. There are no mattresses, no chairs, just the metal floor. Some of the people pound on the glass, but the pounding makes no sound. A few of them are calling out to us, but their voices are muted by the thick pane.

"The hell do you keep 'em in a cage?" says Reggie. "Can't you give 'em beds?"

"At this point, it doesn't matter," says Rothschild. "They're insane and very contagious."

"Doesn't mean they're not people," says Reggie. He's bristling again, ready to spring.

"Calm down, Reg."

"No, I'm not calming down till somebody opens these. We should put him in there too, and see how he likes it. Tommy…"

"Calm the hell *down*, Reg." I don't need a fight. I just need some footage is all and Reggie had better not get in the way of that.

*

There should be riots.

My dad always tries to tell me I'm wrong about the City. That I'm too young and angry and that I'll find its 'nuance' sooner or later. The other side of the coin, he says. "Fallback isn't bad. It's a tired old man is all, carrying a sleeping child to bed. It isn't perfect, but it's not as bad as you think it is, Thomas."

I wonder what he would say if he saw this. This place isn't as bad as I think? No, Dad. It's much worse.

*

Poplar's hand lights on the back of my arm. I tell Gibbsy to keep filming while I chat with her in an alcove.

She keeps brushing her hair over her ears. "Those people are *watching* us film them, Tommy."

It's a typical Poplar thing to say, but I really don't see why she cares, and I'm not in any kind of mood to ponder it. "That's what we do, Pop. Bad things happen, and we film them. These people are probably glad to see somebody's doing something about all this."

"They're dying," she says. "I don't think they want people watching them through that glass while they're trying to die."

But she's wrong. If I were dying because of what the City did to me, I would want everyone to be watching. The young, the old, the Kennedys and Mycrofts and Poplars too.

*

Whether the film is cranking or not, Reggie keeps talking about throwing Rothschild and Casten into the cells. His face is red, and his neck is pulsing, and he's lost all signs of eloquence.

All the while, Rothschild here is trying to tell him, "That's the whole point. I'm going to help you change all of this. I agree with you."

It doesn't make a difference. That's the thing about Reggie. He'll blame whoever's closest, most times, even if they are trying to help. But it's hard not to side with him right now. Catalyst. Christ, there should have been one of those ages ago.

"We simply can't let them out," says Rothschild. "Some of these people are extremely violent and extremely contagious. One scratch, one bite from them and…well they *will* try to scratch at you, and they *will* try to bite your throats. Opening these doors would be incredibly dangerous. Why do you think there was so much trouble when the locks in 28 failed? Hmm? We had subjects there too, you know, and many of them escaped briefly. These people are quite capable of killing armed men. Think what they'll do to us."

"Which is why you should be in there with 'em," says Reggie. "Right?"

He looks at Gibbsy, who just seems embarrassed by the whole scene, and he looks at me, but I'm not going to egg him on.

Rothschild slaps the glass to get our attention. "Please," he says. "Let me finish. Let me explain. There's more you'll want to hear."

*

Rothschild stands in front of the next cell and the eights roll. The man inside the cell looks every bit as mangled and swollen as the twisted man we met in Triage. His skin is split over his jaw. His shoulders are somehow broader than they should be, and he seems to have difficulty walking, but he walks nonetheless, back and forth in the cell.

"We've been trying to develop a vaccine," says Rothschild. "Some of our subjects seem to respond well to the treatment. They display no symptoms even after exposure to several strains of the Influenza D virus. But as you have seen, not all of them respond well. By this point, there is really no hope for them."

Gibbsy gets closer to the glass…but not too close. He films the man and the smudges and the blood on the floor.

"They are never here long," says Rothschild. "Influenza D is typically fatal. The vast majority of subjects experience…well, not physical mutation exactly, but there are certain parts of the nervous system affected in strange ways. Symptoms appear to be similar to those of encephalitis lethargica, but this can be incredibly misleading. Subjects at this stage are every bit as intelligent and reasonable as any of us. But at the same time, they all exhibit a peculiar change in behavior. As Influenza D progresses, the subject communicates less and less with *unaffected* humans. They simply choose not to speak with us. And soon they die."

Rothschild moves to the next cell where four men and two women sit quietly on the floor, staring at us. Their faces are bandaged, but in all other ways, they seem fine.

"For a very small percentage of subjects, the swelling and nerve damage actually grow less severe. They don't heal, and they still exhibit a mutilated affectation. But they do look more normal, I suppose, than in previous stages. These subjects, in the more advanced stages of Influenza D, rarely speak at all, but when they do, there's a marked hostility and dissension in their behavior toward unaffected humans. They do not explain themselves to us, and they seem to understand one another's thoughts, somehow. I'm not suggesting they can read minds, no, but they're very good at reading one another's intentions, I guess you could say. In any case, they are incredibly aggressive toward us. It's as if they hate us, for their own private reasons. They mean us harm and at this stage, they are quite brilliant. There's a name for those affected at this level, a name you probably know very well."

"Crackjaws," says Gibbsy.

"That's right. We've all heard the stories of their cleverness and their contagious nature, of course."

But it doesn't make sense to me. "They don't look like Crackjaws are supposed to look."

"They will," he says. "If they live. These aren't well developed, and most of them won't survive long enough to become what we think of as the typical Crackjaw. But they're certainly a version of it."

"Is that why people say Zanzibar was a lie?" I ask him.

He nods. "Yes, I suppose that is what they mean. Crackjaws did not create the Spanish Flu, like people used to claim. They didn't simply crawl out of hell and build a disease. No. It was always the other way around, as much as we tried to hide from it. We created Influenza D to use against the only enemies we had at the time— regular humans. And *some* of the sick became Crackjaws. You see? It's our fault. A new weapon always breeds a new enemy. But that doesn't matter. Everyone assumes that anyway, and I don't think it would surprise anyone."

Dr. Casten, who has been quiet this whole while, lets out a troubled breath. "Even if they do survive…we have to slaughter them of course. None of this is the point, Rothschild, is it? The illness isn't the point."

Rothschild jerks his head toward Casten only slightly, like he doesn't want to be seen doing it. "No, not in this case."

*

Rothschild shows us through Autopsy 2. We film the cadavers, the tissue samples, the distorted shoulder blades, the enlarged femurs, the goddamn elongated fingers. A skull rests on a shelf at the back of the room. There are no eye sockets.

"What about the people who don't get sick?" says Poplar. She's shaking her head, halfway between laughter and rage. I try to touch her shoulder, but she moves away from my hand. "They just go back to living life in Fallback?"

"No," says Rothschild. "They don't. Once they've been cleared, they are assigned as crewmen for the Drowners. They go to the surface. This is what I want to say into the camera. Can I say this into the camera?"

Gibbsy finds a better patch of light. Rothschild sits on a stool and looks into the lens. Poplar is shaking so hard it pulls her breath to tatters. I've never seen her this bad, and I don't dare to touch her.

"Not all of the men and women who apply for work aboard Drowners are vaccinated first. Some of them *aren't*. Some crews simply serve aboard the Drowners, complete their surface excursions, and return none-the-wiser, living examples that the excursions aren't hopeless, so that we can continue to recruit new crew members.

"But those who *are* injected and appear to respond well to the vaccine are escorted onto the Drowners thinking they will be collecting air samples or specimens or salvage from the safety of their clean-suits. The moment they reach the surface, the Hectors force them out of the Drowner completely unprotected. Into the open air. That is when we really learn whether or not the vaccine works.

"Within two days of exposure to surface air, every subject yet tested has shown symptoms of Influenza D, even though they seemed to have been resistant prior to departure. You see, the vaccine has been one-hundred percent a *failure*. We don't know why. After five days on the surface, the subjects are forced onto the Drowner again and brought to Fallback and are subjected to some necessarily brutal tests at the hands of Mycroft's scientists in Cellular Transmutation. None of them ever return to the populated city."

Suddenly those big cages near the Drowner docks

make sense. Poplar's probably thinking the same thing. I wonder if she's thinking about her mom. About her being brought back in one of those things, insane and mean as hell and nothing like the mother Poplar had known.

"Of course," says Rothschild, "I've been to C-Tran and seen some of the subjects. Many of them refuse to speak to us at all, and some of them tell us that during their exposure to the surface environment they heard 'seductive voices' inside their heads telling them that this is no longer a world for humans. The same message, rattling in their skulls, as if the virus is talking to them. This is important work we do, the vaccine study. But I can't say we've made much progress."

Reggie drags the doctor by his collar toward the door. "Tommy. Where's the peg? It's important work? Like hell. Where's the peg?"

I'm tired of dealing with Reg. He needs to calm down before he gets any more notched. "Here take the goddamn peg and do it already." I throw it at him.

Reggie scrambles for it, scratching along the floor

tiles. He gets a better grip on Rothschild. All the while, Dr. Casten does nothing. He rubs his nose.

Reggie looks at the rest of us, face getting redder by the minute, and he pauses there at the door. He pauses just long enough to give Rothschild a chance to twist away from him and get to his feet.

The doctor strikes Reggie across the cheek, and the boy goes to the floor. But Reggie isn't down long. He's like a spring, that kid. The second he hits the tiles he's up again, pushing Rothschild away. The doctor swings an open palm and leaves a welt that Reggie won't notice until later. The two are against the wall now.

It's Gibbsy who tries to pull Reggie away first, but he's not having much luck, so I have to go help him and pretty soon we've managed to drag Reg back a few feet. Just enough that the doctor can stand and straighten his coat.

"How come you're being such a child? I'm trying to help you. I don't need you barking at me, I'm a grown man, and I've seen more open veins than will ever wake you in the night in a cold sweat. Barking at me. I'm trying to help you. This city. All that's left of us. Of us!"

"He's not the kind of guy you push," I tell Rothschild. "And you pushed him."

"Ah. I pushed him, did I? Well, fine then, I pushed him, but I'm not the kind of man you drag around by the throat either. We need level heads, not maniacs. Why couldn't it have been adults? Tell me that, will you? Why do we have to deal with children on a night like tonight?"

I don't want to explain it to the guy. It should go without saying, but he doesn't have a clue about things. And he's calling *us* children. "Seems to me, all the adults around here can't look this thing in the eye, is why. Now quit pushing my pals and let us do what we do. If we want to put you in the cage, we'll put you in the cage, and it's not like you don't deserve it."

Rothschild knows what I'm saying. He rubs his throat. He says, "Mycroft will do worse things to me than that. Don't worry. My punishment is coming soon enough. There is no way out of this city."

"What we should really do is put Mycroft in that cage. Why in god's name haven't you tried to do something about him, if you're so against all this?"

The doctor is still shaking. He finds a place to sit and waits for his breathing to slow. He says, "I'd love to agree with you, but this city wouldn't survive without Mycroft. He's a brilliant man."

Brilliant or not, I think we would be better off without him, after all I've seen tonight.

Rothschild leans against the wall. "It's true, he doesn't mind wasting lives to accomplish important things. We all know that. But he has done many great things for this city."

"Like what?" I ask him. "You just said you've made no progress."

"I mean other things," he says. "You should know, Fallback was not meant to be submerged. When Kennedy and his men began capturing the Crackjaw barges, they intended for this to be a floating city. It was Mycroft who told them that it wouldn't work. Mycroft knew how dangerous the surface would be, even at sea. Even back then. He was the one who figured out how to make it all work. The arbors, the mines, everything. I'll tell you a story. You can film this if you like."

Gibbsy primes Cassandra and the doctor stares once again into the lens.

"Mycroft knew that we would need geothermal power to survive here. He knew of an operation in Cape Town with enough equipment to make it possible, but he said he needed two ships to retrieve everything and bring it all to Fallback. He told Kennedy about the drills, and the fittings and Kennedy gave him two ships and two crews.

"A month later, Mycroft returned but with only one of the two ships. They say he had a smile on his face, but the crewmen couldn't even bear to lift their eyes. When Kennedy asked him how many men were lost, he said one hundred. When Kennedy asked how much of the equipment was lost, Mycroft said none of it. Kennedy was surprised. He demanded to know why Mycroft required two ships if one was enough to haul all he needed. And Mycroft told Kennedy that he needed the other ship for a *distraction*. And so it was.

"The other crew had been told to make their way up the coast to the far end of Cape Town. They were told to retrieve three drill rigs, and they were given exact coordinates. But what Mycroft did not tell them was that there were no rigs at those coordinates. What he did not tell them was that they were being sent into the heart of a Crackjaw fleet. And they did not survive."

We stare at the man for what seems like ten minutes. Rothschild closes his eyes.

"That's all I have to say."

Gibbsy lowers Cassandra, and she hangs by her strap from his neck.

*

We change the reels even though we've got nothing left to film for now.

"You can still get home," says Rothschild. "You will need to go quickly. There is a way out of here, at the far end of Quarantine, along the rails if you're careful. My keypeg will get you as far as that, and then you will have to do some squirming. But it can be done. It can be done if you go quickly."

Rothschild looks at the map with Gibbsy and me, and he shows us the way to Quarantine. It's a long ways away, but it's the only place we can break through.

"The Hectors will be looking for you," he says. "By now Mycroft will have gathered them back from C-Tran, and there will be an entire *army* combing the halls. I don't have any weapons for you but here's a satchel with vials of sedative and a syringe, if you need it. Half of the cylinder is enough to put *anyone* to sleep, if you can get the needle close enough to use it."

We cram Rothschild's satchel into the backpack. I don't thank him. I should, but I don't want to have to use that syringe on anybody.

"What about when we get home?" I ask. "They'll come looking for us no matter what."

"Probably," he says.

"Well…what do you suggest? I mean…,"

"I don't know," he says. "You'll have to be clever and find clever friends."

He's talking about the Barkers. It's like a burr in the palm. A sliver of metal from a damaged rail. A blink of pain that makes you not trust the stairs.

Even if we do find a place to hide, the City has ways of tracking you down. They've been known to shutter whole blocks just to starve-out the folks they're looking to find.

"HINGES AND BROKEN CHAIRS," Reel 1 of 1, 8mm, 16fps

Vats of molten steel shine white against the darker shapes in the frame. Halos of light surround the channels and the places where it drips from the molds. Men are pushing heavy carts or hauling at the chains.

The camera follows a thin sooty man down the steps. He keeps looking to the right and to the left, but he never shows his face.

The scrawny steelworker opens a door marked "Scrap," and the camera follows into the scrap bay where a thousand crumpled shapes litter the floor. Old doors, engine blocks, pipes, hinges, and broken chairs.

In the back corner of the bay sit a few old girders and hulls and spools of telephone wire. Things salvaged from the surface, useless now except as scrap. Among them stands a cage, three feet by three feet and nine tall, with a hook at the top so it could be hung from a chain. An old burnbox from before they started using electrified plate metal. The bars of the cage were severely rusted, and much of the metal has flaked away. The kind of rust brought on by sea air, by surface air. Salt is crusted in some of the nooks.

Soot covers the roof of the cage and some of the bars. Parts of the floor have been preserved from the rust by an oily residue that must have been burned fat, scorched against the metal. A handprint can be seen outlined there, still slightly black against the rust. Long fingers and a thumb bent oddly backward.

EIGHT

As soon as we're in a clear hall, I pull Gibbsy aside and say, "That guy ain't altogether up-and-up, is he?"

"Who, Rothschild?"

"Well, both of 'em."

"I don't know. I, uh, I don't know Tommy…I guess."

I remind Gibbsy about what Corporal Dunning said the last time we saw him. How he was going to check with the boys in Quarantine. "Doesn't sound to me like a good way out if there's boys to be checked with there…"

Gibbsy rubs his neck, the way he does, and gets his hair out of the way of his face.

"Where's the map?"

He pauses, as if he doesn't want me to look at the map at all. But all it takes is a tilt of my head, and he's unfolding the damn thing.

"What are you looking for?" he asks.

"Something I noticed last time we had it out. Here. Records Office up in Sector 25."

"Records Office," says Gibbsy. His tone is downwind.

"I wasn't sure we would be able to get close enough to 25 but look where Quarantine is, and what with the doc thinking we can get there unseen and all...well what are you looking at me like that for, huh?"

"Poplar's going to be upset, Tommy."

"She's never upset."

"No, just, the way she's been tonight, with all this,

and every time you want to do something that seems like a bad idea she kind of sighs about it."

Gibbsy doesn't have to tell me that. I've got ears. But I don't like the way he's putting things, either. "So, what has 'seemed like a bad idea,' Gibbsy? What have I done tonight that didn't need to be done, considering you and me, we both know the worst thing we could do is to turn a blind eye?"

He says he doesn't know and we leave it at that.

*

He's right about Poplar. She doesn't like the idea of a detour, so I start reasoning with her before she can say word-one.

"It won't take long," I tell her. "He didn't tell us everything he should have told us."

"So all the answers will just be spread on some table?" says Pop. "You could look through a thousand drawers and maybe not find anything worth finding the whole time, and meanwhile there's an *army* headed our way."

"You never know. It's worth a shot."

"No, it isn't 'worth a shot.' You don't need to do it."

I tell her, "Yes I do," and I mean it. There's a city full of people with no idea of what Mycroft and the others are doing. "They need to taste the salt in the water, Pop. And what about your *mom*? Don't you wanna know what happened to her?"

I'm expecting a slap in the face, but Poplar doesn't slap me. She just turns and leans against the far wall, shaking. "She's dead, and she'll stay that way."

Maybe Pop doesn't care, but I do. That's always been the difference, I guess.

I try to tell her that Quarantine might be an even worse place to go, and the records office will have some answers as to how we can really get out of here, but she just says, "When you can't win, Tommy, you lose more by fighting."

I guess there's nothing more I can do so I bite my tongue. She's numb. Everybody's numb. Living in a place like this gives folks an I-just-don't-give-a-shit kind of attitude that I don't understand. Maybe it's on purpose. Maybe the City goes out of its way to keep people from feeling anything. I wouldn't put it past them. Maybe there's a whole City office whose job it is to make sure everyone is depressed. It would make their lives easier, that's for sure. It's hard to know if you're being lied-to when nothing matters to you.

Me, I'm sure not happy, but I'm not depressed either. What I am is furious. I just wish Poplar was too.

*

I finally convince her to wait here for ten minutes and if we're not back by then to scurry along to Quarantine and whatever fate that will bring. We find a swabby vault for her to hide in, and just as the rest of us are gearing to scram, Gibbsy says he should stay here with Pop.

It knocks a bit of dust into my eyes, to hear it. Nobody should be left all alone here, even as tough as Pop is…it's just, if I'm going to be combing records, I'd rather have Gibbsy handy and leave Reggie back here. But I'm not about to raise the issue.

They nestle in among the brooms with the dim yellow light bulb swinging naked overhead, tossing shadows this way and that. Tall jars of fluid shiver as we brush past the flimsy shelves. Reg and me, we tell them to be quiet, and we slip out.

Ten minutes. It will probably take longer than that but hell, they won't leave right away. They'll wait a little longer if necessary.

*

The hatch opens to the smell of roses. The whole junction fills with that sweet foreign air.

On the map, Sector 25 looks just like any other science wing with labs and test chambers marked here and there. But in person, this place looks nothing like Triage or Pathology, or any other place in the industrials, for that matter. It's filled with flower pots. Lining the balconies, filling concrete troughs, and hanging from the concrete ceiling. Roses mostly, with drip irrigation coming down in thin pipes.

The hall is open to the next deck. Long balconies with wrought iron rails line it on either side. Anybody up there would have an easy time seeing us down here. The door hinges are wrought iron too, and the doors are made from carved wood. They still have those FR slots, but the doors are…fancy and old-world, and completely out of place down here in Fallback. The goddamn place looks lovely as all hell, to be honest.

"The Christ is this place?" says Reggie and I couldn't have said it better. The loveliness of Sector 25 strikes us both as very, very insane.

*

"Which room's got the skinny?" says Reggie. He's squinting. We pass a few little alcoves with old oil paintings in nice frames. I've never seen one in person before today. Pictures of angels and things like that.

"Down here to the right." I've got the map folded into a neat square in my hand so that we won't have to wrestle with it on the move and make all sorts of undue noise. It's the Barker's map. I grabbed it out of the backpack by mistake, meaning to take the maintenance skits, but it's been accurate enough so far. Besides, the place seems empty as a drum. So far.

We scuttle from awning to awning, hiding from the balconies. Most of the rooms we pass are test chambers with floor-to-ceiling windows, but the lights are off. In some of them, we can see the glimmer of odd machines. Engines or cutters. The records office is a hundred yards away, past a bunch of dog-legs and checkpoints.

Reggie has been playing with that syringe. He filled it with sedative and keeps twirling it in one hand. I wish I could tell him not to worry about it. It bothers me that this place is so empty. It bothers me that Sector 25 doesn't even have a name.

The hall widens ahead, and we peek around the corner. A screencheck booth sits against the wall just past the L, tilting its thick glass at us. The booth is empty, and the lights here are dim. A painting hangs from the wall. A broad old canvas with Christ himself reeling from the stab of a spear.

We skirt nice and careful past the booth and through the next room, which is some kind of jabber den with plenty of switchboards and radios. Some of the radios hiss. Just static. This room is vacant too.

For half a second, the radios jitter and a voice solidifies from the noise, clean as a chime. We haven't heard from Mycroft in awhile, so at first I think it's him on the PA again. But no, this is a spec radio, and it isn't Mycroft's voice. Maybe it's the Colonel's. "Eleven, 80 degrees, frost."

I can't guess what it means, and it goes back to static just as quick as that.

The map shows another long hall past this one, a small clerk's office, and behind that is record storage. Not far at all.

But this is as far as we get. I twist Rothschild's FR peg in the lock, but the switch goes red, and the godforsaken thing stays latched.

"Son of a bitch."

"It's not *o*pening?" says Reggie.

"No. Shit, he must not have…I don't know, *access* to this place. Or clearance or whatever. Goddamnit."

I'm so mad I almost hurl the peg at the ground.

"Well, why the hell'd we come all the way down here, Tommy?"

"I don't know, Reg. Why's the doc's peg not get us through that door? That's what I want to know. He's a top dog, right, and his peg should trip the lock same as the others."

Reg says, "Maybe this ain't his turf. He ain't a gardener."

Hearing that reminds me of something and my face goes pale. Reggie must have noticed the blood drain from my cheeks because he's looking awfully confused right now.

"Come on," I tell him. "We need to go back for our pals. I shoulda brought Gibbsy. He would've noticed by now."

"Noticed what?" says Reggie.

"You saw this place. What's it look like, a garden? But what kind of garden?" The paintings, the statues, the air full of pollen, the iron bars twisted like vines. "The Machinist, he said something about it, didn't he? Something about a graveyard gate. Let's get Pop and Gibbsy. And we need those keys the Machinist gave us too. To hell with Rothschild's. There's a door around here somewhere the Machinist wanted us to find. This is the way home, Reg."

*

It's been long enough now, Pop and Gibbsy are probably wondering what to do next. Me and Reggie, we move as fast as we dare, under the roses.

"Surprised we haven't run into your buddies yet," I say.

"My buddies," says Reg. "Barkers wouldn't come in here."

"No, they'd rather send a buncha kids, yeah? They sent the right buncha kids, but that doesn't mean they did the right thing."

Reggie lifts his hands and says nothing.

"Jesus, Reggie. I mean…good god, this is a big goddamn deal but what bothers me is none of us *knew*. If I'd known where they were sending us and why, maybe I'd have come down here without a fuss and done a better job of it."

"Doesn't matter," he says.

I love Reggie, but I don't think he understands why I'm on edge. "Even if we get out of here with our skin, I guess the Barkers will try'n lay claim to the reels, like they do. And it's not that I want my name on something like this, but if they get clumsy and the Bands come looking for whoever shot this, the Barkers'll know who to send them to. If I'm gonna risk the burnbox, I wanna know the lay of the land first and not go in blind, right? We're dancing on their strings right now. Have been all night."

Reggie tries to tell me they're not that smart. On some level, I agree with him, but underneath it all the

Barkers are an *organization.* They're just like the City. It doesn't matter if they're all morons because when a bunch of morons get together and start worrying about what all the other morons in the room are going to do, there's sure to be trouble. We still don't know what happened over in the docks or C-Tran, with the doors. We still don't know what all that radio trouble was about, with the Hectors. And the Barkers…we still don't know why they sent us down here in the first place.

Maybe they don't know either, and that's a scary thought.

*

Just shy of the Pathology hatch, Reggie shoves at me, like he has something to say before we go back to fetch the others. "Tommy," he says, "you gotta stop bottle-feeding Gibbs like you been. It's making me nuts. Remember that time he said I'm not half as smart as a rivet, just to be a bastard? Couple months back."

This isn't a good time for rubbish. "You're smarter than a rivet, Reg, but Gibbsy's on another deck. He said that because you hit him, is why, 'cause he asked if you were 'Okay.'"

"He's not as smart as you think, Tommy. And what if he is? What does he do, just standing there staring at everybody, listening all the time without actually *doing* anything for anybody?"

Maybe, but when Gibbsy watches something, his gears are sure as hell spinning.

I start walking again so I can put this whole thing under the grate. "Reg, all *you* do is make a lot of noise and get notched. You don't do anything *either*. You just go around making sure everyone knows how notched you are. Remember the lilac bush?"

I can tell he's annoyed by the way he tilts his head back. He remembers. It was about a year ago. We used to get steamed dumplings sometimes at Queequeg's in Dollrand Markets. They had this lilac bush under a drip and a sun lamp, but it was in pretty bad shape because the drip wasn't giving it enough water. Reggie kept saying how they should take better care of it and if it was his plant he'd take great care of it. One night we went down to Dollrand late, so he could take the damn thing home.

The place was empty. We could have just grabbed the plant and walked away but Reggie, he thought it would be an even better idea to stand there shouting, "Wake up, assholes. They're my flowers now." Then he tugged at the drip tube that had been watering the lilacs. The hose broke away from the wall and water started pouring on the ground. Spraying everywhere. "You wanna save water, assholes? It's all yours. Drink 'til you drown."

We ran, trying to carry those goddamn flowers between the two of us. Reggie, he's always doing things like that, and I just get fed up sometimes.

"Every time we're trying to do something worth doing," I tell him, "you just run out there and shout 'drink 'til you drown' thirty goddamn times. That's all you ever do. It doesn't help."

He doesn't say anything, and we keep moving.

*

Going through the hatch, I'm nervous. I don't care so much if Pop is still mad. It just bothers me that Gibbsy stayed with her. He never stays behind, ever. This is a guy who follows me into the john once in awhile, even when he doesn't have to piss or have anything to say. He'll just come in and lean on the counter and wait sometimes.

I peek around through the stacks of chemicals and buckets, not sure if Gibbs and Pop are still here and not sure what I'll see. But they are here, and all they're doing is leaning against opposite corners looking at us. My stomach stops fretting for once. I don't know what I was worried about and I don't want to think about it. And besides, I knew they'd wait longer than ten minutes.

"Hey, hey, mops and brooms. We're going home." I punch Gibbsy's arm. They both look at me like they just woke up from a death nap.

"You're late," says Pop. "You find any precious top-secret records?"

"No. But what I found is better. I found a better

way to get home."

"What? What about Quarantine like the doctor guy said."

Poplar's eyes go wide, so I tell her about the graveyard gate. "Just like what's his name said. The Machinist. He said this key peg would work on the graveyard gate, and we found it. That was a hint. Right Gibbsy?"

He shrugs. "Rothschild said to get through Quarantine as fast as we could, so…"

"So the doc didn't know better," I say, "but I guess there's more than a few Hectors in Quarantine 'cause of what our buddy Corporal Dunning said. The Machinist knows something Rothschild doesn't, is what I mean."

Poplar grabs a scrub brush from the hook next to her and starts slowly flicking the bristles back and forth over the corner of a shelf. She doesn't believe a word I'm saying. She always acts bored when she thinks I'm lying to her. And most times there's nothing I can do to turn it around, but I've got to try. Me and my indivisible charms.

"Look, here, I'll get out the skits. Have a look at this, citizen with the bright red hair."

She won't step closer to the map, so I unfurl it under her nose with Gibbsy leaning close to hold the other corner.

"We went up this, and down here. All this is stone and iron with flowers everywhere. I mean everywhere. And this? A big iron gate and the room past that has no sign on the door or anything. All these statues and things in there, just like they used to put in the old graveyards topside. I know you know what that means."

Poplar says, "Why didn't he just tell us to go this way, if that's what he meant?"

"I don't know. You tell me. Maybe he didn't want the other Barkers knowing he was helping us?" It makes some sense to me, at least.

"No, I mean the doctor. Why wouldn't he say to go this way?"

"You think we can trust Kennedy's toadie?" She gives me a deadly glance and looks away, so I modify the statement. "Okay, so even if we can trust him, how's he supposed to know we have a key for that? As far as he knows, this place isn't an option. If he even knows about it."

She still isn't looking at me. She's still brushing the shelf. I take the brush out of her hand and drop it, and Gibbsy says, "Tommy." But I'm not trying to be mean, she just needs to pay attention. I'm trying to help her, I really am. I back to the middle of the room and I start doing ballet dips or whatever they're called. Like a swan. She doesn't smile yet.

"I guess that's a furnace room," I tell her. "See what I mean? They call it the graveyard because that's where they take all the bodies, and they burn 'em up to get rid of 'em. Which means…there's a dust ladder like they've got coming out of the mines and I bet we can get out that way without anybody noticing us. That's my guess anyway, and you have to admit it makes sense. All those flowers are somebody's idea of a joke, but if you ask me that room is where they get rid of the dead, and the Machinist's key gets us in there, and out of here. Once you think about all the details and all the things you know, it all makes sense."

She's still not smiling so I get down on one knee and I take her hand and start to sing low and soft, making it up as I go. "My fair lady tall and bright. You...said there was something about the Machinist you liked. Clearly, he cared whether or not we lived tonight, and..."

She puts a hand over my mouth. I'm half a second from moving my head to the side so I can keep singing my stupid damn song, but then I hear what she must have heard. Someone is walking through the halls just outside this room.

*

It's been so long since we've heard signs of life down here, I hadn't even been listening for it. I only hope I hadn't been making enough noise to be heard through the door.

We wait, and the footsteps wander. Just a single

passer-by, shuffling in an odd and dizzy way, and I think it's that other doctor, Casten. But I don't know why he would be out here, and there's no sense chancing a peek. We wait, like we always do, until the man is gone and we're alone again.

*

"You sure you're not just dragging us along again?" says Pop. "So you can film something you think you should film?"

The way she says that, it's full of teeth.

"First of all," I tell her, "it's *all* been important. Second of all, no, I'm not fleecing you, I just know what I saw, and I know what that Hector said about going to Quarantine."

Poplar doesn't say anything. Not right away. But finally, she lets out a manic string. "Tommy, I'll come with you, but I don't want to hear about my mom again," she says. "I'm not trying to get *revenge* for whatever happened to her, and it wasn't any of my business. She always talked about the cool night air and having funnel cakes at the fair. Like it could ever happen again. She always promised me that the world would get better when I was a kid, and that promise was broken, so there's nothing wrong with what happened to her. She didn't know what I know. There's no such thing as a promise. There's just stuff that happens to you and stuff you make happen to yourself. Ring the havoc bell all you want, we're all too used to the sound already."

"I wasn't going to say anything about your mom anymore. I promise."

"And no more stupid detours," she says. "I either want to go home or get shot dead and get it over with. You can say what you want about Dale Pike, but he'd know what I mean by that. No more detours tonight trying to pull more footage out of this place."

"No more detours," I tell her. And I mean it, too, even though what she said feels like it broke a couple of ribs.

*

"It doesn't say anything about...disposal, or

anything." Gibbsy is scanning the map again. He seems more concerned than usual, but I can't blame him.

"Well, it doesn't say anything else either. I'm saying it *looks* like a graveyard."

Gibbsy stabs at the map awhile longer before bending it in half under his arm as we stand resting in a recess. A couple of vending machines hum beneath the opposite archway. I'm hungry, and I bet everybody else is too, so I knock a few coins through the slots and pull the knobs and walk back to the crew with a few wrapped donuts and a bottle of soda.

Reggie won't eat the goddamn donuts. He says there's butter or lard in them. "Dairy is rape."

"Fine, don't eat, Reg. Starve to death, you picky bastard, while we enjoy our mighty feast."

We're so hungry, we swallow without chewing. And the soda's gone before it can fizz.

*

"I've seen that before," says Gibbsy. We stop in an

atrium, and he sits on the rim of a big fountain staring up at this big tilting frame. It's a painting of a woman with a fur shawl and a veil over what seems to be a very distorted face. "Used to be at the Riley Museum," he says. "A buncha years ago. Whole buncha paintings they took out of Zanzibar, but it's been awhile though…guess they moved it over here."

"Why'd they put that here?" I'm still wondering about this place. About who had the sand to doll it up like this. "She's a Crackjaw, isn't she?"

"I'd guess she is."

The flowers and the paintings and the windows get increasingly elegant, the closer we get to the gate. It makes me wonder, why don't they do this in the rest of the City? Why keep all the nicest stuff at the ass-end of a sector like this where they burn the corpses of tortured monsters? You never see anything pretty in Fallback. The whole goddamn City, except a few places. No roses or lilacs or paintings. I know Gibbsy would agree; he's always saying that. Most of Fallback's nothing much to look at.

It seems to be bothering Reggie, too. He makes a point to piss on some of the flowers outside the gate when we get there. "Hasn't been much rain this year," he says.

Gibbsy laughs and Reggie just glares at him. That's what I mean about those two. Gibbsy, he was just trying to be nice about it, but the way Reggie sees it, that laugh was fake. Now he's staring at Gibbsy and Gibbsy gives one of his smiles and looks away like he hasn't even noticed anything is wrong.

"Hey, Gibbs. Tommy says you didn't want me to come with you tonight."

I don't give Gibbsy a chance to answer. I say to Reggie, "No. That's not what I said. I said we didn't want to talk to the Barkers. You know what I said."

"I know what you meant, though," says Reggie. He's still looking at Gibbsy. "Maybe I didn't want you to come along either."

It'll take a lot more than that to get Gibbsy to talk back. We don't have time for that sort of thing, so I tell

Reggie to shut it off, and I hold the gate open and tell everybody to march.

The walls rattle just a tiny bit as a tram passes somewhere overhead, a few decks above us.

*

The crematorium door stands wider than the three of us together. It's got those thick rivets like they use in bulkheads and the FR lock sits flush in the wall. Everything about it seems heavy, brutal, and indifferent, just like a furnace or a tomb should look I guess.

The hall is otherwise a dead end, but so many flowers hang from the lamps, you'd almost imagine you could push through, into a wooded glade like you hear about in stories. A statue leers through the vines, an old marble thing with a shattered face. Maybe that's from Zanzibar, too. Looking at it, past all these shaking leaves and creepers, it almost makes me dizzy. It makes me want to just sit down and stare, and I realize how dog tired I am, all of a sudden. I don't know what time it is, but the bells will chime soon enough I'm sure.

Somewhere back there closer to home.

"Gibbsy, you see that? Think it had a Crackjaw face once?"

"Yeah," he says.

I don't know why it matters. I just get this feeling, like I can hear a thousand people muttering and crying and growling. An image in my mind. A long room filled with folks sick and dying. Clawing at each other's eyes. Clawing at each other's throats.

"Where's that peg we bought?"

Reggie starts rummaging through the backpack. "Which one?" he says.

"I don't know. Same one that got us into the docks."

"No clue," says Reggie, "I mean where's that list they gave us. It said what's what."

But I don't know where that old slip of paper went either…it's probably hell and gone now.

Reggie just starts sliding a few pegs into the slot, one after another. They all give the red light.

"He shouldn't do that," says Gibbsy. "Too many bad tries and the whole sector goes red."

"It'll be fine," I tell him.

Gibbsy starts to get nervous but the next peg Reggie tries gives us the blue, and we're in.

"Christ. See?"

The big crematorium door clicks, rumbles, and slides into the wall.

"Let's get to gettin'."

Before any of us can take a step, the lights go out. All of them. Another goddamn blackout.

*

I can hear everyone breathing. I can hear the distant bump of some oblivious tram and another sound too. A soft sound that scares the hell out of me. The unlatching of doors. The quiet click of disengaged FR locks, behind us, in front of us, all around us, all unlocking at once.

In the darkness, a frail hand touches my shoulder. "Tommy," says Poplar. "Let's turn around and go."

*

The lights come back, and for a minute we just stare through the doorway, past the vestibule. I'm expecting a big furnace room but all we see is the crook of a wide hall that angles away from us to god knows where or what.

"Shit. Hear that?" says Reggie.

"Hear what?"

"Guns," he says.

And he's right. A faint wave of shots echoes from somewhere past the bend, far enough off I have to tilt my ear to catch it. It lasts a good couple of minutes before petering out completely.

I tell my friends, "It was our fault."

Somehow, we unlocked all those doors when we came to the docks, and now we've done it again.

I almost don't notice the mark on the vestibule wall, the symbol scratched into the paint. The shepherd's crook. The goddamn Herds.

Poplar is tugging my sleeve. "Tommy," she says. "Come on."

I do my best to ignore her. "Those gunshots? That'll be the Barkers, Reg. Your buddies, sneaking in the way we're supposed to be sneaking out. I'd bet my jawbone on that one, youngsters."

"Hell it is," he says.

I don't understand it either, but that's the way it's got to be. Somehow, I don't know, the Barkers knew we would get through to here, and they needed us to open the doors from *this* side for them. Or maybe we were just a distraction. I sure as hell don't know but I'm notched over it, wide into the red, and I'm not turning-tail until I find out what's what.

I don't say anything to Poplar. I just look at her,

and she tilts her head as if she knows what I'm thinking.

"Eights, Gibbs. Start cranking. Wake-up our old gal Cassandra."

He's too wide-eyed to hear what I said. He inches back a bit toward that statue.

"Eights, Gibbs. The camera."

But he *doesn't* get the camera, so I have to fetch it myself. Cassandra has a fresh reel, still loaded from when we left Pathology, and I start cranking as I step through the vestibule and toward those frantic gunshots.

We've been walking into the haze all night, and I feel like everything is collapsing slowly behind me. Eventually there will be nothing left. I'll never be able to make anyone care. There's no use trying to explain it to them anymore. They won't listen. They won't start caring about what actually matters.

My pals are hesitating, following me but not following me. If I weren't grinding my teeth right now, I might ask them the Question. I would ask them, what's so great about saving your own life if you live in a dishonest world? "At least we're alive," they would say. But no, "alive" is not the word for it.

*

The hall twists again just ahead, and a body slumps in the corner. A Hector. He isn't moving, and when we get close enough, I can see why. He has been shot in the face. The wall behind him is scattered with bone and blood. His hand grips a pistol, and it looks for all the world like he did this to himself.

The four of us stand over him, and I'm thinking about the Barkers and wondering how many of them are storming into the place, right now, to where a guy like this would lose all hope.

"Tommy it'd be better if we weren't here," says Pop.

"They don't have anything against us; we did 'em a favor."

"Tommy..."

"Probably shake our hands, the bastards, and tell

us 'good job'."

She strokes her cheeks, the way she does, which means she's done with the discussion and we move on. I barely notice that the sound of gunfire has stopped.

*

The hall puts us into a slit bunker filled with guns, including a couple of floor-mounted Plug-20s, both pointing out through metal slots at the next room. I've never seen a goddamn bunker like this. Not for guarding dust ladders.

The others stay back while I peek past the glass, at a wide span of a room and a thick blast-shield. A big red and white metal slab with a redbell spinning over it. It's the same kind of shutter they use in the gas mines.

I'm expecting to see a big huddle of Barkers, but I don't. The room is empty except for one Hector, collapsed against the blast-shield, with his arm severed at the elbow.

Gibbsy rushes through the bunker's gate and across the metal floor. He steps clear of the spreading pool of blood and leans over the Hector. I'm right behind him, filming everything.

"You okay?" says Gibbsy. It's a stupid question, but the Hector is awake and seems calm. His arm is bleeding-out slower than I thought a wound like that would bleed and as I get closer, I notice the tourniquet he has tied around the stump, using his belt and some cloth.

I don't know where that missing arm is. I guess it's on the other side of that blast shield. Meanwhile, the Hector is out here sitting cross-legged, yellow, cheeks sunk, and the arm he's got left is holding a strap tied to the blast-shield to keep himself upright. He's swaying like a tram-ginny, and he's sweating thick droplets to mix with his blood.

"Pen is broke," he says which makes so little sense, I guess he's in shock. It's a hell of a struggle for him to say much all. He keeps taking these deep perforated breaths every few words. "You gotta get out. He could open it."

With the camera close to his face I ask him, "Are

they trying to get in here? Tell Cassandra. Tell the eights."

"Get the flood-checks," he says. He's on the verge of passing out. He doesn't know what he's saying.

I knock on the blast shield. The strap he's holding, a gun strap I guess, is actually tied to both handles on either side of the seam, like he's trying to keep the damn shield closed with it.

I ask him again about Barkers, and he just gets more confused. He says something about how the strap won't hold long. His voice is dizzy now with a delirium that keeps getting worse. "Locks are off, he'd just have to push it open."

"He?" I ask him how many guys are out there. He just shakes his head, wincing. I ask him if he's the only one here. I keep filming.

"Everybody else is dead," he says. "All our guys plus the extra guys they sent. All gone." It's hitting me now that something is wrong here. Something other than what I thought was wrong.

"The Barkers or your guys? Who's dead? Tell the camera. How many Barkers are still out there?"

The Hector gives me a pained, baffled look and I repeat the question. Slower this time. He still doesn't answer. The shock, I guess, or losing blood like that.

"Can we get out through here?" I ask him. "Is there a way out of the goddamn industrials, or what?" But he thinks I'm insane, so I shake the guy and say, "Can we get out of here through there?" and I knock on the blast shield. It seems to bring him back to his senses and clears his eyes a little.

And what he says next has no hint of confusion to it. No hint of shock. He says, "This is a cage."

A cage. I don't know if I say it out loud or just think it. A goddamn cage. I can feel Poplar's eyes on me now, looking at me and then looking away.

"A cage, a cage for who?"

And the Hector says, "For him. For Blankface."

Almost by itself, my mouth moves to repeat the

name but my tongue trips over it, and nothing comes out. This isn't the first time I've heard that name tonight, and it's like having the valves all shut at once. Boiler shrapnel in the scalding air. I half glance at Poplar, but I don't really look at her. Just long enough to see her arms are wrapped around her ribs. I'm wrong about things more than I think I am, is what she would say to me right now if she could.

This isn't a place for incinerating the corpses, and it isn't a place to dump the ashes. There's no way through here to any kind of dust ladder, and there are no Barkers trying to pry into the industrials from the other side of this door.

It's a cage, a dead end. It's a prison, and we've been epoxied in to opening the goddamn doors and letting out whoever is trapped on the other side. It makes me so dizzy to think about it, I almost fall to the floor.

I lean against the wall and shut my eyes and try to think.

*

Blankface.

I don't care anymore. It doesn't matter if I'm right or wrong or if we've been swindled. There never was a way out of here, but I don't care. I'm filming anyway. Somebody needs to lay out the facts, so it might as well be me. Somebody needs to talk to the people, and I've got the camera. I'm going to use it.

"Friends and citizens of Fallback, this is the second time we've heard that name tonight, and no one seems really happy to say it. *This* soldier seems to know something about it and so let's ask him, shall we? Who is Blankface?"

The Hector looks at me as if noticing the camera for the first time. "I don't know…"

"Not *supposed* to know, friends and citizens. Right? Not *supposed* to know. Can we assume he was asked to risk his life here at this post and never once was he supposed to know why?"

From the back of the room, Poplar is yelling at me to stop horsing around. But I'm not horsing around. I'm talking to the People, and I'll keep talking to the People, whether the hell she likes it or not.

"Tell the good citizens what happened to your arm."

He looks up at me and shakes his head. "This strap won't hold him. He'll come out here I promise. This won't hold him."

I point the camera at the gun strap. "What he's saying, citizens, is that this thick old strap isn't enough. That someone named *Blank*face will somehow bust that strap and kill us like he killed all of the other poor soldiers. What is he? Is he a *Crackjaw*? Well, let's watch and see. Don't you want to see old Blankface for yourselves, friends and citizens? Don't you want to see what this goddamn City is *hiding* from you? Don't you want to know why the Blackbands never let you breathe? Why you have to watch those Bulletins? I think Blankface might have some answers and I want to see him as much as you do."

Now Reggie is yelling at me too. Goddamn

Reggie. Let him yell. I don't have to explain myself to him or Pop or Gibbsy. They're all staring at me like I'm crazy, but the fact is this *City*'s crazy, and I'm done lying down with its boot on my throat. It's time to stand up, for god's sake, and turn on the lights. I know I won't get home alive and I know the City will destroy the reels. But whoever kills me, they'll learn something before they do it. That I won't stop filming until they cut my throat.

"The flood-check," says the Hector. His face is pale now, but he's still calm.

"That's what the City *does* to you," I say, filming the Hector's arm and the blood. "Here's this poor man on the verge of death and all he can do is tell us to turn off the camera and leave. It isn't fair, friends and citizens, that they make us act like this. And over there, that's Poplar Meer, whose mother was killed by the City, and she doesn't even care. And there's Charlie Gibbs, who gets sick every time he tries to eat his lunch, but he'd never do a thing about it. And then this poor Hector, he's still trying to *protect* whatever secret is on the other side of this heavy door. Well, I'm not going to leave. I'm not going to turn a blind eye, friends and citizens. You can always count on Tommy Molotov and his trusty gal Cassandra to let you taste the salt in the water. Let's see what the City has to say for itself. Let's give Blankface a hand..."

I stand and reach for the gun strap. I'm going to open the godforsaken blast shield, and I'm going to film the whole thing. Reggie is shouting, and I'm not listening. He's coming back from the bunker with a goddamn Lebanov, and he's waving it around.

My hand touches leather. I start to unthread the strap, but something is wrong. I can't feel my fingers. I can't feel the brass of the clasp. The camera drops from my other hand, and my whole body is going numb.

As I turn my head, I see the half-empty syringe in Gibbsy's hand. I see Reggie, all but a blur, as he reaches over and punches Gibbsy in the face, sending him to the ground, and when he lands he loses the empty syringe which breaks into a thousand shards like a burst boiler while Reggie starts to kick him in the ribs.

And then I sleep.

"A SMALL CRUTCH," Reel 1 of 1, 16mm, 24fps

A pair of legs step into the frame. One of them has been amputated and replaced with a prosthetic. Next to it stands a crutch.

A filtered voice from behind the camera says, "How did you lose your leg?"

"It was crushed off, like, in a junction hatch," says another voice. This one is muffled but not altered aside from that. A young boy's voice.

"Why were you caught in a junction hatch?" says the cameraman.

"Because it was too crowded," says the boy. "The Blackbands, they told us to get out of the screencheck place where you wait, because someone said something they didn't like. I didn't hear what. Everybody scrunched up to the hatch, and they started shutting it before I could get all the way past it. I couldn't go back either. Then someone pushed me, and I fell."

The camera does not show the boy's face.

"And the Blackbands didn't care."

"They shut the hatch before we could all get out," says the boy.

NINE

The dreams are vivid. The dark playgrounds from my youth. The "parks" with metal walls. I follow a girl into a hospital room that somehow faces the markets and we sit together on a hospital bed. Before I can ask what her name is, she leaves me, and when I turn back to the bed I see Gibbsy lying there, his skin burned to tatters, his lungs and stomach showing through his thin abdomen, his eyes shattered as they flicker at the ceiling.

In the dream I start to cry and sob, calling for the doctor to come and fix Gibbsy, and then I collapse in the corner gasping, "I'm sorry, I'm sorry. What didn't I do?" and the doctor comes into the room carrying a bone saw.

Gibbsy tries to scream through his brittle lips.

*

When I wake up, I'm covered in crackly blood. I don't think it's mine, but I feel like hell, and I start looking around to see if I'm bleeding.

Gibbsy is sitting next to me. We're in some small office, behind a desk. I don't know where, but we're surrounded by plants and paintings, so I guess we're still in sector 25. One of my pals has wedged a coat rack against the door on this side, like somebody's going to try to get in here.

The lights are dim. Reggie paces past. He's holding the Lebanov, and he's sweating.

"How'd I get here?"

"Dragged you," says Reg. "Heavy bastard. Your glasses broke."

I try to stand but my limbs seize, and the spasms feel like ten-thousand volts.

Gibbsy's face is red, and his lip is bleeding. "How many times did Reggie smack you?"

Gibbsy shrugs. "I can't blame him."

"Goddamn stabbed you with a syringe. Course I smacked him."

Gibbsy says, "Are you still mad, Tommy?"

I'm so groggy, I can't decide. I guess Gibbsy would have felt bad if he hadn't done it. Tranq'ed me like that. I guess I don't know what I was thinking, trying to open that blast shield, and Gibbsy would feel awful if I had let myself get killed. "No, Gibbs, I'm not mad. You fellas *dragged* me out?"

"Yeah," says Reg. "Practically passed out, too. Heart's still beating like a piston."

Gibbsy nods. He's been sweating too, from the looks of it. His shirt is damp. I don't know how far they dragged me, but it must have been a long ways.

"Well I keep telling you bastards I'm an asshole, but you always seem so goddamn surprised. Put the gun away, Reg."

"No chance," he tells me. He doesn't skip a beat.

"How long was I asleep?"

"A half-hour, maybe," says Gibbsy. "I looked around the records place," he says, pointing. "Just over there. Doors are open now."

That makes me sit up straight, spasms or not. "Shit, you find anything?"

He nods. "Not much, but, well, here."

He pulls a wedge of papers from his pocket and smoothes it all. My eyes hurt too bad to read. "What'd you find?"

"Wasn't any mention of Blankface," he tells me. "But it talks about the Quarantine ward. It's filled with people from the city hospitals, moved over. Influenza D. Says people are getting sick without the doctors making them sick, sometimes. The Spanish Flu shows up sometimes in hospitals."

I'm not surprised. Fallback really is a coffin.

"A whole ward full," says Gibbsy.

"No mention of Blankface."

"No," he says.

"I'd say he's buddies with the Barkers, but they can't be that psychotic, can they? Trying to set a Crackjaw free like that? I hope that strap holds…"

Gibbsy and Reggie go quiet, and Reggie stops pacing. They know something I don't. "What?"

"We saw him," says Gibbsy. "When we were dragging you out. He tore that shutter open even with the strap on it and…there he was, wearing a suit and tie and tapping his fingers together. A man without any eyes."

A goddamn man without eyes. "A real, hand-to-god Crackjaw walkin' the halls."

"Yeah."

"Tried shooting at the bastard but I missed," says Reg. "Too far away. He just…stared at us. But without eyes. Yeah. Stood by that Hector just letting him bleed and didn't follow us when we dragged you out, thank Christ. God knows where he is now."

"Doesn't matter."

"I don't know," says Reggie. "There was a shitload of dead Hectors on the other side of that blast shield, what we saw of it."

"Like a theater sort of," says Gibbsy, "with a big cell in it he must have come out of when the locks went away. There were all these rows of benches around the cell like for people to sit in there and watch him. Instruments and things."

So they had him under the scope.

"We're not getting out of here alive," is all I can say. Now I know why my pals wedged the door in here shut. We've gone and done the worst thing we could've done. We let loose a monster.

*

My head is too full of waves to talk much. We sit awhile. Now and then somebody says something, and I'm not always paying attention. But it's getting better.

"Been thinking about it," says Gibbsy. "All the statues and paintings and flowers. I've been thinking about Donovan Square, how it's different than the rest of the City and how it's…I don't know, got art like this place does. The architecture. I think that was the original Fallback, the parts the Crackjaws built for their own cities before the raids on the barges. The Crackjaws used to live in places like this. The rest of Fallback's all just pieced together from their, like, basements and factories."

"Crackjaws have fancy tastes, is what you're saying."

"I guess so. But what I'm saying is, this place is old. Maybe that Crackjaw is one of the old ones too. What did Rothschild say about those back there? Not 'fully-developed.' Maybe Blankface is the real thing. He's one of the bad ones. A thousand times smarter than us and mean about it. Maybe Mycroft's been torturing him all these years not just to learn how to cure the Flu but to figure out how to keep the city going."

Gibbsy's right, most of this place is beyond any of us. It makes me think of the Machinist. He had eyes, but he was probably a Crackjaw of some kind. And the peg he gave us shorts-out whole grids for some reason.

Maybe there are more like him than we know about, out there and "free." It makes me shiver.

"Lucky this one didn't bite our throats. Blankface."

Gibbsy shakes his head. "Lucky."

Something's been bothering me, and as my head starts to clear, I realize what it is. I grab Gibbsy's arm. "Where the hell is Poplar?"

Gibbsy just looks at me. Reggie says, "I don't know."

"She left," says Gibbsy.

"When you were doing your JFK voice," says Reggie.

"What, she left? Before you knocked me out? The hell'd she go?"

"I don't *know*," says Reg.

"She just left," says Gibbsy. "Out the way we came. We tried looking for her, but she's gone."

*

My legs aren't working very well, but I can walk. The more I walk the worse I feel, but the nerves are starting to wake up, and I can move fast enough.

"She could be anywhere."

Gibbsy shakes his head. "I think I know where she went," he says.

"Quarantine?"

"I was telling her how to get there," says Gibbsy. "When you guys came out here to the records office without us. She kept asking. She didn't think Rothschild was lying to us, said it wasn't fair to think he was anyway."

Jesus, Poplar. But hell, for all I know she was right. Maybe Rothschild really does want us to get this footage out into the world, and he was trying to make it happen. I hope so.

The three of us stand there at the door, not one of us daring to move the coat rack out of the way. I can picture him standing out there. Blankface. Staring at the door even though he doesn't have any eyes. Waiting for it to open.

*

Years ago, I had a crazy idea to try and get some film of this tagger named "Petal." A true graffiti artist, real slick, never seen by the Bands, never seen by the punks. Petal had been painting walls after curfew in some of the City squares on I and J, and used to do murals of old city streets and vistas, like you would see if you still lived on the surface. Right onto the walls of Fallback. They were pretty good, too. Not realistic, but more convincing than a realistic painting can be, if that makes sense. Surreal, or abstract, but...accurate. Standing in Sterling, you could almost imagine you were outside in some geometric world, as the path zigged down a flowered spiral slope.

I finally caught up with Petal in Bamph Commons. The place was empty, and I was hiding between the beams, waiting with Cassandra, almost falling asleep. Echoes like the dripping of water. A shadow like scorched glass. If I had been looking in any other direction, I would not have known Petal was in the room.

Here came this huddled figure in a hood with a bunch of stencils and paint cans. The mural went up fast on that mottled wall between the pillars. In less than ten minutes, I was faced with a grand scene. A bunch of old buildings on the streets of a lost city. And past the city, a purple sky and a setting sun in the shape of a gearwork. On the street were a dozen scattered toys for absent children.

Petal was gone again as quick as that. Footsteps on wool, barely touching the ground. Then I realized I hadn't even filmed it. I'd been so struck by the scene, I didn't even think to hit Cassandra's switch and roll the eights. There I was, cursing myself, when I heard a sound that I was hoping I wouldn't hear. The clicking of keys. A Blackband key belt, like the captains wear.

That put the hurry into me. It was time to dissolve.

The plan was to catch the dark trams—the ones they don't watch much—so maybe I could sneak into H without having to wear-out my shoes. A couple of other folks got on at the same platform as me, some drunks and some swabbies and pipe twisters and such. Just regular joes, none of them Blackbands. No rattling keys.

The problem was, I took the wrong tram. I was in a panic after hearing those keys, but the line I had boarded was about to take me further away from H after the next bend, and then it would wheel me back in the opposite direction. I started to panic. I kept looking at the route line. I was sweating.

As soon as the tram reached its next stop, I stood and reeled out onto the platform. I skulked around until I found the routes posted in a shifty corner. The first thing I noticed was that there were no more trains coming through here tonight. I wasn't happy about the idea of walking home on foot, but that's what it had come to. I practically ripped the chart off the wall.

Then I heard those keys again. The Blackband. Click, click, click. Right behind me.

It took me awhile to get up the nerve to turn

around, but when I did, I didn't see a Blackband at all. I saw a girl smiling like she was trying not to laugh. I remembered seeing her coat near Bamph. She had boarded the train from the same place as I did but I must have assumed she was older because of the hour.

She held up a copper ring full of keys, and she said her name was Poplar. "I been watching you get madder and madder and been wondering how much madder you'd get."

I didn't care how pretty she was, and I said something about the city being a jumble, and she asked if it was really the City's fault. "You're damn right it's the City's fault," I said. And the more I said after that, the more she laughed, until I finally just asked her, "Do you live around here? Know how I can get to H?"

"I don't know," she said, "I was supposed to stay on that train."

She'd gotten off at the wrong platform just to watch me fume, the crazy damn skirt. I decided the gentlemanly thing to do would be to walk her home.

We stumbled through the dark and dripping tunnels, turning away from every light or sound we saw or heard along the way, stopping to swing on the swings of abandoned parks where the ceilings were too low. I told her about Gibbsy and how if he had it his way, they'd let him come and clean and polish the whole damn place and make it sparkle.

Poplar said she liked the place the way it was. "Kind of like an old man smiling," she said. "All those wrinkles from smiling his whole life."

Then we were off again. Running through the crackling vickshafts with our hair floating in the static fields, giddy from the late hour but not the least bit tired, quick, quiet, whispering through parts of the City so empty we couldn't imagine that this was not our world. Just us and the tin crickets.

When we got back to K, we talked for awhile outside her apartment. I said something about Kennedy, and she laughed and opened her backpack to show me what was inside. A hooded cloak and a spray nozzle and a bunch of paint cans.

When I caught my breath, I smiled and bowed and said, "It's so good to meet you Petal," and she curtsied and went home. After a while, I went home too.

It seems like forever ago.

*

The intercom sputters for the first time in a long while, and Mycroft coughs through the tinny speakers.

"You came to open his cage, Tommy. I don't care one way or the other. There's no way back to the world, anymore. The halls are filling with a thousand guns. Stay in there with him if you want."

For a minute I think Reggie's going to shoot the speaker, but he doesn't. Instead, he kicks Gibbsy's foot.

"Well how 'bout it?" he says. "Any way out of here he doesn't know about, genius?"

"I don't know what he knows or doesn't know, though."

Reggie starts to say something, but I tell him to shut it off. "Will the two of you just stop falling in love for a minute and seven-by-seven."

"Seven-by-seven?"

"Yeah, Reg, eyes and ears. There's probably no way out. Let's just find Poplar at least."

"With Blankface out there," says Reggie.

"With or without him out there."

Reggie shakes his head and doesn't say anything else. He just looks at the door like he'll shoot the first person to unbar the damn thing. "C'mon Tommy."

"We tried to find her," says Gibbsy. "We looked…"

"She out-ran you. We know where she was going so let's catch up already. If that Crackjaw is smart, and we know he is, he's far away from here by now, right?"

"I guess."

"And Poplar, maybe she found a way out, for god's sake. Then everybody'd be happy."

Reggie starts waving the tip of the gun and pacing

again. "Or she's dead already."

"Either way, hell, let's join her." And I mean it. It's all there is left to do.

The two of them stare at me, and I'm not sure they're convinced anything's worth the effort anymore. Or maybe I don't care.

"We can't stay here," I say, and there's no arguing with that.

*

Sector 25 is still and empty, and the roses shiver as we slip low and quick through the halls. On the run up, I figured it was even-odds this place would be dripping with Hectors, but it isn't. Anyway, Hector's aren't the reason I'm holding my breath right now.

We skirt through the sector junction and sit low in the Pathology screencheck booth wondering whether or not we should trip the floodchecks for 25 before we move on.

"Go on and seal it," says Reggie. "She got out

before we did."

"Yeah, probably." But what if I'm wrong? What if she doubled-back, started feeling bad and came back to find us? "No way to know what Pop's thinking one minute to the next. That's the thing."

But we have a bigger problem than that, and we all know what it is. If a Crackjaw like Blankface gets out into the world, there's no sense leaving the candles lit for *anybody*. We'll all be dead sooner than later. I'm probably right about him getting out while we were holed-up outside the records office. But maybe he didn't. He could still be in there. We need to seal off, even if that means trapping Poplar too. It's a goddamn shell game, but we've got to make the safe bet here.

"Why did he let us go?" I'm wondering.

Reggie says, "Hell, we sprung 'im and he was grateful."

"I doubt that."

"Well, I don't know. Ask Gibbsy if you wanna know."

But Gibbsy doesn't know either. "I don't want to see that guy again, whatever we do."

"So how sure are we that Pop got out already?"

Nobody says anything.

"Alright then, for the record: I think I notched her enough to where she's halfway home by now and won't be looking back."

The boys make no move to counter, so I swing the big iron floodcheck breaker from up to down, and we watch the redbells spin. We stare past the whining pistons half expecting some quick figure to come tumbling through at the last second. But nothing does, and the hatches hiss into place unobstructed, to be opened by no easy means.

We're as safe as we can be now, but it isn't saying much. If I'm wrong and we meet up with Blankface in the halls ahead…there would be nothing to do about it. But at least now there's some small reason to hope we won't.

And there's still some small reason to hope we'll

find Poplar, too. I can live with that. Maybe we can pick up some hint of her along the way to Quarantine before things corrode any more than they have.

*

The last time we were in this hall, we had just come through the sixth gallery. We had said goodbye to Rothschild and watched the door close. Now that same door is open again, and an old woman stands against the jamb, looking at us.

At first, I don't notice her. She's just a sliver of a glimpse, and I almost walk past, oblivious, but the image begins to resolve itself in my head until I stop mid-step. We're being watched.

The crone is utterly still just standing there...just *staring*. Her eyes flicker. I don't know how old the woman is, but her hair is gray, and her throat is bandaged, and the bandage is flecked with blood. Her cheeks and eyelids are swollen, almost shut. Her hands are cracked and raw, the fingers longer and twitchier than they should be. A ruined angle grips at her tilted spine.

"The other doors," says Gibbsy, just a whisper. He points past her, into the gallery. From here I can see at least one observation cell is open and empty.

"The goddamn locks."

None of them are working here either. And how many of those cells did we pass when Rothschild was showing us around? Dozens. Now they're unlocked too, and Blankface isn't the only Crackjaw loose in Fallback.

"Tommy, don't let her touch you," says Gibbsy.

The woman holds up one of her brittle hands. "You're Tommy," she says. Her voice is raspy, thin, stripped, like it's struggling to hold back a cough and a laugh and a scream all at the same time. "Aren't you?"

Before I can register the question, another odd shadow lurches in the peripherals, somewhere to the left of us near the stairwell. It's gone as soon as I turn my head. In front of us, the woman hasn't moved at all.

"Poor you," she says. "Being human isn't what it used to be."

She waits for one of us to speak but none of us does. My voice is snagged in my throat.

"Are there any bullets in that gun?" says the woman. "Do you know how to operate it?"

I glance at the stairwell again. A shadow brushes against the wall. Someone is at the top of the flight, tapping the step.

"Let me show you," says the woman. "Come here. You won't get far without weapon or wit." She comes closer, just a few feet, holding out that hand of hers with the long and crooked nails. One scratch is all it would take. That's what Rothschild said. One scratch.

We move away from her. We're not saps, and we're not about to give her the gun, no matter what she says. We know better, and I guess she can tell how scared we are. Every step we take backward, she takes one forward.

All the while, footfalls echo from the stairwell. She's got a friend pacing over there. Another Crackjaw. Maybe more than one. I'm thinking about the Lebanov in

Reggie's hand.

She says, "Soldiers are coming, and I can protect you from them. Give me the gun."

"Don't, Reg. I mean it. She gets that gun, and she'll kill us, trust me."

She takes another few steps, forward and to the side, and we keep backing away, not taking our eyes off of her. The problem is, she's pushing us closer to that other Crackjaw. Toward the staircase, bit by bit.

"There's a better way to live," she says.

Reggie doesn't waste any more time. He points the gun downward and shoots at her leg, nicking the side of it. The Lebanov is much louder than the S8s. It kicks against Reggie's hand.

But the woman is close now, and her wound isn't deep. She reaches out with one quick hand, snatching the barrel of the gun and tugging at it.

Reggie's got a good hold, and he's still got his finger under the trigger guard. Bullets pelt into the

Crackjaw woman's chest and shoulder, and she twitches and falls. It takes a second or two for Reggie to notice what he has done, and he just keeps shooting, spraying bullets into the hall and finally prying his hand away from the grip.

Everything is quiet now, but it feels like the whole world is pounding, fast and white-hot in my temples.

Gibbsy is saying something. The words are a shattered puzzle. It's like they're struggling up from some deep place. "You've got blood on your arm. You've got blood on your arm." He's pointing at Reggie, and when Reggie finally notices, he wipes the blood on his pant leg like it's just plain water. I can't tell if he's in shock or just scared.

Behind us, the tapping in the stairwell has turned into footfalls. Whoever was there, he's running up and away from us now, and we stand huddled together waiting for the echoes to die.

When true silence comes, it is quickly broken. Someone calls to us. Somewhere past the dead old woman, past the corridor, from somewhere along that pale observation gallery, someone is speaking. A man with a rusted voice.

"How many more bullets do you have? You don't know, do you?"

He begins to sing some song I've never heard before, and his voice is joined by a dozen other diseased voices, muttering and singing with him.

*

We pour down the stairs, trying to stay quiet. The rails groan when we take the corners too fast and sometimes my shoulder scrapes against the cinderblock, scratching dust from the grooves, but I'm not willing to slow down.

I'm not sure where we're going, just that we don't want to go anywhere near those Crackjaws and we don't want to go upstairs and meet whoever was tapping his foot a minute ago, either. Downstairs is the only place left to go.

Gibbsy ducks into a switchpass. It seems like a

good enough idea, so we hide in there for a minute to get our bearings.

"You ever shot a gun before, sheriff?"

"To hell with you, Tommy." Reggie is used to this kind of abuse. It's like flinching for him, now. He's a died-in-the-wool flincher, this one.

"How many of those shots actually hit her?"

"*God*, Tommy. To hell with you. The hell'd you tell me to do that for, anyway? She didn't do anything to us, and you don't know for sure she would have."

"You're the one who shot her, not me. Beat yourself up."

Reggie backs off. The fact is, he would have killed that Crackjaw without me telling him to, and he knows it. That's what I mean about him being a flincher. For all his don't-tread-on-me bullshit he sure does a lot of stomping around and never bothers to notice who *he's* treading on because he's too busy flinching at something.

"How many bullets *do* you have left, anyway?"

"I don't know. How the hell can you tell?" He tilts the gun this way and that and taps the clip. "Probably not a lot," he says.

Probably not a lot. But it doesn't matter. There wasn't any point bringing a gun in the first place. Part of me doesn't even mind that I was too rattled back there to start cranking the eights on that crone. The fact is, we won't get out of here alive. Not with every Crackjaw cell in Pathology open and every Hector in the industrials looking for us too. I guess I'm starting to come to terms with that. I just want to see Poplar is all.

We wait, breathing, listening.

"I don't know. What do we do now, Gibbs?"

"Find Poplar."

"I know. *Where* do we go from here to get there?"

Gibbsy points to the floor. "Downstairs." He starts looking around the walls of the switchpass like mad. For what, I don't know, but pretty soon he's tugging at a thick wire, coming out from one of the breakers. "Hold on, let me just…"

"Electrocute yourself?" says Reggie. "What are you doing, smart man?"

I don't want to hear it. "Let him do his thing, Reg. Gibbsy's going to do his thing."

Gibbs finally tugs that wire free and stumbles back against the wall.

"What's that?"

He coils the damn thing and throws it on the ground. "Says pneumatics. Like for the doors, so they won't open when you push the lever? Not sure how many it'll stop-up, but maybe it'll slow them down."

"Can't they just slide the door into the wall with their hands?"

"Yeah but I guess it might take longer to do is all."

Yeah. I guess it might. It'll take longer for us to open them too, though.

*

Gibbsy knows the way, but the *Lebanov* goes out

first, with Reggie close behind it. "Hell," he says. "Here's another one."

My pulse trips. A man stares at us from the end of the corridor, staring with a tilted head just like the woman upstairs. Except, this guy's face is covered with blood and it drips as he stands there, completely naked and swaying on his toes.

Reggie lifts the gun and holds it steady in front of his eyes. I'm thinking, *don't miss, Reggie, and don't waste too many shells for hell's sake.* But he doesn't even fire.

"Wait," says Gibbsy. "Look."

"At what?"

"Some kinda cable," says Gibbsy, pointing.

Now I see it too. He's right, a thin strand of, like, duct-wire is looped around this guy's neck, and it leads up to the ceiling where it's tied-off against the base of a vent. His feet are just barely touching the ground. He's not standing at all, he's *hanging*, and the bastard is dead as can be already. Some poor Hector. A goddamn decoy.

"Tommy," says Gibbsy. "They're trying to get us to waste our bullets."

*

Quiet, low, and fast. None of us dares look up. None of us dares look out along the corridors that we pass at each landing. We just keep moving. At MM we see a sign for Quarantine and cross over to another stairwell, passing through a pneumatic door on the way, pushing it with our palms, inching it halfway into the wall and sliding it shut again. Gibbsy loops a cinch tie. These doors have no knobs, but they have little braces at the bottom, slide-catches so they'll stop at the wall without banging against the machinery. It won't open very easily, not without somebody prying at it.

"Alright, good enough for now."

"Says Quarantine's on L." Gibbsy points at another placard on this side of the door, listing nearby wards. "Either she went through there or was scared off and came back this way or went someplace else."

"I guess there's Hectors aplenty."

Gibbsy shrugs. "Probably worse than that too," he says. "With the locks shorted like this? Whoever's quarantined is probably wandering around too. Maybe it's not that bad."

I don't want to think about it. About Poplar being surrounded by all those coughing, angry, twisted maniacs. I don't want to think about her getting sick and turning into something she was never meant to be.

"What do you mean someplace else? If Quarantine spooked her where would she go next?"

"Back this way, probably."

"Where else *could* she go, though?" I ask. "Show me on the map. Not this, not the Barker's map, the map you got from wrench bucket. The real map."

Gibbsy lifts his hand to do that very thing but stops short, and his eyes go wide.

"What's wrong? What?"

"Pop's got that map," he says. "She had the backpack."

Reggie and I blink a few times.

"You're just now telling us that?" says Reggie.

"I didn't notice until now. But she had it last. The map and all the pegs too."

"Madre de dios."

"What's that mean?" says Reggie. "Not madre de dios, shit. I mean what does it mean for us with her having all that stuff."

"Reg," I say, "it means we need to put a rope on that girl before the locks come back online."

*

Two more flights to go but for now, we're crouched on the stairs, listening. Always listening, always still. Everything is noise, and nothing is useful. Too many rushing vents or yawning steam pipes or buzzing lights, scratching at us from every angle.

That's how it is. Not just here but everywhere. The City is always filled with noise, no matter where you go. The echoes of someone muttering, senseless, mad. The wake of the trams. Even in those drooling, remote corridors, you'll always hear the steam and the electricity and all the things that gnaw this place to bits day after day. Sometimes you can even hear the shriek of the rivets as the ocean above tries to crush us all.

*

"Quarantine." The word is painted in red across a set of doors. I press the lever, and they slide apart, splitting the word. Whatever Gibbsy did to the pneumatics, the effect wasn't very wide-spread. We listen awhile from the vestibule.

"You hear someone shouting?" says Gibbsy.

"No." But maybe I did. I heard something. Maybe a voice, maybe not. My hand hovers over the inner lever, waiting. I reach for the camera, to bring it around front.

"Don't," says Gibbsy.

"What?"

"Cassandra. The eights," he says. "It's just, it wastes time, is all. But we can film after we find her?"

"Wastes time?"

He's right. He always is. So I sling Cassandra by her strap, over my shoulder, and I pull the door's lever.

When I see the floor of Quarantine I almost wretch. We can't even see the tile. It's covered with blood, and the fresh dead are sprawled in all directions. Regular folk riddled with new bullet holes. Arms and legs twisted and splayed. Quarantine is a slaughterhouse.

"We better not touch anything," says Gibbsy. "The blood, the bodies. These people were sick."

The foyer is wide and long and lined with windowed cells. Mid-way, the floor slopes up a hard ramp and takes an L. More than a dozen hallways feed into this place. They're lined with cells too, and a veranda looks down into the foyer with another level of cells above this one. Probably thousands of them, and thousands of corpses too, now.

Past a ruin of overturned carts and gurneys and rolling cabinets, someone is gasping and crying for help. We crouch low, behind the mess, and I lift my head just enough to see an arm waving above the bodies. A Hector steps out from past the L and levels an S8 at whoever is waving that arm, and the Hector puts an end to the crying and the begging, and the arm falls.

I guess they've been told to shoot anything that moves. Easier that than trying to wrangle a mass of diseased monsters back into a bunch of unlocked cells. But the term "monster" seems pretty versatile in a place like this, I guess.

It bothers Reggie more than anybody, and it's all we can do to hold him back as the Hector steps out of view again. "Sweep up," says Reggie. "You dumb lopes. Sweep the place clean." But he calms down soon enough and stays quiet while we look out at the massacre.

"You see okay without your glasses?" says Gibbsy. "Poplar out there? Hiding or anything?"

"The glasses were ornamental, Gibbs. How'm I supposed to see Poplar? She could be anywhere." I'm just hoping she's not one of these bodies and I don't have to tell Gibbsy or Reggie that for them to know it's my chief worry. "If she's *hiding*, we won't find her without us being spotted too."

"What about up there?" says Gibbsy, pointing to the veranda. "If we crawl and stay out of sight."

"Alright, might as well."

Reggie pulls himself into a crouch, but Gibbsy just sits there for another few seconds. "I'm tired, Tommy."

So am I.

*

The second level cells are mostly empty. We crawl past a few that aren't—bodies lie bleeding on the floor or hunched over benches. The Hectors have swept through here already.

Every now and then I shimmy over to the edge of the veranda and peek at the corpses below, looking for those shoes of hers, hoping not to see them. She's smart enough, she wouldn't just wander out in front of the Hectors. But I don't know. If she thought this was the only way out, she would have tried to sneak through and maybe would have been pinned-down somewhere.

We haven't passed the bend yet, and I can't see the Hectors, but I can hear them talking through those filters. The words are jumbled, as far away as we are.

Reggie grabs my ankle, and I twist my head to look back at him. He thumbs toward the cell next to us and mouths a word I can't quite read.

I scoot backward on my stomach until I can see through the door. Two boys lie at odd angles bleeding on the floor. One of them is older, and his body is blocking the door open. He has been shot through the throat and through the chest, and his skin is already pale. The other boy is maybe only eight years old, for god's sake. And he's still breathing.

He knows we're here, but he's struggling to keep his eyes closed so we'll think he's dead. If he's sick, he doesn't look it. But I don't want to crawl over the other boy's blood to find out.

"We're not going to hurt you," I whisper. I don't know if it's loud enough for him to hear but I'm not going to say it any louder. "What happened?"

He opens one eye, just a slit, and looks at me and closes it again. His face pinches-up, like he's trying not to cry.

"Don't do that, don't do that. Stay quiet. You'll be okay. What happened?"

He doesn't answer me.

"Is this your brother?" They both have the same hair. The boy manages a nod. "What happened?"

But he won't answer me. He won't open his eyes.

*

Reggie used to have a sister. Seeing this little kid has me thinking about her. She was older than us, maybe thirteen when we were eight. A true original riot punk. Reggie used to tag along with her when she went places. Me too, sometimes, and she'd always get notched and tell us to go home unless we wanted the Blackbands to get us. She was the one who got us thinking about the City in the first place, and what fascism is, and the underground. No surprise, she disappeared one day, and Reggie's parents never really talked about her after that. To this very day, even.

I remember Reggie wearing one of her shirts for a while after she was gone. This torn-up old thing she had written on with an ink pen. He kept saying, "Let 'em try and haul *me* to the burnboxes. Let 'em try." Just an angry little kid. And I think he actually wanted it to happen, back then.

There was a cartoon of Kennedy his sister had drawn on the back of that shirt. I always liked what she'd written under his face, "Friends and citizens, I must ask you to chain yourselves to the anchor." I wrote that on one of my shirts once, too, but my dad made me throw it in the incinerator when he saw it.

*

The kid won't budge, and maybe it's safer for him to just play dead anyway. We crawl ahead, past a dozen other bloody cells, stopping to look over the edge now and then.

When we reach the L, we stay out of sight away from the rail. The others stay back while I inch forward and see the nest the Hectors have built.

They've strung barbed wire across that whole end of the foyer, and there must be five or six Hectors standing behind it with Lebanovs and Carsten-Ws. Ready to shoot anything that moves. Past that is the door, Gibbsy was telling me about on the way here. It leads to the tramway, and the tramline goes back past the city hospitals. A dedicated line just for this. Just for Quarantine. If we can get through that door, we can make our way into the world again. But we can't get through that door. Not with fifteen goddamn Hectors standing there. If she's smart, Poplar didn't come this way, but you never can tell.

For no reason, I can understand, five of the Hectors line-up and march away from the nest, toward us. I roll back away from the rail, hoping to hell they didn't see me, and in half a minute I can hear them veering away, moving along the foyer. A couple of shots are fired at god knows who.

When I get up the nerve to peek out again, the Hectors have started moving all of those crash-carts around, pushing them to the walls, covering the near bodies with gurneys, clearing the floor of the taller debris so they'll be able to see the whole length of the foyer I guess. But the thing is, they don't go back to the nest when they're done. They check past those double-doors—the ones we used to get into the place—and they nose around for awhile in the vestibule.

From the looks of it, they're fixing to stand guard down there, which is bad news for us if we ever need to get out the way we came in. I guess I'm hoping we *won't* need to, but none of that bothers me nearly as much as what they do next. Three of the Hectors start walking up the stairs to the veranda.

"We need to move. Gibbsy, Reg. Now. Quick."

*

Ahead to the right, the veranda meets with a small corridor that leads away from the foyer rail, past more cells. If we can get there before the Hectors reach the top of the stairs, we should be able to swing out of sight, but it won't be easy. We don't dare stand, and we can't exactly crawl *fast* without making a racket, so for awhile I'm sweating like mad.

As soon as I'm close enough, I grab the edge of the wall and pull myself into the corridor. Nobody's shouting yet, but we're sure not in the clear either. I wait until I can reach Gibbsy's collar and I yank him into the corridor, his feet kicking behind him. Reggie is on his heels.

Moving away from the veranda railing, at last, we're able to stand and walk, stooping, striding past blood-streaked glass on either side. I'm not sure where this will take us but anywhere is better than that veranda right now. And hell, Quarantine's supposedly big enough, maybe we'll find another tram platform someplace that isn't as deadly crowded.

The cells are mostly empty now, but the glass is still smudged so I can imagine they were full before the locks failed. Every other one has a body still in it, riddled with bullets. I don't know what to think of that. From the looks of the place, all the folks who left their cells are no longer up here—they're probably down in that pile of bodies after trying to make a run for the exits—but the folks who *stayed* in their cells are dead anyway. They probably didn't even try to open their doors. Maybe they were too sick or maybe they knew they'd be killed for doing it. And here they are, dead just the same.

I guess I shouldn't be surprised. It would be just like the City to gun down a man for trying to escape and then gun down another man for staying put.

I'm so busy trying to imagine what the whole scene was like when the chaos hit, I don't notice the Hector stepping out from the cell in front of us. Before I know it I'm off my feet, blood spraying from the bridge of my nose where he has hit me with his gun. The blow sweeps my feet out from under me, and it seems like ten seconds before my back hits the grating.

The Hector steps past me so fast I barely notice. By the time I'm able to roll over and get to my knees, he has already taken the Lebanov out of Reggie's hands, and he's pointing his S8 at the whole lot of us.

For longer than I'd care to count, I'm thinking he's

going to shoot us. It takes quite awhile, in fact, for me to realize he's pausing longer than he probably should and his jaw is tilted like he doesn't know what to make of us.

"Get in the cell," he says through the filter. He motions. We crawl through the nearest door and sit against the glass. "Stay there."

Then he kneels close to us with the gun pointed at the floor, and he lifts his mask. "How did you get out from under Mycroft?" says Dunning. The corporal shakes his head, and I think I'm just as surprised to see him as he is to see us. Now that I think of it, he said he'd be coming to Quarantine. But that seems like forever ago. "Stay on in here a spell," he says. "'N lay down like you been shot."

*

We can hear him talking to the other Hectors on the veranda, but the words aren't clear. He shouts, "Two and three are clear," to the men in the barbwire nest, and one of them shouts something back that I can't make out. The discussion isn't lengthy by any means, but it seems like a night and a day to me before Dunning comes back alone and takes off his mask again.

He comes into the cell with us and sits on the bench. The floor is bloodless, thank Christ, but whoever was in here must have thrown up in the sink within the last day or so and the smell is still here even if the rest of it has turned to shattered clay.

"What's the story, Mycroft put you in here?" He's not looking at us. He's looking out through the glass.

"Is there someplace we can hide?"

"What do I look like to you?" he says. He looks me in the eye long enough for me to know it's been almost as bad a night for him as it's been for us. "Yeah, well, nobody'll come up here so don't twist around too much about it. We've got a little time, anyway. I'm guessing you know more about whatever's going on tonight than we do, so let's hear it. I wanna know what you know. Did Mycroft put you in Quarantine?"

"No," I tell him. "We came here on our own."

I don't know why I bother. For all I know Dunning

is just going to shoot us in a minute or so anyway. He turned us over to the Bands in the first place, so I can't expect much in the way of compassion from the guy. But I tell him everything, anyway. About Rothschild and about Blankface and about us being the ones who shorted the locks. I tell him about the Machinist, too. "I think he's a Crackjaw," I admit and Dunning nods along the whole while, almost like he's not paying attention, but I know he is.

The whole tale comes spilling out so fast I don't know if the corporal even catches the high points. I'm sure I glazed over a few things anyway. But not the important stuff.

"So that's why we're here. Any chance she came through here and lived?"

"What?"

"Poplar. The girl. She woulda come in the same way we did. And if she did, what next?"

"What next?" says Dunning. "I don't know what next. Well. She would have looked like anybody else to us, and she would have been shot like anybody else. Unless she did a good job staying out of our way. We swept through here like a flood."

"Son of a bitch pricks," says Reggie.

"Yeah, well, I guess that's what we are," says the corporal. "We don't need you to tell us that, and we sure didn't need you coming in here with that camera. We'd be better off if you'd never done it."

I almost lose it when I hear him say that. It's just the kind of shine-on you always get from a Hector or a City suit or a Blackband. Always talking about how you should leave well-enough alone. But there is no "well-enough" here. Not in Fallback. "No, you wouldn't have been better off. You would have been worse off because none of you woulda had this reminder of what pricks you are. Even if we don't get out of here alive at least, we made the point that *some* of us won't dance no matter how pretty a dress the City wears. Any way you look at it, it's still a fascist bitch and I ain't bringing a single goddamn flower. That's more than…"

"Kid, if you talked less you'd be able to say a hell of lot more."

Dunning leans his head against the wall and laughs. It isn't much of a laugh, but I get the sense he needs to let it out anyway. "Some kinda dance that'd be," he says. "Way I see it not a lot of folks are on the floor these days. That or else the music stopped. I keep wondering why you don't think we've all been where you're at. Hell, the City doesn't have any real friends at all I'd guess."

"Maybe," I tell him. "But if everybody really hates the way things are, they sure don't complain much. Not in a way that matters."

Dunning takes the butt of his gun and starts scratching at the wall, making some kind of mark. It's the shepherd's crook again. My joints shiver. Dunning taps the mark with his knuckles. "You notice that anyplace else around here?"

"The Herds?"

"The Herds."

"Yeah, a couple places, but what does that even mean? Who are they?"

"Bunch of us," says Dunning. "Some soldiers, lab staff, a few doctors, and some of the Bands too. Anybody who's not too afraid of the city to whisper behind its back. Regular folk chipping away at what guys like Mycroft think is the way things should be. Trying to find out what's really going on behind the shutters. Trying to get some idea of what we should know but don't.

"Half of what you told me tonight, I had no idea," he says. "We don't ever get the straight story around here, not even when we're marching into a turbine. You might not be surprised to hear it, but it was Mycroft who shut down the spec tubes and jammed our radios, so we couldn't talk to each other all night. Blindfolded us. He was afraid some soldier, out cleaning up this mess, would find out something he wasn't supposed to know, and he'd chirp it out to the rest of us. I only just found out about that, but it would've been nice to know before all this happened."

He waves a hand toward the corpse-jammed foyer.

"Sometimes the Herds catch wind of these things, and sometimes we don't. We do what we're told and go where Mycroft wants us to go; but one thing you learn real damn fast is, if you see the crook on your way there, you'd do best to be careful." He taps the wall again. "This means keep your eyes open, it means there's trouble ahead, and it means keep your ears open too because you might hear something we can use to piece it all together. It means something important's been kept from you."

I guess I can vouch for that. We've sure walked into some snares tonight that I wish I'd seen coming. It's got me wondering how much of what Dr. Rothschild told us was true. Then again, he's the reason we're not with Mycroft right now, so maybe I'm wrong. I don't know.

"If old Grovesner hadn't had his neck on a leash all night," says Dunning, "things might've worked out better for you. I'm sorry about that; we just didn't know enough. A lot of blood hit the floors tonight. A lot of my pals died in C-Tran when the Crackjaws got out, and now a lot of 'em are dead here too. Hell, here you opened the one door in Fallback you just don't open, and I'm the one who feels bad about it. I guess it wasn't your fault. Somebody just outsmarted the whole clutch of us I guess."

"What now?" I ask.

He sits thinking it over for half a minute. "Well…I don't know. I doubt you're sick, so I guess you'd best get out of Quarantine before that changes. If you go, go quietly. Not a lot of these other boys are friendly, and I can't help you much if they notice a couple of live bodies like you jitterbugging through the blood."

I ask him about the tram tunnels, about the City hospitals at the other end. I ask about maintenance shafts or access panels or conduits or any other way we can slip past the Hectors. The kinds of things Poplar would have been looking for if she came through. I ask him if there's any chance she found a way past all this and if she did, how can we. But he shakes his head.

"We've got guys on every pipe," he says. "Most of the guns we've got left are down here making sure nobody slips out into the world. Anybody sees you they'll shoot you. Hell, anybody sees me with you, I'll have to shoot you myself to let 'em know I'm still doing my job. Lotta triggers waiting around down here, and my guess is if your girl came in here at all she either got shot or backtracked. But the thing I'm thinking is Pathology's spread to hell on the roundups and full of holes. Well, she coulda gone that way."

"What, the way we *came* from?" I ask. "We won't get through there alive and it ain't your Hector pals I'm worried about. Those doors are open. That place is filled with Crackjaws, one kind or another."

Dunning starts to put his filter on again. "Yeah, well. I don't blame you if you're scared. But you won't get through here alive either."

*

The way Dunning tells it, we should be able to get back to Pathology easy enough. They don't care much about that door since it just leads further away from the public sectors, which isn't encouraging. Four or five

Hectors stand between Pathology and us, but Dunning doesn't think it will be a problem.

"They'll be dropping nineteens here in a few," says Dunning. "That'll get 'em away from where you need to be. Keep an eye on those boys, and when they start shooting, you scramble, okay?"

"Nineteens?"

"Small caliber," he says, and he pulls a chromey from his vest, just a little snubbed barrel thing like they sell in the track halls. "So we don't waste good ammo. Anybody doesn't look dead enough we go ahead and shoot 'em through the skull just to be sure."

"You...shoot the dead folk? Jesus."

"H Christ," he says. "But we'll be busy enough you can excuse yourself from the table, and nobody'd know. Okay?"

"Okay isn't the word."

Dunning skirts out to the veranda while we stay back in the empty corridor.

*

I figure I've got a half a minute to kill, so I get Cassandra ready and inch back past the cells, away from the foyer, looking for a bit of carnage to film.

The back of the corridor ends at a nurse's station. A long counter lines one wall with fixtures hanging over it and cabinets against the wall on the other side, full of jars and boxes of medical supplies. A big chart of Quarantine has been tacked beside the x-ray glass, but I can't make much sense of it from here, and I get the sense it would take some time to decipher.

The floor here is as bloody as anywhere. What really gets me is that I can see one of the nurses, sprawled over the counter with about a dozen red holes in his smock, and I'm wondering if it was Dunning who shot him.

Reggie pulls me back before I can start cranking. "Don't be a son of a bitch."

"The hell, Reggie, look at this place. They did this. The City did this. All on account of these people were sick. I bet none of 'em were even *trying* to escape until the Hectors started shooting everybody. And those nurses? They weren't probably sick at all."

"So you wanna show the riot, and some kid'll see his mom or dad dead in a hall," he says. But he doesn't get it. He never does. And now he's starting to sound like Poplar.

"That's exactly right, Reg. They killed a thousand people tonight. We should show *all* the kids what the City does to their moms and dads. I'm filming this."

Reggie looks at me and at the camera, and I start cranking.

"I should just go downstairs and kill the pricks like they killed these guys," he says.

"I thought you were a vegetarian, Reg."

"Animals never shot a thousand people for nothing."

I'm about to thank him for proving my point, but Gibbsy puts a stop to the conversation. He doesn't tell us to shut it off or anything, he just coughs and asks if it's time to hit the ground floor yet. And he's right—we should be keeping an eye on that.

I put Cassandra over my shoulder and crawl to the edge of the veranda again, just enough so I can see down the foyer to where the smaller bunch of Hectors are cocking pistols. Dunning is with them when they start walking the floor putting bullets in the twitching skulls.

*

We're crawling again, low and slow, while the chromies pop in the foyer. One and then another. The Hectors step while we slide. They shoot, and we flinch. But nobody can see us up here, and Dunning hasn't done anything to clue the rest of them in.

I look over the edge now and then to make sure all's well, if you can call it that, and sure enough their eyes are down, watching the bodies, shooting the ones that might be just pretending to be dead. This is the kind of thing I should let old Cassandra in on, but the boys don't seem to be taking kindly to her lately, so I don't even try to think of a way to do it.

Halfway down the veranda, I look out again and I flinch, but it's not because of the gunshots. It's because I see a pair of shoes I recognize, and suddenly my whole body is twitching like a cut wire. Poplar is lying next to one of the cells. She's down there on the floor with all these poor corpses and my stomach lurches, almost ready to vomit. And her eyes open. She's alive.

I don't think she's injured, but she can't see me, and I can't exactly let her know we're up here. I kick Gibbsy, and I point. Something about the way the air stills tells me he has noticed her too.

She must have gotten in here when the panic was high. Must have made it this far and just laid down with the dead so she wouldn't get shot. She would do that. She's smart enough to know to do that.

I scoot to the side and Gibbsy crawls up next to me as best he can.

"Can we get to her?"

Gibbsy whispers too low for me to hear.

"Wave something, or, I don't know, get her attention?"

But I know it's no use. She's looking at the Hectors. The guys with the pistols getting closer and closer, putting bullets in anybody they're not sure about, and if they see her, they won't be sure about her either. They'll make sure.

"Gibbsy we need to get her out of there."

"How."

"I don't know."

Reggie's behind us, probably wondering what's going on. When he sees her his face drains to ivory.

The next thing I'm wondering is if maybe we can somehow get Dunning to stop all of this, but that doesn't seem possible either. He's down there shooting just as many sick folks as the others. Doing his job.

"Gimme the gun, Reg."

Gibbsy looks at me like I'm a monster. Like *I'm* a monster. I'm not the monster.

Reggie's in a panic, and I can't say I'm not halfway there myself.

"Reggie…" He's not listening. "Look, Gibbsy, I'll try to miss," I tell him. "A couple shots over their heads is all, to get 'em curious, yeah?"

To be honest, I don't know if it'll work. If it'll draw those Hectors away and clear the room for Pop. But maybe it will. Maybe just long enough she can figure out another plan. I don't know.

"Might be the only way," says Gibbsy.

Reggie gives him a confused nod of appreciation, and mouths the words, "I'll do it," and that's that.

*

We try to signal Poplar, to give her some idea of what's about to happen. She doesn't see us. She's watching the Hectors, shiny-eyed. I can't stop looking at her.

"We have to crawl past them first," says Gibbsy. "Or we won't make the door."

It's good logic but hell, if we wait too much longer, they'll get to Pop before we can do anything. They're only about twenty feet away from her now and even though they're moving slow down there, body to body, they're moving a bit faster than us crawlers.

"Not a second later. Reg, you hear that? We even up and that's when we make our ruckus and be ready to run."

Reggie nods, and we slither as fast as we can over the metal veranda, edging the odd body now and then, sticking to the wall when we can. Below us, chromies pop like kids throwing bolts at the tuns.

They're ten feet from Poplar now. No, less than that. Not a sound but the pistols.

It's time for us to go.

*

Shots from the Lebanov echo against the top of the foyer and deaden on the carpet of bodies. Gibbsy and me, we start to run first, ears raw from the sound of five other guns returning fire. Bullets ping against metal, fast as the fingers can pull. I'd guess we wouldn't have gotten ten steps if they'd been holding automatics.

I overstep the stairs and practically fall down the whole flight. Stumbling to the last with Gibbsy on my heels. Behind us Reggie's face is pale, glistening as he clambers for the rail. Something small arcs through the air and just misses him, sticking to the wall. A sticky bomb. He sees it too and tumbles sideways. His weight breaks the banister, but Reggie's a tough bastard and stands up almost as soon as he hits the ground. The sticky bomb sends shrapnel our way, but we're in good enough cover to avoid it.

I peer out through the rails of a gurney. The Hectors have holstered their pistols in favor of S8s, and they're coming this way, moving against the wall, deliberate, precise, and fast. A couple of test shots puncture the door behind us. When we don't return fire, a couple more bullets come past, and I can feel the air move.

"Reggie, come on. Just get low and run it. Gibbsy, get the door."

Reggie angles the gun around the shelves and fires toward the Hectors. Nothing hits home, but the men crouch low and halt. Reggie tumbles across the floor to the door with us.

"Shut it Gibbsy, shut it."

Another few shots punch the puckered door as we squat in the vestibule.

"I'm outta bullets, Tommy."

"Yeah, well, maybe we won't need 'em."

"I doubt it," he says. "They're all coming. Every one of them."

"LIVESTOCK," Reel 1 of 1, 16mm, 20fps

The stockyard is long and arched like an old hangar. Forty by twenty. Six pens divide it, and the straw seems to sparkle like spun gold under the vicious lamps that line the ceiling, mimicking day. Three of the pens hold cattle and one holds several goats, utters full of milk.

The camera does not move. Its angle is odd, from the top of a shelf, as if wedged there.

A man enters the frame from the left wheeling a tank and a hose. He fills the troughs with water and takes the tank away.

He comes back with a barrow full of alfalfa, fresh cut from the wet halls. He uses his hands to toss it into the pens. When the barrow is empty, he takes it away, and he comes back to watch them eat.

The livestock stay away for half a minute, glaring at the alfalfa. Glaring at the man. Then they come to the troughs and drink, and they eat. All except one.

One cow steps toward the alfalfa but steps back

again and lowers itself to the ground. The man coaxes it. He goes into the pen and holds alfalfa under the cow's nose. It turns its head away.

For awhile the man stands there staring at the cow. He starts beating its haunches with his palms and then with his fist, and he goes out and fetches a switch and beats the cow with that too until blood seeps into the fur. The cow inches away but not far. It doesn't ever stand.

The man crouches in the pen and holds his hands over his eyes and starts to sob.

TEN

Two flights and the Hectors are still coming up the stairs fast after us. Reggie is as quick as hell and isn't slowing, but my chest shakes like a generator and Gibbsy is lagging already. I stop to look down over the handrails, partly to rest for a second and partly to see how close the Hectors are.

Only six of them now. The others must have gone off in another direction to head us off from somewhere else. That's what worries me. We need to lose those pricks somewhere in the halls. Sure, we're fast. Sure, this is what we do every night. But these are no Blackbands.

"That door over there. Reg, back here."

We veer off, hoping to get out of earshot before

the Hectors realize where we went. The door at the next bend is tied shut with Gibbsy's cinch, and he stoops to unwind it.

"Crackjaw freaks are out there," says Reggie. "Probably waitin' for us."

Gibbsy stops what he's doing and looks up at me. "Tommy?"

"What?"

"The Crackjaws."

"I don't know, Gibbsy. Yeah, they're out there. You wanna chance it with them or chance it with the Hectors?"

Reggie reminds us that the Hectors have a bunch of guns.

"Can't we just double back?" says Gibbs. "Hide, let 'em pass? The Gopher."

I don't know. I really don't. It feels like we're wasting a bunch of time, but I really don't know. "A bunch of those pricks are unaccounted-for, fellas. That's fine by me, but the whole point is we need to be dragging these boys *away* from Quarantine, not back into it. I don't want them stumbling into Poplar just when she's trying to find a crack to crawl through."

Gibbsy glances from me to the door and back again. He's still crouched there with the cinch in his hand. "Tommy…"

Reggie cuts-in, "Tommy I'm outta *bullets*."

Gibbsy keeps looking from one thing to the other. He keeps looking at *me*, for Christ's sake, as if I have anything more to say about it. "I guess at least we have a chance," says Gibbsy. He's practically wheezing.

"I'm outta *bullets*. I'm *out*."

Reggie's not articulate, but I get what he's saying and so does Gibbsy if his pale eyes are any clue. The only reason the Crackjaws didn't swarm after us the first time was because they didn't want to get shot.

"Reggie, I don't know. Just…act like you're *not* out of bullets. Act like the clip's full."

*

Pathology feels thick, like running through water. For all its quiet it doesn't seem the least bit empty. A hundred eyes watching from somewhere. A hundred ears listening. Every gaping door seems to have an odd shadow wavering just out of view.

If the Hectors are still following us, they're stepping awfully soft now. Maybe we lost them, but the chances of that aren't great.

Gibbsy gets his bearings and takes us upstairs to the far end of that sixth autopsy suite. "We'll be close to where that woman's body is," he says, listening at the exit. "Close to where those other Crackjaws were. But if they're not expecting us to come from this direction we can maybe slip through there before anybody sees us."

"Maybe. Unless that's where Rothschild's cooling his heels, though. Him and...the chemist guy, Casten. If they had to hole up someplace, it'd be there, and they might have blocked the doors."

"I do hope we see them again," says Reg.

"What, so you can beat 'em to death? That I'd like to see, son."

We step into the dark hall, where a deformed and deranged man stands to greet us.

"Are you going to shoot me?" he says. That rusty voice again. We've heard it before. Something about his tone tells me he knew we would sneak back this way. He knew to wait here for us. Somehow, he knew.

The Crackjaw is tall in an elegant way. He bounces on one toe like a dancer. He's very slender with curved hands that almost reach to his knees. Another step closer and he could probably swipe at us with those long fingers of his. Those diseased claws. He only has one eye, and the other is bandaged, and he's wearing a wrenchie's jumper. Reggie is pointing the Lebanov at the guy's face, and it seems to be enough to keep him at bay. For now.

Three or four others come from the cells to stand behind him, against the wall, watching us calmly. The dancer hops to the other foot. He bows.

"Are you going to shoot *all* of us?" he says.

Reggie's temples pulse under a film of sweat and white skin.

Gibbsy says, "We don't want to shoot any of you. Soldiers are following us."

The dancer of a Crackjaw stands still and twists his crooked chin toward Gibbsy. "You're not soldiers."

"We don't want to shoot you. You didn't do anything to us."

"We don't want to be shot, either," says the dancer. He steps away, toward his friends, and gestures to the opposite wall with a flourish.

A couple of double-doors hiss open, not fifteen feet away, and another bunch of broken figures limp into the passage. They're dragging a struggling man in tow.

He's sick--that much is obvious--but not like the Crackjaws. I can tell he hasn't turned sour yet. Maybe he's one of the ones who never will, one of the ones that'll just die from the flu. He looks terrified though, gaunt, bleeding from one nostril and coughing. The dancer points to him.

"Bite their throats," he says. "Charge forth. Infect. Into the valley of Death rode the six hundred. While the world is full of troubles and anxious in its sleep. You…don't understand."

The man with the bloody nose looks at us and shakes his head. "I want to lay down."

The dancer pins him with a hard stare. "You'd rather murder these children." Then back to Reggie. "If this…man steps close enough, will you shoot him? He's not clean."

Reggie is in no mood to talk, and Gibbsy misses the beat. "He comes any closer, we shoot *you*," I say.

"Me," says the dancer.

"You."

"We don't want to be shot."

"I know."

The dancer looks at the other Crackjaws and back to me. "Why aren't you holding the gun?"

"He's a better shot."

"Is he? We have friends who are…mad. Who don't care about the whither or whether of guns. They've killed soldiers who thought they could keep them at bay just by pointing a muzzle at them. And now you're pointing one at us."

Reggie is visibly shaking now, so I take the gun from him. He doesn't fight. The dancer takes another step away from us.

"Yeah, well, we'll shoot *you*. Anyone comes any closer, whoever else gets shot you get shot too."

The dancer says nothing. He tilts his head as if listening to a whisper from the empty space beside him. He arches his spine, touches his hands to the floor, and springs backward in a mute cartwheel.

I tell him, "Have your boys move away from the door."

"Someone else is coming," he says. "Not one of us."

The dancer wanders toward the far end of the corridor, not taking his eyes off of me. The others follow, in the same direction, leaving this exit free enough that the three of us edge toward it, pivoting.

"How many bullets do you have?" says the dancer. "I don't think you have any."

Before I can say another word, that far end of the hall erupts. Bullets spin past. The Hectors are here. The goddamn Hectors caught up with us. A few of the freaks spin spraying blood, hit by the scattered lead, red flecks against the walls on either side. They run for the alcoves and intersections, but we're left in the open.

"Shit, Tommy," says Gibbsy. He tugs my shirt, and we slide to our knees at the door, waiting for it to open while the bullets pock the metal over our heads. The pneumatics hiss and we slide away while the Hectors kill whatever else they can see.

Gibbsy cinches the slide-catch. His knot is sloppy, but it's the best we can do.

*

This autopsy suite is a longer room than I remember, segmented but not broken, pacing the gallery. We breathe softly, listening for Rothschild or Casten, or more of the Crackjaws. But we hear no voices. No shuffling steps.

"Musta been ten Hectors out there," says Gibbsy. "Maybe everybody from Quarantine."

"Maybe."

We jog past the splattered tables and odd jars despite our goddamn raging lungs. Our dry throats.

Around the next pile of desks is a familiar face but it isn't looking at us or at anything else in the world. The old man, Dr. Casten, slumps against the wall beside a shelf filled with collarbones. Jawbones and wrists, chemically cleaned, deadly white. Casten's throat has been slit.

"I'd guess that was done with a scalpel, friends and citizens." I crank the eights and tell the people of Fallback what I think of justice and betrayal. Or whatever this was.

*

The Hectors have moved into the next gallery right alongside us. We can hear them. The gunfire is all but muffled by the walls, but we can hear it anyway. Part of me is glad to have them here, and part of me knows they'll be coming into autopsy soon enough and we won't have any place to go unless we hurry. Unless we stay low and fast and quiet.

"We gotta double-back," says Gibbsy.

"Who says they're not at that end too?"

Only a couple of ways out of here. We make the wrong choice, we get shot. Or our guts get spilled by the mobs.

"What if we hide in here someplace?" says Gibbsy. "Those drawers." He's pointing to the cadaver drawers where they keep the corpses for study.

"The Gopher."

"The Gopher," says Gibbsy.

"I'm not getting in one of those," says Reggie.

The far wall is full of them though, and I guess most are empty and we could just crawl inside. They'd never know. "Just for a minute, Reg."

"Fine. Shit. But I'm not shutting mine all the goddamn way."

*

The first one I open has a body in it, and I shut the drawer without a touch of grace. We find three that are empty, and we stand there staring at them, nervous as hell about climbing into those long dark spaces.

"Just a minute," says Gibbsy. He goes to every drawer, twisting the latches open. "If the handles all face the same way," he says, "maybe the Hectors won't think anything's strange."

"Some prize melon you've got there, Gibbsy." I sock Reggie in the arm for good measure, and we shimmy into the nooks.

*

The walls of the drawer are slick and clean. My

hands slip on the metal, and it takes a good effort to pull my drawer shut with me in it. Reggie and Gibbsy had it easy…I shut theirs from the outside, but here I am slipping my palms against the chrome until the crack shuts.

It's a good idea. I'll give Gibbsy credit for that. All we have to do is wait. Once we're in the clear—once the Hectors stream past oblivious—all we'll have to do is kick against the back wall and the drawers will slide out. Gibbsy already put it to the test. But in the meantime, we're stuck in these things waiting, trying to listen for the Hectors, hoping we'll be able to hear them clearly enough to know when they've come and gone. Hoping they don't get suspicious and open the drawers looking for us.

From in here, every sound in the world sounds like stones in water. The scratching of wires. Already the close darkness is turning my stomach, lifting my hairs. In the drawer next to me, Reggie bumps against the tin walls, making a hellish rumbling noise. What the hell's he doing in there? Trying to get cozy. Tossing and turning. He needs to settle down before the Hectors come through and figure out what's what.

I knock against the wall of my drawer, trying to get his attention but he keeps struggling.

"Reggie, shut it off, or they'll know you're in there." But he can't hear me. He's panicking, and it's getting worse.

Then his drawer slides open.

I tap my feet against the back wall and push my own drawer a few inches clear. I can't see him, but at least I can breathe a few words into the air. "Reggie, Jesus."

"Tommy, I can't, goddamnit. I'll do what I can. This is dogshit."

"Reggie?"

He's getting out of his drawer. He's leaving.

"Reggie?"

I wedge my hands against the slick walls and push

until I can grab the lip of the drawer above me and slide myself all the way out.

Reggie is gone. His drawer is fully open, and I can't even hear his footsteps anymore.

When a door opens at the far end of the autopsy, I think for a second that it might be him. That he might be coming back. But he couldn't have gone all the way down there. That's where all the Hectors are. And now they're in autopsy too. Here I am sitting halfway out of the wall, and next to me Reggie's drawer is fully open. They won't have to think too hard about what's going on here if they see this.

I can hear the rattle of the Hectors' gear and my hands are slipping against the lip of Reggie's now empty drawer.

Finally, I get some leverage, and I ease the damn thing shut, but that still leaves me out in the open, and it will be even harder to shut my own drawer now that my hands are sweating.

Inch by inch, hands smearing on the metal, I move

the drawer over its rollers and into the wall. When the lip touches the seal, all I've got left to do is remember to breathe. But I'll have to do that quietly.

*

Something brushes against the outside face of my drawer. An elbow, maybe, as one of the Hectors edges through the room. Fabric scratching against steel. Or maybe it's a gloved hand, gripping the latch. I stop breathing, and I close my eyes.

Whatever it is, it scrapes past, and for a moment a dense metal edge slides across the drawer too. The tip of a gun. And then nothing.

*

We've been waiting in the quiet dark for more than ten minutes. The air in my drawer is muggy and thick, and my chest aches for a cooler breath. I'm wondering if we shouldn't just stay in these things for awhile and get some rest. Maybe the Hectors and Crackjaws would never get wise to it. I could probably sleep, as tired as I am. Maybe that's a good idea.

Really, I'm just hoping Gibbsy is okay. The truth is he's probably doing better than I am right now. He can be a pretty steady hand.

I remember when he first started going to Chalcenor. He kept showing up late to Home Room. Turns out the Blackbands had been giving him trouble, coming through the H screencheck, since he lived out of the sector. He had the papers and everything...they just didn't believe him some days, depending on whether or not the Band at the cage was being an asshole that morning. I shot some footage of it one day. This was before Gibbsy and I really knew each other. I left home early that morning and sat there on the cleared bench with Cassandra peeking out from my backpack while the Bands harassed poor Gibbsy. All he did was hand over his papers and look at the floor and answer their questions.

Me, I would have probably said something stupid to those bastards and gotten my face cracked. But not Gibbsy. He's a real steady hand. Always has been.

*

Sleep just keeps sounding better and better. But the longer I lie here thinking about it, the more anxious I get. These things could be air-tight for all I know. Could suffocate us. Or those Crackjaws, as clever as they are, maybe they would sniff us out. Maybe the Hectors would. Maybe we would miss our chance to get out of this goddamn part of the industrials what with all the chaos out there. If the Hectors get hold of the place again, maybe they'll figure out how to lock the doors and Poplar's got the keys still. And Reggie. Reggie's out there alone.

No, we can't stay here.

I push the drawer out as slowly as I can, and I peek into an empty autopsy room before inhaling a cool lungful and swinging my legs onto the tile.

"It's just me Gibbsy," I tell him as I open his drawer. "Nobody else here. We need to move."

His face is pale and clammy.

"Where's Reggie?"

"Bolted. I don't know where. We need to go."

"Where? Same way."

"Well hell, we can't double back. They're going to be watching that nest. Just…same way we were going and hope we don't run into the back of that crowd. Gibbsy. Gibbsy, buddy, we're okay."

*

In the hall lie three disfigured bodies, bleeding over the floor. Among them is one Hector whose throat has been cut all the way to the bone so that his head is against his back. I can almost imagine his blood having a different color than the diseased pools swelling beneath the bullet-ridden Crackjaws.

The dancer must have survived the battle. He and a few of the pals of his are still around here someplace, fled but not far. The dead Hector's guns and bullets have been stripped away from his body and the bloody footprints smeared beside him are those of bare feet. Elegant toes. Graceful steps. The Crackjaws have guns too, now.

*

Wherever Reggie went, I have no idea. And whether or not we bought Poplar enough time to get someplace safe, I don't think I'll ever know. It's just Gibbsy and me. Goddamn City. If there's ever an idea spreading through the corridors that they didn't invent, they snuff it. If there's ever an unchecked camaraderie, the City lets out a flood to scatter the billposts. There are no accidents in this place. There are no coincidences.

People disappear. Friends are separated from friends. Mothers are injected with disease and locked in cells where they grow sick and die.

We listen at every door, and we move quietly through the halls. Twice we've had to take the stairs to avoid a rushing crowd of Hectors. What worries me most are the shuffling sounds and the heavy breaths that we catch only now and then when all else is still. The disfigured men have been following us. I don't know why they haven't just surrounded us and cut our veins.

"Where is your friend with the gun?" A rusty voice from the stairwell. And we sure as hell do not answer.

*

We keep moving. Down one flight, through another autopsy room, and back up again to a vestibule, sandwiched between galleries. The lights are dim here. The metal doesn't gleam like it does in the galleries. There are more shadows, and nothing is sterile.

We lean against the doors to the next gallery, same as always, but the sound through these cracks isn't one we've heard before. Clicking, like metal tapping against metal but in a pattern. A circle.

"What is that?" says Gibbsy.

I don't know. Something in the goddamn next hall is all I can tell, so I listen at the crack. It almost sounds like footsteps. Drawing close, fading away, drawing close again. Click, click, click.

"We can't go this way," says Gibbsy. He has gone from red to pale.

"We can't go back out that way either, for Christ's sake. The hell's the matter?"

The clicks and clacks circle, come back again. Gibbsy inhales. "Remember those dogs we saw?"

Yeah. I remember.

But we can't just sit here anymore. I can hear the Crackjaws muttering. They've been following us, keeping their distance, and I can tell that a few of them at least are listening to us from the bottom of the steps we just climbed. I guess they'll get brave enough to climb them too, before long.

"What are they waiting for?" says Gibbsy. "They know we don't have a gun, don't they? They know it's just us."

"Maybe. Maybe they're not sure."

"I don't know," he says.

But on the other side of the door, the dogs are still pacing, maybe three of them, growling every now and then.

"Well the dogs probably wouldn't care even if we *did* have a gun," he says. Maybe it's true.

I'm thinking about those big, calm mutts. About that story Casten told. About the guy who tried to keep one as a pet.

A voice comes slithering from the stairwell behind us. The dancer. "What will you do now? Come back to our welcoming arms? Or traipse among the glistening hounds? We'd rather think of you as men of reason than wasteful children, and we can use all the wise friends we can get."

I'm not going to answer the prick. I lean close to Gibbsy.

"Shit, I'd rather try my chances with the *dogs*, Gibbs. Those pricks are laughing at us. At least the dogs're straight-forward about how they feel."

Gibbsy nods, but I don't think he's convinced. He doesn't want to go out there. Neither do I, to be honest. But we don't really have time to think about it.

"Any ideas?"

"No. I don't know. Those Crackjaws…."

"Hell Gibbsy."

"I don't know," he says. "Either way we're dead. We go back, they'd shoot us. We go through there; the dogs'd go after us I bet. I think the Crackjaws want to see us eaten is what. They hope we open the door."

Some of his color is coming back, but he's grinding his teeth like mad. Sitting still like this, the pain is coming back into my joints. I need some rest. A big part of me wishes we had stayed in those cadaver drawers.

"We're already at the front end of the ward," says Gibbsy. "Triage was just past here."

"The dogs, then, Gibbsy. That's all there is to it. Cross your fingers."

"They're crossed. All ten of 'em."

I press my hand against the door so that it won't slide so fast into the wall. Trying to hush that pneumatic whoosh. I don't know if it'll make a difference.

A dozen or more dogs stand in the hall. They're

facing the far end, and some are still wandering away as if something down there had tickled their fancy before we came into the gallery. But now their attention is on us. They all turn to look.

The two dogs closest to us stand and stare, very still. They've tracked blood over the floor, but I'm not sure whose blood it is. Or maybe it's dog's blood.

Further down, a few of the dogs whine and scratch at the door of one cell for a bit, almost like they're trying to get back *in*to the goddamn thing. But pretty soon they give up on whatever's behind the glass and sulk toward us instead. Others gather out from open cells. Maybe two dozen now. It's a congregation of hounds. A gathering of teeth. They're here for us.

Me and Gibbsy, we edge to the right, toward a little side corridor and god knows what else. Maybe we can try to outrun the dogs along these back rooms and not get swarmed.

The dog closest to me is bigger than I think a breed like that should get, whatever it is. A German shepherd I think. The hind legs quiver, full of spring and deadly tendons. But even he is not the biggest dog in the room. Not by any stretch.

A crooked monster clicks out from the nearest cell. He must have been a Great Dane once, but he's not anymore. Not if you ask me. His fur is covered in blood and sweat and froth. In his mouth, he grips something rigid and pink. A human jaw bone picked clean.

We haven't shuffled more than a few steps toward the corridor when they start to growl. All of them at once. That's what scares me most. It wasn't just one dog who got the others started on growling…it was two dozen low growls all rumbling across the hall at exactly the same time.

We back toward the narrow corridor, inch by inch. I keep expecting the closest few to spring, but they don't. It's like they're waiting for the others before they make their move. Hell. I don't know. I get this silly idea, and I start fishing in one of my pockets for this old billfold I carry around, and I take my papers out and put them back in my pocket, and I throw the billfold down toward the middle of the hall.

The dogs watch the leather spin overhead, and they watch it land. But they don't chase after it. All those eyes turn back to us.

It's time to run. I just don't think we can outrun them.

"Gibbsy, move slow. Real steady."

He doesn't answer. I can hear the shiver in his breath.

The further we back away, the deeper the growls get. Rapid like a room full of band saws.

I'm staring so hard at the dogs, my eyes are starting to go dry. I almost don't notice when the figure of a man steps out of the cell at the far end of the gallery. But there he is. There past the dogs. It's Reggie.

"Hey, assholes! You want blood, I got plenty. Drink 'til you drown."

He fires a shot at the ceiling from a little Pentreb revolver he must have found on some dead Hector and the dogs turn their growls to him instead of us. They shuffle away from Gibbsy and me, bit by bit, and Reggie does just like we were doing, edging back slowly. He's got the gun held out in front of him, but I think little Pentreb won't do much harm to this crowd.

Reggie hits the door and fires one more shot, and now the dogs are running for him. But they don't get to him. He shuts the door, and the pack breaks against it, barking and baying so loud my ears hurt.

Me and Gibbsy...we run too. Down that little corridor as fast as we can go. A few of the dogs notice and they give chase. But we don't stop until another door has closed between them and us and the cinch has gone to the slide-catch.

*

The corridor lets us into a broad lab filled with tables and burners. Tubes running along the walls and benches all over the place, but not like in autopsy. These have glass tops that light up from underneath for looking at slides I guess. No...x-rays. A few have been left out on the tables, here and there.

Behind us, the dogs scratch at the door. For a minute I wonder if maybe they're smart enough to pull the lever, but with the cinch, it wouldn't matter. The door stays good and shut.

"Their skeletons change," says Gibbsy. He leans against a chair looking at one of the x-rays. "Change and sort of change back. Some Crackjaws look like freaks. Later the ones who survive it all almost look normal, except the head. "

"Goddamn pricks." All these x-rays of dogs too, going through some kind of mutation from the Flu. It's notching me up just to think about it. About Rothschild and Mycroft and their chums torturing dogs and sick folks all these years, and them not knowing what the hell they're in for. I don't care what good it could come to or what sort of cure they could make of it. They shouldn't have been using goddamn dogs to do it and people neither.

"I'm tired, Tommy. Tired as hell."

"Me too. We can't just sit here."

"Just for a little while…"

"No Gibbsy. Not just for a little while." I'm tired too, I really am. Looking at Gibbsy leaning there, drooping, I want to sit down. "But not here," I tell him, and I point to the corner of the room. "Not with them."

A pile of bodies has been stacked here. Hectors, bleeding over the floor. Their suits are torn, and some have lost their masks.

"Why'd they stack 'em like that?" says Gibbsy.

"Couldn't've been the dogs. The Crackjaws? Why do they do *anything*? Christ, I don't know."

But it's creepy, to look at that. Like they were building a hut out of bodies just for fun or something.

"We shouldn't stay here, Gibbs."

"I really need to rest, Tommy."

"Okay, just not here."

*

We move to the next lab, and we shut and cinch all the doors, using the last of the ties from Gibbsy's pocket. There were more in the backpack, but Poplar has that. It worries me. I'm not sure how many more doors we'll need to keep shut between here and wherever we're going.

Gibbsy collapses against the wall. We're in a meeting room of some kind, with a big conference table in the middle. Chairs have been scattered in a panic to every corner. There's blood in here too—long handprints on the walls—but no bodies. One wall has a window looking out on the adjacent corridor and still more blood. More meeting rooms just like this one, all up and down the place. I can see the flicker of a projector in one of them, just across the way. It has been overturned on its table and is showing smudged slides of god knows what.

"Get up. Gibbsy. We can sit for a second or two, but let's get away from those windows for god's sake. Through there. Goddamn storage room, maybe?"

"Yeah," says Gibbsy. "No, I can keep moving."

"The hell you can, your face is purple. Go on and sit in there a second."

It's a small door, set back in the corner, and the word "Storage" is stenciled on the face of it. We don't exactly have to be geniuses to know what it is.

"I'm okay," wheezes Gibbsy. "I just…we need to walk slow for a while."

"Fuck, Gibbsy, go in *there* and sit down for Christ's sake."

"I'm alright."

"Just go sit down for awhile."

I push him by the shoulders and follow after him. The storage door isn't pneumatic. Just a good old-fashioned hinge-and-handle job. Gibbsy pulls it toward him. And everything after that seems to move in slow frames.

I see the Hector on the storage room floor, bleeding out, the blood soaking into a box of files, the shattered goggles, the eyes opening behind them. The shepherd's crook is drawn on the inside of the door. My eyes move down to the gun in the Hector's hand. It jerks upright and fires. I hear the first shot, and I see the blood pulse out from a new hole Gibbsy's shoe. I hear the second shot, and I feel the spray on my face. Gibbsy's shoulder jars back. It's a glance of a shot, but he hits the wall, and his legs whip forward, kicking the door shut again.

Blood streaks over the outside of the door. Speckled over my arms and my shirt. Gibbsy is wheezing.

*

They say that which governs least is best. A city that is willing to kill its own people for any reason is guilty of the worst of crimes. Of governing the one thing that shouldn't be governed at all. Of taking something that can't be given back. This is what happens when a City gets used to the thought of its own power. It stops feeling responsible for anything that doesn't feed it.

It's so close I can almost touch it, that moment

when I should have told Gibbsy to keep moving instead of opening that door. But it doesn't matter how close a moment is. When it's past, it can't be redone.

*

I film the door. When I get up the nerve to crack it open, the Hector is already dead. His blood and Gibbsy's blood meet at the sill. I film the Hector anyway and the Herds' mark on the door, and then in a breathless choking spasm, I bash Cassandra against the table behind me, and her lens shatters.

I don't hate myself for doing it. I hate myself because for a second I care more about breaking the camera than about what just happened to the best friend I ever had.

"Gibbsy, what do I do?"

He points but he can't get any words out.

"What, tie-up your ankle? Like a tourniquet?"

He nods, so I take his belt, and I cinch it mid-calf until the bleeding slows as much as I dare slow it.

"We gotta keep moving. Can you get up on your good leg?"

"I...where's the..." He's pale, and his eyes shiver in their sockets.

"Where's what? Come on, I'll get under your arm, and we'll go."

He makes some effort to push himself up. I hoist him by the armpit, careful not to slip in the blood or anything. I get him up on the good leg and we start to hobble but he screams like the air coming out of a tube, and he goes to the floor again.

"What? Did you hit your foot on something? What? Gibbsy, tell me what to do."

But all he can manage to do is breathe faster and point at everything and nothing.

*

I used to go on long walks with my dad when I was a kid. Tunnel to tunnel, hall to hall. He used to love looking at the City. All the tired pump housings and crippled half decks, and the big GT pipes with the wrinkled wire cages all around so nobody'll get too close, and all the fittings shaking like they're palsied. We'd always go before curfew, but he liked the deadhalls anyway. He liked the quiet.

"Look at that," he'd say. "Tommy look at that, the way all these valves dilate on their own. It's from the pressure. Simple," he'd say. "Brilliant. Things like that, you've got to think about how beautiful they really are. Most people would call this place dingy."

But him, he was dazzled by it, the way folks used to get dazzled by cut jewels I guess. All this Crackjaw ingenuity, he couldn't get enough of it, my old man. I'd bet he still goes on those walks sometimes but not as much. Some of the wonder has been crushed out of him probably. Maybe he shouldn't have had it in the first place.

I remember this one time we were down on HX and nobody was around, so he found this old bureau somebody had left there, and he dragged it over against the wall and climbed on top of it. "Come up here," he said, and I did.

He had this screwdriver with him, and he started taking one of the ceiling panels off. I bet if there'd been Blackbands walking through right then he'd have been put in a burnbox for awhile, just for unscrewing that panel. But this place was empty as a vickshaft, and I could actually hear the dust coughed out to the floor.

He set the panel aside and lifted me up into the ceiling. "You see that up there, that little box with all the wires?" he said.

It was a clumsy metal box, bolted to the bulkhead.

"Looks out of place, doesn't it?" he said. "The wire's already corroding, the metal is a different color than all the other stuff here. Rougher edges and all that. The Crackjaws didn't make that, didn't put it there. It doesn't belong there. You know what those wires do? They patch into the PA feed. Into the speakers. It's a timer and every night, it tells the speakers in this Wedge to chirp. That's a tin cricket."

I'd never seen one before, but I was old enough to

know there was something about the chirping I didn't like. My dad, though, he said even though the tin crickets weren't meant to be here, there was something lovely about the fact that somebody had thought to wire them into the ceilings of Fallback.

I remember saying, "Nobody even knows what a cricket is. It's not like we won't know when to go to sleep."

"Some of us remember crickets," he told me. Just the kind of thing he'd say.

For all my shouting, for all my noise, for all the Riot Reels I've shot, and all the times I've called the City on its lies, I haven't been an honest person either. Just more of the same chirping. Totally dismissible. A sad imitation of something that might have mattered in the now dead world.

*

Gibbsy is still bleeding but not as bad anymore. And he's not shaking as much either, which is a good thing.

"I can see if there's a cart or something."

We're nestled away at the back of the storage room now, behind some shelves, in the dark. I was able to drag him that far, which isn't saying much, but the pain of being jostled practically killed him.

"I should just stay here," he says.

"No, you shouldn't. I'll find a cart. Gotta be one somewhere."

Gibbsy reaches to tap my arm. "You…you can't sneak through here pushing a cart the whole time," he says. His voice is so tired. It's breaking my goddamn heart to look at him. "Maybe when things calm down. You can tell somebody where I am."

"What do you think they'll do, take you to a hospital? Patch you up? Christ, Gibbsy, they'll skin you for a trophy."

He doesn't have anything to say to that, and we're quiet long enough for me to feel terrible about it. "Maybe I can find somebody friendly. The Herds or whatever. But who says you'll last that long? Look at this."

"I'll be alright. It doesn't even hurt anymore." He smiles so I'll know he's kidding around but it's still got me knotted-up, and this is no time for a sense of humor. "Tommy," he says. "Don't be mad at Poplar, okay?"

"What, for leaving us? I know. She did what she needed to do. I'm not mad."

"Don't be."

"I'm *not*, Gibbs. I'm not."

I guess it's true. I'm mad, just maybe not at her. "If I'm mad at anybody it's me. Talking you all into coming down here. I know you didn't want to. Hell, Gibbsy, you could've said you didn't care about getting even with those pricks in Processing. You could have just said that."

"I guess I did kind of want to get even, is all," he says. He's lying though. He wouldn't have thought to do anything about it if I hadn't been nagging him all day.

"Well, I wouldn't have listened to you anyway, Gibbs, so it doesn't make any difference. Either I'm right about things, or I'm not done trying to be. I keep telling you guys I'm an asshole, but…"

"Nothing'll change until we change it."

Somewhere in the hall, fingernails scrape against metal. I shimmy up to where I can see past the table and through that half-window of the meeting room. A lurching clump of shadows passes and moves away and is gone again, like some kind of psychotic patrol.

"We can't stay here."

"I have to," he says. "Just block the door."

I don't want to do that, but I don't want to sit here arguing either. Gibbsy's right. He's going to have to stay here, and I'm going to have to move, soon and fast.

"Did you know she can sing?" says Gibbsy.

"Who, Pop?"

"Yeah," he says. "That time at the flashrant at Thrustein's, after you got mad and left. She took the mic except instead of ranting she started singing some song she must've made up with your name in it. I think she was trying to get you to come back, but you didn't hear."

"No, I didn't know that."

"She sure can sing," he says.

"*Could* sing. Past tense." I feel like a bastard the second I say that. Gibbsy looks at me like I'm a bastard, too, which makes it a thousand times worse. "Naw, maybe she got away from Quarantine when we caused all that noise. Think she could've?"

"I don't know. Yeah."

Me, I'm not so sure. The funny thing is, all I can think about right now is how I wish I'd heard her singing that day and gone back. Things like that, it's almost like you're not meant to know about them until it's too late to fix any of it or set it right. Just like I wish I'd left Gibbsy home tonight.

"Hey, Tommy though, I still would've come with you tonight if I knew what was going to happen," he tells me.

"You'd have still come huh? I doubt that."

"No," says Gibbsy. He's sweating so much. He

looks so cold. "I mean it," he says. "Somebody *needed* to do what we did. I wish we knew. I wish the Barkers and them had told us about all this instead of tricking us, but I still would've done it even if I knew I wouldn't come back."

"To hell with that. You're just trying to make me feel better about leaving you here, and I'm not going to feel better. We didn't accomplish anything tonight, Gibbsy. We wasted all we had on nothing. You think having Blankface on the loose is a good thing? I'm no fan of the City, Gibbs, but it's the fact they had a bunch of Crackjaws down here in the first place that's all wrong, not the fact that they weren't letting the worst of 'em roam free. I don't even know why he'd kill all them Hectors and then just let us go, but he did, and that's probably not a good thing either. For whatever reason. Shit, we can't win unless we get out of here, but I'll tell you this Gibbsy, we can't get out of here unless we lose."

The knocking of a blunt hand on metal shuts me up. Those wayward Crackjaws have come back. Probably circling the place. One of them shouts down the muffled hall, maybe the dancer.

"Someone, I see, has passed this way but gone no further. Sing, sing! And we'll fly to thee."

I go still as a stone, but Gibbsy reaches for my sleeve. "The last thing they are is dumb," he whispers.

"I know."

"Those guys'll come in here sooner than later, Tommy."

"I know. I know."

Like it or not, it's time for me to leave. And I'll have to make some noise when I do.

*

I don't have any way to lock the storage room from the outside, and we don't have time to ponder the matter either. I bury Gibbsy behind a bunch of boxes and cover him with drop cloths.

"Don't move."

"I won't. I'll listen. I'll be okay."

I tell him I'll try to find somebody with the Herds or something. Not Mycroft or Rothschild or their goons, but somebody who'll bend a kind ear to the situation. Then I crawl out into the meeting room and shut the door behind me.

For almost half a minute, I can't pry my hand away from the doorknob, and I can't breathe.

The Crackjaws are pacing away from me again. Four or five of them. The one at the back of the group, he's the dancer. One shoulder droops and that arm twitches at his side.

They're looking through all the windows, into the meeting rooms, but they're not going through any doors. That same sly caution we've seen all night. Gibbsy's right. They're not stupid. Not at all.

But the dancer, he's lagging, and he keeps turning around looking this way. The others have practically left him behind.

I slip under the table and out into the hall on my hands and knees. I want to get this guy's attention, but I don't want him to see me coming out of this particular room. I don't want him to think to check in here when I'm gone and find Gibbsy.

The best thing I can think to do, actually, is go into another meeting room altogether. Then I'd just have to knock something over and take-off running when the Crackjaws come to see about it.

I crawl along until the hall T's and move past the corner and in through the side door of the room with the upset projector. The dancer is not ten feet away, now, and he's moving back in this direction again.

I don't want to let him get too close. You never know what'll happen when trying to draw somebody off…it's good to give yourself a cushion. Some extra space. I should know, as many close calls as I've had.

I sit leaning against the half-wall under the window as he passes, and I give him another five or ten steps before I kick the table, rattling the projector. Its mottled square of light flickers against the dropscreen. Some fuzzy image of shattered bones.

I'm on my feet before the dancer can turn all the way around but he sees me soon enough, squinting with his crooked, ruined eyes. "Come out!" he says. "Sooner or later we must all grow-up. Become something better than we were. Why not now?"

But before he can say another word, I'm out through the other door, running past the next few windows, zigging and zagging through the crisscrossed halls away from his buddies. But when I turn the next corner, I can see he must've had more buddies than I thought. Lots more.

Five of them stand waiting in the corridor, staring at me as I come into view, with not a hint of surprise among the lot of them. The closest one is near enough, he reaches for me and misses by maybe an inch or two, is all, as I skid to the side trying to avoid him. But he's not the one I'm worried about.

One of these guys…he's big. Not tall, but wide, half-naked, covered in blood, and bleeding from a couple of places where he's been either shot or stabbed or whatever. The other four, they're no prizes themselves, but they practically look normal next to this big Crackjaw. And him, he looks fast. He looks like he could catch most anything on legs if he wanted to.

"Stay here, you'll be safe with us," says the dancer. "The men will shoot you if you try to leave."

The last thing I want to do is stay. I tear-off across the tiles and into a long, low sitting room with a sunken reception desk and overturned chairs. They're following me, but I'm doing my best to stay ahead and out of sight. Turning here, turning there, doubling back through windowless rooms with enough doors to make a difference. The Snake. The Aftershock. The Priest. I'm making too much noise, but this is as quiet as I can be.

Every time I'm in an open hall, I hear them scrambling after me. Sometimes I step out in front of another unsurprised Crackjaw, and more than once I have some near misses. This place is crawling with the twisted bastards. And I'm guessing they know where I'm going because they're always ahead of me. Pinching-off halls and forcing me into another waiting crew. I can't get twenty feet without hearing that big Crackjaw behind me, gaining in the straight runs and not slowing much when I try to shake him.

I need to find some quiet way out of here, or this won't last much longer. First things first, I need enough time and space to think of a plan, so the next time I see a fuse box, I slide to a stop and pop the goddamn thing open. Flipping a few breakers, the halls go dark. But not all of them. I sprint toward the dimmest corners and then I move on out toward the light again.

I think this'll slow them down enough, maybe I can take a second or two to get the lay of the land and figure out where I'm at and where I need to be. But that's when I trip.

My hands hit the floor first, sliding along the smooth tile, blistering the palms instantly. My wrists almost crack trying to catch myself, but even that's not enough to stop my chin from hitting, and I start to bleed from the white-hot gash.

Behind me, a bell is ringing. Every time I move, it rings louder, and it doesn't take long for me to figure out why. My legs are bound with wire. Thin filament. I can barely see it, even now. The Crackjaws must have stretched it across the hall to slow me down. The springy, sticky wire has broken loose from where it was tied to a vent on one side of the hall, but the other anchor-point is still taught. The wire over there is spooled around an old caster broken off from a chair, and hanging from the caster is a small bell that they must have pieced together from other parts of that same chair. Goddamn clever bastards.

I'm quick to free my legs and unspool some more of that wire. When I've got enough slack, I'm off down the hall again, trailing it behind me, ringing that bell so that whoever's still following me will go toward that sound instead of listening for my footsteps.

And when I've gone around the next few corners I tug hard, pulling the wire free, and I reel it in around my arm, so they'll have no trail to follow. The Ghost.

*

I'm trying to think of what Gibbsy would do if he

were with me. What he'd say and where he'd go. All I can think is, I need to find the washrooms. If I can find the washrooms, I can find the pipes, and when you're cornered, that's the best thing you can do. Maybe I can get into the wet wall and follow the pipes right out of here. Maybe.

The Crackjaws are near enough, I can't really slow and wander. Their feet scream on the tiles. Their voices mutter and bounce around odd corners. All I can do is guess...so I guess, and I run.

*

I must have a sprinkle or two of luck left, because it isn't long before I see a restroom sign on one of the walls, pointing down the left hall. The whole stretch is clear of Crackjaws, for now, so I sprint and pass the men's room and duck into the women's room since it's closer to the far end of Pathology. Closer to where I want to be.

The lights in here are bright. Blinding almost, after all those dimmed nighttime runners out in the corridors.

It doesn't bother me, though.

I round the L looking for an access hatch. Usually, they're under the sinks, and I'll need to unscrew a latch probably, so I've got my little knife out already.

The problem is, the hatch is blocked. I skid to a halt just shy of a glistening pond of new blood. I almost fall into it, but I don't, and thank Christ for that because it would be the end of me. Leaning there under the sinks are the remains of two Crackjaws whose throats and bowels have been slit and spilled, and I guess it wasn't Hectors that did it. It was other Crackjaws.

They must've known I'd come through here and they must've known I'd never dare touch their blood. They must want me to find some other way out of here. They're pushing me somewhere. They're herding me into a snare, but I'm not going to let them do it.

*

The stall panel bends under my leaning weight, and my foot slips a little on the rim of the toilet as I push against the ceiling grate. I shift back to steady myself.

The room is almost too tall for this, but not quite. Bracing one arm against the metal panel I reach up and push one corner of the grate up and out to the side until it teeters, and when the edge droops I twist the whole thing and pull it down off of its rests. Then I pull another grate, and a third for good measure. Dust sifts from the thin wire conduits that lace the naked ceiling behind the grid.

The grates are about an inch and a half thick and heavy enough that I don't think I'll crush them. I drag all three over to the L, and I lower the first one into the blood, careful not to get my hand wet. Hell, I don't know if you can catch the Spanish Flu just touching blood like this, but that's what they tell you and I'm not going to take any chances.

Standing on the first grate, I put the second one out further into the blood, like stepping stones. The third one gets me close enough to the sinks, I should be able to reach the hatch.

Now I just have to figure out how to get the corpses out of the way. Their clothes are soaked, and I can smell the copper. I think about maybe lassoing them with Cassandra's strap, but I don't want to abandon the camera, even if it is broken. And I'll need my hands free.

I feel silly standing on the grate. I could probably stand in the blood for hell's sake, and it would just get on the bottom of my shoes wet, but I just don't want to touch it, not even with my clothes, and my stomach is welling up again from all I've done tonight, all I've ignored and all I've wrecked and all I'll miss.

In the end, I resort to pushing the poor dead bastards aside with the end of a waste bin. The halls outside the washroom are quiet for now, but I'm not taking that as a point in my favor just yet. I've still got to loosen that smeared hatch, and there are four screws between me and the crawl.

My penknife is small and unsteady in the screw heads, and I can't really put a hand out there to steady the damn thing from slipping. It's slow going. One screw drops without a sound into the gelling red below.

I'm working from the bottom up. That way the hatch won't tip into my face and splatter blood into my open eyes. I hope.

After the third screw, the hatch swivels downward on that last pivot, scraping the wall, shrieking. I half expect I'll hear it echoed from the hall by the howls of deranged men. But the Crackjaws must not have zeroed my trail yet. And as the hatch finally lowers away from the pipe crawl I feel for a second or two like I've got some reason to hope.

But I won't be able to cover my tracks this time. If they come in here—and they will come in here sooner than later—they'll know exactly where to pick up the trail. I move fast, through the crawl, on hands and knees, trying not to lean against the steam. Trying to see in the dark.

*

I hit the wall so hard I can see flashes of white in the pitch black. I hold my head, rocking on my knees. I don't know how far I've gone, but the crawl has ended, and the pipes bend and dive into the floor, leaving no gap to follow. I can't even turn around, it's so tight. I'll have to back up, feeling against the wall for the last hatch.

It isn't far. I trace the outline of it with my fingers, and it occurs to me I won't have any way to turn the screws from this side. I'll have to bust it down, but I might not even have enough space to get a good punch at it. Plus, it'll be noisy as all get-out so I won't want to be pounding against the thin metal more than a time or two. It'd be like ringing a dinner bell.

For a while, I crouch there listening at the hatch. Somewhere past it, water is dripping. Another washroom maybe. Nobody is moving around out there, that's for sure. Or maybe they're just being quiet.

Christ. For that matter, there could be somebody sneaking up behind me in the dark, not making a sound, just a few feet away, ready to drag me by the feet back to the gang.

The thought of it starts to panic me. Right now, I feel like there's no hall wide enough in all of Fallback. Must have been how Reggie felt, in that cadaver drawer.

I twist my waist, trying to give my elbow a

running start, but I'm gun shy. I need to hit that hatch square in the middle. I shuffle back and forth until I think I've got the right spot. I wind up, and I hit it so hard my entire frame shivers.

The damn thing doesn't move. And the echo stretches back along the pipe crawl to god knows what set of mangled ears.

This won't work. Hitting with my arm—it won't work. I've somehow got to get my legs against it, but the only way to do that is to lie back and scoot my chest under the pipes.

At first, I'm thinking, there's not enough room. But my head squeezes past, and my shoulders too, and I have to exhale, but my chest fits under the pipes too. Meanwhile, I'm trying to find the hatch with my feet. I've got the edge of it, but I need to move over just a little more.

When my forehead first touches the steam pipe, my whole body bucks against the tight space, trying to pull away, but I can't move. I'm stuck against that heat.

I've got to start kicking and just hope my face isn't blistered by the time I'm done.

Two, three hits against the hatch and I can feel it bulging away from me. I can hear the wail of the screw threads. And then, pop, it's off, skidding across some hard floor.

Pulling against the lower water pipe, I scramble feet first out of the pipe crawl. Out of the dark space. And before the light blurs my vision, I'm sure I can see hands and a face coming up toward me through the crawl. A skittering, twitching, clicking mass of limbs just four feet away.

I scoot forward, legs flailing, shoulders rocking, hands pawing at the slick tile. It's like I'm moving an inch a minute and can't get traction, and my wrists are always just a half a second from being grabbed and dragged back into the dark.

But I'm clear now. I roll away. My eyes adjust, and my ears stop hissing from the red-hot pain, and I can both see and hear that the crawl behind me is empty.

*

Water drips from a busted showerhead. Dozens of them in here. It's a locker room. Just as vacant as anywhere else in this place.

The first thing I do after I convince my legs to start working again is I drag a half-section of lockers over and block that hatchway. The lockers are empty, and it wouldn't be hard to push them out of the way from inside the crawl, but it's better than nothing.

I'd best keep moving, right on through and out the next door, but I can't move. I'm going to fall to the ground if I don't sit first, so I sit on one of the benches, propped on my arms folded in the crease of my waist.

The dented hatch cover is at my feet. Lying there, not moving, pretending to be dead, waiting, scared, not sure what to do next or where to go or if there's anything that can be done or anyplace to go, and if I had a gun right now I'd put a bullet in the middle of the hatch and kick it to the corner of the room where it won't matter anymore. Not to anyone in the whole world.

My insides are caving in like an empty can under a boot. I don't know if I'll throw up or not. I don't care. I might as well. Jesus, I'm tired. Sitting still like this isn't doing me any good. It's just making me think about the things I can't do anything about, and it's slowing me down.

On the wall in front of me, someone has written something on the tiles with machine grease. It's a phrase I've seen a thousand times. A phrase I've said a hundred and never really, really understood. "Zanzibar is a lie."

It bothers me, seeing that again. Mostly because it doesn't make any sense anymore. Who cares if Zanzibar is a lie? That place is long gone now, and it was a long time ago, and it was a huge mess, so what's to lie about? One should never bother with old dead things. That's what's bothering me, I think. More than anything. It's that people think anything is worth hanging on to. That there's anything precious enough to stick in a jar at the back of a cupboard. Old photographs, is all, and things like that should be burned or torn to pieces. If you're going to forget something, let yourself forget it. The important things won't let you forget them, so it makes me sick thinking how worried folks are about forgetting the unimportant things.

Then I glance at the far end of the locker room, and none of that seems to matter anymore.

I'm in trouble.

I'm not alone in here after all. The first thing I see is his suit. A dark suit with an orange tie, sort of like Kennedy wears, or the other bigwigs. But this guy's face is nothing like a human face, and it's not like those other Crackjaws either. The guy's goddamn jaw is *filled* with needle-sharp teeth, and the lips don't close over them. He has no hair, and he has no eyes.

You see pictures sometimes or read about them, and Crackjaws never seem to look the same, but you can always tell they're Crackjaws somehow. I've seen mangled men tonight, but they've looked nothing like the stories until now. Here in front of me…here's what a Crackjaw really looks like. If he had eyes, he'd be staring at me right now, but somehow, I don't think he has any trouble knowing I'm here. Watching me with that eyeless face.

Blankface lifts his hands to his mouth and moves his fingers like he's playing some instrument that isn't there. His mouth doesn't move, but I could swear to Christ I hear flutes, all around me.

I keep thinking, "He's in my head, he knows what I'm thinking," and any minute now I'll hear his voice in my skull telling me to cut my own throat over the drain and die here on the tiles. But there's no voice in my head. He's saying nothing to me, for whatever reason, and now I can't hear that flute anymore either.

I'm too scared to move, but after a good minute of just staring at the fucking Crackjaw, I get the sense I should leave.

"Go on and kill me if you're gonna."

He doesn't say a goddamn thing and he never will.

"Go ahead. Go ahead. I helped you out, but I wouldn't't've done it if I knew I was doing it, so you don't need to do me any favors. Go on and break my mind over your knee already if you're gonna."

But he just stands still playing a flute that isn't there.

Scared or not, I've got to do something. I've got to get out of here. I stand up and edge past the lockers, past the benches, sure with every step that I'm about to die. I edge to the nearest door and through it, without daring to blink. And as soon as I'm out of sight I start to run.

The strange thing is, I don't know how I worked up the nerve to do that. Half my mind is still screaming at me, "Don't move," but I'm moving, and fast, and I don't look back.

"THE BANNERS," Reel 5 of 8, 16mm, 24fps

The transformer station fills a wide expanse that opens like a vat at the end of a very narrow hall. Chain link barriers surround it, locked with thick brass plates so old they clearly do not belong there.

Wires feed into the towers from the turbines in upper Geothermal and feed away from the towers into the city.

At the center of the transformer station stands a redbrick building with cross-frame windows, two stories tall from the floor to the roof of the expanse. Some of the windows are stained-glass, blue, various colors lit from behind. Now and then a shadow paces past one of the windows.

The camera does not pass the gate but comes close to the chain links, focusing on the transformer towers. Banners have been hung from them, like flags. Despite the fact that they are hung on City property, they are not the City's typical darkened version of the American flag. A bold ark and three circles have been painted on them.

Not like any flag that could be hung legally elsewhere in Fallback.

ELEVEN

I come to a full stop in a mess of a lounge where the chairs are overturned, and one of the lights has been shattered. Bullet holes pepper the wall, but there isn't any blood. Rumpled on the floor in the middle of the room is a yellow track shirt from Chalcenor High School.

"Reggie? Reggie."

A strange murmur struggles up from somewhere at the end of the lounge. The denting of tin. A low cabinet shimmies, and the door slides away, and Reggie crawls out shirtless, clutching a gun in each hand. His hair is matted, a flap of a mohawk tilting to the side.

"The hell *happened* to you?"

"I'm fine," he says like he's ready to hit me. "Didn't want to wait around. Didn't want to come out unless it was you." He picks up his shirt and shows it to me and puts it on.

"We gotta keep moving, kid. Come on. God, you're an asshole."

Reggie shrugs. "The hell you all needled for?"

"Blankface is back there." My face is sweating, and Reggie notices, but he doesn't say anything right away.

Then it sinks in with one hell of a splash, and he asks where Gibbsy is.

I don't know how to put it. There's no way to make it sound like something it isn't. "I had to leave him."

"Shit...Tommy. Leave him where?" He sees I'm serious and he goes pale. "Tommy...we gotta go back for 'im. I heard 'em talking, they're gonna seal off the place."

"We can't go back."

"Shot where?" says Reggie.

"Reggie, Blankface is back there. He was. Gibbsy, he was shot here. In the foot, bad. He can't walk." And then I almost lose it. "Some *prick* of a Hector was there, dying on the floor. I mean the guy's lying there about to die and what does he *do*? He fucking thinks we're Crackjaws and shoots, and what the fuck difference was it supposed to make? This Hector's dying anyway and shit, two minutes later he *was* dead, and if you're dying you aren't supposed to goddamn *worry* about something coming along to kill you, to where you'd even think you needed a gun. It's like *every*thing else."

Reggie puts his shirt on. "Well is Gibbsy dead?"

"No, he's okay, but he can't move much. And don't tell me we need to go back and get him because there's no way. He'll be fine."

"Fine, with his leg shot."

"The foot. Shoulder's grazed too, but yeah. Fine." I tell him again, there's no way back through there. Not the way I came. "We just have to leave him. I know."

For a minute I just stare at Reg. My throat's trembling like mad. I point to the guns in his hands. "What about you? You run into trouble?"

"Found these," he says. "It's weird, I don't know. Haven't seen a live Hector in ages. Just them dogs. Some of them Crackjaws."

"Well," I tell him. "We been lucky, so let's go on and keep being lucky for a while."

"Son of a bitch," he says. "Yeah, let's go."

*

I asked Poplar, once, why she never tagged anything with a bona fide message to it. She just did these murals or big stencils of poetry. I mean, no matter what the graffiti was, the City would have put her in Mocap if they'd caught her. What would it matter if she put Kennedy's face on a wall with "Crackjaw Rule" written on his forehead, or something like that? People were talking a lot about Petal back then, when she was tagging a lot, but none of her graffiti ever *said* anything.

It was just there. I told her she was wasting her audience. I told her, "You've got their attention. Do something with it."

Poplar gave the same answer she always gave when I asked her why she doesn't care about whether joes got a fair shake in Fallback. She said, "If you tell somebody what you mean, they wonder if you're lying. If you make them guess, they don't."

I wonder how she would feel about that now.

*

If something's going to happen, it'll be here. This is it. This is the choke-point for Pathology. The place where all of the scattered halls converge. No more honeycomb, just the one door out of here back through the sector junction to Triage.

And now that door is directly in front of us but the last time we were in Triage it was crawling with triggers, and I'm guessing they'll be watching this place from behind a good dozen iron sights. Sure, I've got some reason to hope the whole place has been scattered to hell and gone what with all the chaos. The Crackjaws have been doing a damn fine job of keeping the Hectors busy, and we've slipped through the holes so far, but this is different. This is ground zero, the one foothold the Hectors would not want to lose.

It bothers me that this place is empty. That the sector junction sits there at the end of the corridor, all alone, unmanned, still as the grave.

"Just means they're on the other side of it playing dead," says Reggie. He's probably right.

"What else are we supposed to do?"

"How should I know?"

There *is* nothing else we can do. We creep toward the junction, listening like always, eyes twitching for any bad sign, watching the side doors. Watching the booth, the empty benches.

I'm thinking about what Reggie said, about how the Hectors were talking about sealing off Pathology. Locking the junction. And maybe the reason this place is so empty is that they already have sealed it off, and we're trapped in here until god knows when. The redbells aren't spinning, but that doesn't mean anything. Maybe they've already pulled the lever. Maybe it's all over, all done, no use doing anything but sitting and waiting for someone to come along and slit our throats.

But when Reggie tries the junction hatch, the handle spins, and the door opens, and we both breathe again. My ears catch the tail end of my heavy pulse as it eases. We edge through and shut the hatch behind us. We cross the junction, spin the next hatch, and we're out again. Back to Triage again and, Jesus, I can barely remember the last time we were here.

The memories come back real fast when we see the screencheck booth. It is very much occupied.

Mycroft rests his forehead against the glass and as he smiles his breath spreads a bit of fog. Rothschild is with him, leaning back in a chair, and he jumps to his feet when he sees us, reaching for something on the console. Mycroft and Rothschild. I'm not surprised.

The booth is much further away from us than the

nearest corridor, so I figure we've still got a chance to scram. "Don't stand here, Reg. I don't want to hear what they have to say."

We sprint out of the cage and cut diagonally across the floor. But that's when our luck leaves us. Two Hectors come out of the corridor five feet away, and the way they're bearing down on us with those guns, I guess they knew we would try this. My shoes skid and shriek over the glossy tiles. I can see myself in the Hectors' amber goggles, falling backward.

The first thing I do when I hit the ground is I grab for Reggie's arm. I don't want him lifting those guns and getting shot for it. But he has already dropped them. He knows better.

Redbells splash over the walls, vanish, and flood the place again. They're spinning, and I'm starting to realize what Rothschild was reaching for, in the booth. The junction is now shut. He has pulled the floodchecks, and Pathology is sealed. And to be honest, I'm not one-hundred-percent sure we're standing on the best side of that hatch.

*

"Where are your friends?" Mycroft stays in the booth. Even when Rothschild comes out to stand behind the Hectors, Mycroft stays behind the glass and stares at us and talks through the mic. "The other two?"

The Hectors have collected Reggie's guns already, and they've got us on our knees with our hands clasped overhead. The colonel, whatever his name is, he's with these two, watching them watching us. At least back in Pathology we could hope for a few Crackjaws to come along and scatter the situation. But no, not now. We can't scatter this one. We're caught.

"Did you leave them behind?" says Mycroft.

"Your boys killed 'em is what it was." I'm not going to tell this prick about Gibbsy. Not Mycroft.

He leans into the mic again. "Colonel, then, if you'll call Billingsly and have the locks reset..."

My eyes flair when I hear that. I don't know what in Christ's name he means. "You did that to the locks? You could reset them?"

"Hmm? No, you disabled them," he says. "But we figured out very quickly how to fix the grid after that."

Rothschild steps forward and keeps looking from us to Mycroft and back again. "He means we didn't want to lock you in there. We wanted to wait."

"We need to ask you something," says Mycroft. "Let's bring them back to the tables."

*

They march us out of screencheck single-file with a grim, faceless Hector on either side and the colonel tailing behind. Mycroft is leading the way, but Rothschild is close enough that I can start giving him hell for how tonight has turned out.

"You're not a good liar, man. You should find another hobby."

Rothschild gives his head half a turn. He's twitchier than he was last time we saw him. Jumpier I guess. Closer to the brittle edge. "Well, I'm sorry if you were *offended*. Everything I said to your camera was true, you know. I don't like to lie, but you weren't honest either, you have to admit. We had to find out the truth the hard way, but that's not the way we wanted to do it."

This makes me mad enough I start to lower my arms without thinking about it, and one of the Hectors hits me in the ribs with the butt of his gun, reminding me to return my palms to the top of my head. "Find out *what*? That it was us who shorted the locks? You already knew that. You knew it before we knew it. Christ, we told HIM everything we knew. All you had to do was listen to us in the first place and not string us along and play some big game with us and all this mess. Go ahead and shoot us now that you've got us. We said all there was to say."

Rothschild starts to reply, but Mycroft jumps in ahead of him. "There were a few details you left out," he says, not bothering to turn. Not bothering to explain.

Me, I'm just wondering why they haven't shot us yet.

*

On a shelf in the corner of the room, all that's left

of our film is smoldering in its own canister. Mycroft burned every frame. It's all been for nothing.

"I want to ask you about the Machinist."

He is shining a penlight in my eyes, one and then the other. We're back where we started with these two. Back in that glass Triage cell. The strange thing is, we didn't pass anybody on the way here. Last time this place was crawling with folks, but I guess all those Hectors were sent off to the next ward when the locks went down. Where they are now, god only knows. Dead or trapped, probably.

Mycroft has us strapped to those metal chairs this time, with big leather straps so tight around my wrists, my fingers are going numb. The colonel and those couple of Hectors are in the cell with us too, muzzles at the ready, just in case. Ready to pull the trigger if we don't sit still.

To be honest, I'm more worried about the chrome tray next to my table. A neat line of tools glimmers in the fluorescent washout. A scalpel, some pliers of some kind, an empty syringe for taking blood, I guess, and another syringe full of a pale, almost pink liquid.

"What did he tell you about our...about Blankface?"

"Didn't say anything about it. I already told you what he said."

"But that isn't true," says Mycroft. He's been shining that light at me so long now, even my free eye is seeing spots.

Rothschild, who has been leaning against the glass for the last little while, comes close to the chair now. His face is red. "How did you know where to find him then? Tell us that. I never said anything about Blankface or where to find him, and yet you proceeded directly to his door with a peg designed *specifically* to short the grid. You've called me a liar, well I'm calling you a liar now. We had to see what you and your Machinist friend planned to do. We had to let you off the leash to get a better idea of your intentions, and it worked. It's incredibly important that we know who we're dealing with. You're putting lives in danger. Do you realize that? The whole City…"

He runs out of breath and doesn't finish. He just goes back to leaning against the glass.

Mycroft swivels on his stool and starts shining that light at Reggie now.

"We *didn't* know there was an ever-loving old-soul Crackjaw in there. We just didn't. The guy, the Machinist, he said something about a graveyard and that place looked like a graveyard, and we thought it was the way out. That's all. We thought it was the way home, but it was just more rust in our eyes is all."

Mycroft swivels back to me for a moment and smiles. "It always feels like your own decision, doesn't it? When someone else gets in your head and takes away the other options. It always feels like your own decision." Then he goes back to shining at Reggie.

I'd ask him what he's driving at, but I'm still notched by what Rothschild said. "And you keep talking about us putting people in danger, being here, but you should say that to your buddy over there."

Rothschild comes back fast, his breath caught and then some. "You're simply in no position to say that. No position. I know the things that happen here are cruel. I know that. But they have to happen. The whole human race is blinking out of existence, and it would be gone already if it weren't for us holding the line. Mycroft, tell them what you told me when I first came to work here. Tell them what you've seen. They don't have the slightest idea how close we've come to extinction."

But Mycroft doesn't say anything.

"This man," says Rothschild pointing at him. "Is the thread by which we're holding on. You're in no position."

Looking at Mycroft, it's hard to imagine I owe him much of anything. That's what they always want you to think. That the pricks in power are in power because they deserve to be. Like they've got something the rest of us don't. And that's the biggest lie. We're all the same, and the only thing different about Mycroft is he's enough of a prick to think he's special, and insane enough to make everybody else think so too.

He's reaching for the tray now, and he grabs the one thing I'm hoping he doesn't grab. The scalpel.

"You see what I mean," I say to Rothschild. "That's not something you do unless you don't care about whether people live or die."

"I need to check the optic nerve," says Mycroft. Jesus, he's going to cut out Reggie's eye.

Reggie knows it too. He's squirming, but the cable around his neck won't let him move much. Mycroft even swings a padded headclamp up from the back of the chair and starts to turn the screws.

"Now, Mycroft, you don't have to do that," says Rothschild. "You don't have to do that. We can keep them under observation."

"He doesn't care," I tell the doctor. "Look at him, he doesn't care..."

"Be quiet," says Rothschild. I've really got him

trembling now, but it doesn't mean anything anymore. It's just the last thing I can do I guess. "No, be quiet, there are things that need to be done. I know they're cruel but…Mycroft, he's not even anesthetized, just wait. Mycroft."

"See, it doesn't matter," I tell him. I'm practically laughing now, I'm so rattled. I don't know what's wrong with me. Or maybe I do, and that's the whole problem. "It's like Dunning told us, about how Mycroft here cut off everybody's radios just so nobody'd know nothing they weren't supposed to. It doesn't matter. He'll do it anyway."

Something about what I just said makes everybody come to a quick stop, and they all start slowly turning their heads toward me. The colonel's face is like a drama mask. His jaw is unhinged for some godforsaken reason. He's about to say something, but he doesn't get it out.

The sound of gunfire makes me flinch into the cable around my neck, but I'm too surprised to feel any pain. All I can think about is the gunfire. Right above my head. The colonel's face caves-in, spraying blood over the lot of us. Then one of the Hectors lurches as bullets cut through his chest and into his throat, and he falls backward.

Mycroft is on his feet, but it doesn't matter. A few shots hit his right shoulder blade and his chest, spinning him around. A point on his spine explodes, the tattered cloth rebounding. Scorched edges.

Rothschild is talking, backing away, toward the door. Whatever he's saying, I can't hear. It's like my head is inside a bell. I can't even hear the gunfire anymore as Rothschild's skull splits, spilling one eyeball out before another bullet obliterates whatever's left.

That means there's only one other guy in the room now, the other Hector. The one who did the shooting. The one who killed everybody else in the room without any explanation. I'm trying to twist my head around to see him, but the cable is digging into my throat. Something scorching-hot touches my forehead, and I try to jerk away, cutting the skin even more.

The point of the gun is resting against my skull,

and the Hector stands over me. The ringing has started to fade. Next to me, Reggie is struggling against the straps, making some kind of sputtering sound just shy of a scream.

All I can think about is whether or not I'll hear the gunshot when the bullet goes through my head. Or will it kill me before the sound even gets to my ear? But he doesn't fire. Not yet. Instead, he takes off his filter and his goggles. Corporal Dunning scowls down at me.

Before I can wonder if I should be glad to see him, he's yelling.

"Why'd you give 'em my name?" he says. "Whose boys are you? Whose pullin' your strings? Why'd you tell 'em my name?"

Somewhere in my godawful noisy mind is the answer to that question but it doesn't make any effort to cut through the crowd. I lie there and watch Dunning. I watch the gun.

"Whose boys are you?"

Christ, his finger is on that trigger, and he's

cranked. "Nobody's. You know who we are."

"Did you know they had us out there clearing the way for you? Did you know that? Yeah? After you damn near shot me, and I caught up with my guys in Path, the first thing I hear is we need to make sure you get through. Now, why would that be? Whose boys are you?"

I don't know what to tell him. "They just wanted to see what we'd do. They wanted to see if we'd be able to get into where Blankface was."

"Damn near evacuated the place, all so they could see who's pullin' your strings?"

"Nobody's pulling our strings," I tell him. But it's not true. Not in the slightest. "We…we just don't know."

Shadows pass over my face, and at about the same time, Dunning looks up at the glass front of the cell. Reggie has gone still too. I don't dare lower my chin to find out what they're looking at. Not with that gun against my forehead. But I can hear the shuffling of feet, and I can guess what's going on well enough.

The door opens, and somebody tells Dunning to

back away. He does what he's told. He takes the gun away, and now I can give things a glance. Ten or so Blackbands stand on the other side of that glass pointing pistols at Dunning. The man in the door—the man giving the orders—is none other than Grovesner, but it takes me a few seconds to place his face.

Dunning backs all the way to the corner and puts the S8 on the bloody floor. The fight has gone out of him I guess. Hell, he's outgunned for sure. Maybe that just means he's not insane.

"Madre de dios." Grovesner is kicking at the corpses. "Is that Mycroft? Don't say anything, just face the wall."

A couple of the other Bands come in and put the binds on Dunning's wrists.

Grovesner says, "I don't know what to say," and everybody just sort of stands around looking at the cell for a while, nobody coming up with much in the way of wisdom.

It's a long while before anybody even seems to

notice us.

"Get these two off the slabs," says Grovesner and a couple of his guys work the straps free. Pretty soon we're sitting upright again. He asks us, "This guy shoot Mycroft or isn't it that easy?"

But it's Dunning who answers. "Yeah, I shot all of 'em."

"Well," says Grovesner, ducking a little to get a better look at Mycroft's body. "I guess I don't have to kill you boys, then. But I gotta arrest you."

I know what that means, but still, right now, it doesn't seem like such a bad thing after all.

Somewhere down the hall, the PA is playing the dawnstrings, and all over Fallback our good friends and citizens are rising for another day.

"K to H SCREENCHECK," Reel 1 of 1, 16mm, 24fps

The boy stands in the cage fishing papers from his backpack and handing them through the slot to the Blackband officer. The boy is young, maybe fifteen, and small for his age. He holds his eyes down and sinks away from the gate while the Blackbands look over his identification.

"Name?"

"Charles Gibbs," says the boy. He is nervous. On the verge of stuttering. "Charles Roger Gibbs."

They ask him what his age is. They ask him what his height is. They ask him to describe the color of his own eyes. The boy answers their questions and rubs his mouth.

The Blackband says, "You're permitted to school at eight in the morning. We can't let you through yet. Come back later."

The boy shakes his head. "No," he says, and the Blackband flinches. The boy points through the cage. "It says on the next page, in the middle, 'Permitted through screencheck up to one hour in advance...,'"

All traces of stuttering have vanished, and the boy holds the officer's gaze. The officer waves and folds the papers and hands them through the slot. The Blackbands open the gate and let the boy pass without further question or harassment.

TWELVE

We're bound and blindfolded, moving on foot with a Blackband at each arm. Reggie says something he shouldn't say, and someone hits him, probably in the stomach, and for a few seconds, he's sucking wind. After that, he stays quiet.

I've got something to say too, but I figure I'll be safe enough if I watch my manners. Anyway, it needs to be said, and this is as good a time as any. "We left our friend back there. A kid named Charlie Gibbs."

Nobody says anything at first. Then Grovesner asks me where to find him.

"Lotta Crackjaws back there," I tell him.

He says, "We know."

*

The room they put me in has a door and a drain.
That's it. No benches. No cushions. No *lights*, for
Christ's sake. There isn't even a doorknob on this side,
here in the perfect dark.

I haven't talked to anyone in I don't know how
long. Maybe two days. They give me a scoopful of cold
steamed oats once every so often. Somebody comes
along, opens a little slot in the door, and reaches through
and just drops the oats right on the floor. I'm hungry
enough I lick the floor until I can't taste anything but
metal anymore. The guards don't say anything to me, and
I don't say anything to them either.

I don't know where Reggie is. I haven't seen him
since back in that Triage cell, but from the sound of it,
they dragged him off in some other direction as soon as
we got here. Mocap. He could be in the next room for all
I know. Or maybe there aren't any other rooms like this
around here. I can't hear anyone but the guards and

whenever they open the slot the light that stabs through comes at me so hard I can feel it at the back of my skull, and I can't ever get a good look into the hall without going half-blind trying.

*

This is a bona fide, hand-to-god burnbox. I'm sure about that. The walls, the floor, the ceiling. It's all metal.

It's so cold to the touch, I can't sit in one place for too long. This thin jumper they put me in isn't much help, either. No shoes. Sometimes I warm my hands over that grateless drain hole in the middle of the floor, I'm shivering so bad.

That's not why I haven't slept, though. I can get used to the cold, and I'm tired enough, I could probably sleep. What keeps me awake is thinking about how the floor and the walls could stop being cold at any given second. How they could go from icy to blistering at the turn of some dial, somewhere outside the room. I could be sleeping and all of a sudden, my skin could be fried stuck to the metal, and I'd pull away, bouncing against the walls trying to get away from it, tearing bloody chunks loose only to land someplace hot again.

I'm trying to think of what folks have said about the burnboxes. Trying to think if maybe there's a sound first, to let you know it's about to flash. I doubt it though. I bet it comes fast and without warning. It hasn't happened yet, but it's almost worse *waiting* for it to happen. Wondering when it will. I haven't slept since the Bands put us into the rickshaw that brought us here.

*

Reggie told me once, he hates going home anymore because nobody says anything all night but everybody's waiting for everybody else to say something. I bet he'd go home now. I'd go home now too.

A drain in the middle of the floor. That's the worst thing you can find in a room with nothing else in it.

*

The guards open the slot and tell me to take off my jumper and slide it out through the slot. They tell me again three times before I can actually get undressed. Then they tell me to stick one of my arms through the slot, too, so I do that, and I wince, thinking I'll get hit with a needle or worse.

Instead, they clap a shackle to my wrist so now I'm chained to the door.

This must be it. They're going to burn me without me being able to move around. I try to keep my face away from the door, and I wait for the pain to come.

Ten minutes pass, maybe more, and the metal is as cold as ever. I'm shaking but not from the cold. Sweating too. Footsteps pass back and forth out there, and my eyes are used to the light again so I can see the guards' legs and a few other doors like this one across the hall. Nobody else's arm is sticking out through those slots though.

A deep shattering click makes me flinch so hard I wrench my elbow. I clench my feet as if it'll be any better just being on my toes and my heels. My back is bent like I'm trying to float away. Like somehow, I can turn the room on its side and make a roof out of the wall, so I can just dangle here by my arm and touch nothing else.

But the metal stays cold, and another click from the door means all I'm hearing is the lock release.

"IV65536, step back. The door is opening. Step back against the wall."

The whole slab swings inward, pushing me to the corner. They must have some kind of catch on the hinge because the door locks in place near full open and it won't budge.

I can't tell how many guards are out there, but one of them comes inside the room dragging something behind him. He's wearing full germ gear; I can't even see his face. He's holding a long hose, and he twists the valve and sprays me head to toe with cold water until my lungs hurt from holding my breath. He steps in and out of the deep shadows. Sometimes it's impossible to see where the water's coming from.

I can hear the water struggling down through that

drain pipe long after the guard has gone.

*

This is what they do to all of us, every day. I'm not in any worse a place than anybody in Fallback. We're all lying on a goddamn metal floor waiting to burn. Except when you're out *there* living your *life*, most times you don't even know there's somebody with his hand on a switch that will melt the skin from your bones. Maybe I'm better off than all those folks out there, knowing what I know. Knowing that it could happen any second.

*

It's the same drill today. My hand goes out the slot, they cuff me to the door and push it open, shoving me into the corner. But this time they let me stay dressed and instead of a guard with a hose, here comes some bigwig Blackband with a pile of notes.

He's in germ gear like all the others but I can tell by his stiff shoulders, he's here to ask hard questions. And if he doesn't like the way I answer them, it'll mean blisters for me the second he leaves.

"Where are my friends?"

"Don't ask," he tells me. He starts looking through those notes all clipped together on a board. The light from the door makes a half-figure of him. Just one eye and the other's a pit.

"They alright? Did you find Gibbsy?"

"Don't ask me that," he says. "I'm not here to tell you what you don't know. I'm here to find out what you do know. Okay?"

His voice loses a bit of its fidelity through that filter, but I can hear him just fine anyway.

I tell him I don't know anything that he doesn't know, and he gives me a quick flick of the chin before turning through those notes again.

"When did you first meet Archie Dunning?"

"Who?" I didn't know that was his name. Archie. Hell. "Just that night is all."

More shuffling notes. "This Machinist. You didn't know him either?"

"No."

"Did he mention Corporal Dunning? Did he even *hint* about a contact in the City Guard?"

"I don't think they'd get along, those two." In fact, I'm pretty damn sure of it. The way I see it the Herds've got nothing to do with the Barkers and vice versa. I'd be surprised if Dunning's name was on anybody's tongue before what happened happened.

"You've said you didn't even know how to reach the Machinist?"

"The Barkers know him. They got us together."

The Band watches me for a few seconds, tilting his head. "And...it was this friend of yours. Reginald Stamp. He put you in contact with the Barkers. That's true, isn't it?"

"Reggie's too dumb to know a guy like that."

"You've said he put you in *touch* with them."

It makes me mad as hell, hearing him blame Reggie for anything. "Those bastards used Reggie to get in touch with me. If that's what you mean."

"We could ask him."

"You don't need to ask him. You just asked *me*, and I just told you." I'm trying to be calm, but I don't know if my tone is on target. I haven't slept in I don't know how many days and all I've been thinking about is this metal floor. These goddamn walls. "Did you find Charlie?"

The Band almost shakes his head. "The boy you say you left in the cabinet."

"Is he okay?"

This time he really does shake his head. "We're not going into Pathology until we learn the rest of what we don't know."

Christ, then he's still in there. Bleeding like he was. No, he can't possibly still be alive.

*

I guess I shouldn't blame myself, but it really is my fault. The City keeps pushing, but we still have some say in whether we let it push us too far.

We used to know this kid, Lewis Tobey. He killed himself one night after we'd all gone to the Tuft together. Just killed himself in the tunnel behind the row in hh where he lived.

He was a good kid, to be honest. A horse's ass sometimes but the kind of kid who was always sort of laughing to himself at the back of the room no matter what was going on with the rest of us. We knew him since we were little, Lewis. Since we were boys. He was always like that.

When I heard he died, I thought for sure he got on the wrong side of a couple of Blackbands and they sunk him. But after talking to his brother a few months later, it was pretty obvious he'd done it to himself.

How I knew was, his brother was the one who found him. That must've been hard. His little brother. Royce. Lewis used to give Royce all his old stick jazz cylinders and always used to talk to him about the underground crews who used to jam at Taft or

Thurstein's all night before those places got shut down. Like the Chords. Lewis loved the goddamn Chords.

Why he killed himself, all I've got are guesses. I couldn't understand it. Royce said his dad was kind of a red face, always hissing about this or that, and Lewis caught most of it. Maybe he was rusted all along. But for awhile Reggie thought it was because he yelled at Lewis. That night at the Taft we were baiting the Bands, running around, staying out of reach. After we'd lost the lope who'd been chasing us around for the last ten minutes, we stopped, laughing and falling on the floor in this pipe alley. Well, Lewis, he thought he heard something, so he shut the door we'd come through. Shut it right on my hand. Me, I was cussing and spitting and hollering at my throbbing hand, but when Reggie noticed what had happened, he laid right into Lewis telling him how stupid he was. That was the last time Reggie ever said anything to him.

I kept telling Reggie afterward, Lewis dying had nothing to do with him. And I really meant it. It wasn't Reggie's fault, giving him hell. It was living here in

Fallback that did it. All that water out there pressing in on the City, and the City pressing in on all of us.

Maybe that's how I should be looking at things now, too. With Gibbsy. Even if it is mostly my fault, there's a bigger problem casting the shadow.

They're afraid of something. The City hats. The Bands and all the rest. Ask some random joe in the markets, and he'll say yeah, they're afraid of losing power. But I don't think that's it. It's almost like they're more afraid of people thinking they don't *deserve* to have any power in the first place. Like the only reason they want to be in charge of anything is because they can't handle thinking they shouldn't be.

So they lie and torture and murder their friends and citizens, and they make kids like Lewis think there's nothing worth caring about, and little kids like Royce have to find their brothers dead in the alleys with their smiles gone, and all the while the City tries to tell us day after day we're safe down here, safe from the Crackjaws and the Flu and the lurching shadows that crawl in the sunlight, chewing on everything that used to feed the good people of the world, digging up the old roots with their crooked hands, staring through windows at fields where kids like us used to play baseball and still would if none of it had ever happened at all in those long, long ago days. And they tell us these things and break our jaws just so they can say, "See? I was right all along. See?"

But if there's anything the rest of us need to be doing, it's to say, "No. You were always wrong."

*

I need to figure out what they want me to say.

That Blackband comes back every now and then asking more questions. I don't know his name. I can barely even see his face, just the vague form of an eye from the goggle lens nearest the light of the hall. He asks about the Machinist and about the Barkers. He asks about Dunning and the Herds. He even asks about Mycroft and Rothschild. Why he'd be asking me about them, I don't know.

I keep looking at his boots. Those thick mesh

soles, chord and carbon, insulated so he can have the guards flip that switch out there and put the burn to me without him needing to leave the room. He can stand in here and watch it happen.

"Did Director Mycroft know more about the Machinist than you told him? Was he already familiar with that name?"

"I don't know." I say that a lot when he asks me about Mycroft. I don't know. "He didn't say much about what was on his mind." My cheek is numb from being pressed against the door like this. My wrist is sore from the shackle, and the way my shoulder's wrenched through the door, it feels like it will soon pull out of the socket.

"He didn't give you any idea of what this was all leading to...with the Machinist? About the raid?"

"The raid? You mean my buddies and me. Is that what you call that?"

"The raid."

"He didn't *say* what he'd do next. Just that he'd

strung us along is all. To find out whatever."

I don't know why he's asking me. He probably already knows the answers to all the questions he's asking me. That's the Bands for you, though. They keep kicking long after you've stopped moving.

I ask this guy, "Why do you care? Mycroft was a psychopath anyway. Torture me all you want, but I don't know if Mycroft even believed us about the Machinist in the first place."

The Blackband doesn't give much of a reaction. He takes a step closer. "We're not going to hurt you," he says. "We just need to be sure you're not dangerous. We really do need your help," he says. "Bad things are coming to shape in Fallback, and Mycroft probably knew a great deal about them. More than you think. If you have any idea at all what his notions of the Machinist might have been, we really do need to know."

He stares at me through those goggles, and he's close enough that I can see both of his eyes. Close enough I could reach out and grab that suit if I wanted to and wrap my free arm around his neck, and tell the others to let me loose unless they want to see this guy strangled here in the dark. But he knows as well as I do that I won't.

"I don't know. Nobody ever told us the truth, not once."

"Not once. Well, you tell me…are you dangerous?"

"No."

The Band's eyes flick away like he's thinking things over and he stands again.

"To hear your friends tell it, no matter what happened you kept pushing them. Further and further into trouble. Almost as if you knew more than you told them you knew."

"I was…I didn't want anybody to think I could be backed down is all."

"You were showboating."

"Showboating, yeah. I guess so." It's true. I could

have decided about a dozen different goddamn times that night to turn home, but I didn't. "Showboating at the end of a leash."

The guy almost laughs at me. He says, "Funny," and just stands there.

"What's funny?"

"That's exactly how Charlie put it."

It doesn't sink in at first. That name. I catch a hint of tension in my spine, and half a second later the shock goes rattling through my joints. "Charlie Gibbs…"

He nods. "We found him where you said we would find him. He's okay."

After he leaves, the shackles drop me to the floor, and I stay there looking up into the dark until I sleep deeply enough to dream.

*

My dad is one of those guys who could never get the idea of the surface world out of his head. One of those guys who every March goes down to Patch

Gardens or the Row early in the morning when the misters first sputter, just so he can smell that old springtime smell he remembers. Most of us don't know what seasons even *are,* but some of the older folks like him just can't shake the smell of the air, even after all this time.

Mycroft probably built the gardens, too. I wonder why he never thought to make it snow.

My dad, he never goes down there when it's supposed to be winter.

*

They've moved me to a regular cell now. Our block takes up a wide three-level wedge of Mocap. I overheard that there are at least twelve other blocks and some of them are much bigger than this one. I don't know how many people that means. How many prisoners. The cells are a lot smaller than the burnbox was, maybe just three feet wide, so they've really got us stacked in here.

From the looks of it, we're the youngest guys in

the place, and we've gotten hell for it a few times already. Whispers in the tunnels going to and from the mess hall or the bell commons. There are some dark corners here. Some deeper shadows. Sometimes I think these stripeys know who we are and what we did to get here. Dunning is here too someplace, and I've seen him a couple of times, glaring down past the banisters like he's got something to say.

The guards have put Gibbsy's foot in a splint, but he's still walking on a crutch. His shoulder is okay. First time I saw him, I damn near picked him up off the ground and he was gasping trying to tell me to put him down because it hurt his foot to be doing that. He's still pretty pale and thin, and they shaved his head at some point he doesn't even remember.

Reggie's head is shaved too, so now we all look alike except for height. None of us were burned, and that's a goddamn good thing. I've seen enough scars in this place to know how lucky we are.

Every day, we're let out of our cells for ten hours. Gibbsy is just down the row from me, so when the steel bars slide open, I'm out there fast against the rail to get to him before anybody else can come along and call him a gimp and try to trip-up his crutch. If I walk behind him, he's usually okay. Reggie has always said, if Gibbsy can't take care of himself, I shouldn't go out of my way to do it for him, but Reggie's not the reason Gibbsy's in this place with a bad foot. I am.

We sit at the edge of the mess hall during meals. Me and Reggie, we trade with Gibbsy, fish for rice, whenever we can so that he doesn't get sick. A couple of times he has started to look a bit rashy but nothing horrible so far.

In the bell commons, we take to the benches behind the hoop court and watch all the other blokes play their rough games, throwing elbows and scratching at eyes. I've been drawn into pickup matches a couple of times, and I didn't fare too well. Reggie does okay and plays more than I do since he's tough enough not to mind getting hit now and then. Me, I'd rather sit with Gibbsy anyway. Mostly it's to make sure nobody starts jabbing at him. You have to have a couple extra sets of eyes in the commons.

I can't always be around my pals, though. The guards, they've got us on work detail two hours a day, me washing dishes, Reggie mopping, and Gibbsy is with all the other crippled stripeys assembling mining rigs and polishing bits for the City. That's when I worry the most. When we are scattered like that.

Nights are better. I don't have to look over my shoulder all the time when I'm in my narrow little cell, and I can't get into a jackpot here alone. Nobody can get at Gibbsy or Reg, either, so I feel safe all around. All I can do is watch the dead bulb swing overhead and listen to the drip of the spigot and the gurgle of the drain and try to imagine the sifting crowds at Antrum Market or the Valve Platform where the derelicts still play their one-string guitars.

The best part is, here in Mocap they don't play the tin crickets. I didn't notice at first, but now I can't stop thinking about it. I'd rather be in this cage than out there pretending there's nothing wrong with Fallback. Being here just proves I was right all along and there's something comforting about that.

Whenever I can't sleep, it's not because I miss my old life; it's because of *Poplar*. Whatever else happens, I need to find out if Poplar is still alive.

*

Gibbsy doesn't remember much of what happened after I left him in that supply room. He lost enough blood that he started getting dizzy, and when he tried to tighten the tourniquet, he blacked out completely.

When he woke up, he was still alone, behind all those boxes, but he noticed right away that he wasn't bleeding as badly as before. The tourniquet was gone, replaced by clean bandages. As groggy as he was, he knew there was something strange about that, so he started lifting up the edge of the gauze to see the wound and found it had been stitched shut. All these long purple suture lines. Whoever had done all of that also left a canteen of this sugary water, and Gibbsy drank about half of it before passing out again.

Sometime much later, a couple of Hectors dug

through the supply room knowing he'd be there, and they carried him out to Grovesner and the Bands.

I'm not sure what to make of it. Time was, the Hectors would've just shot him, but with Mycroft gone I guess they came to their senses and remembered to not be pricks. And the guy who stitched-up Gibbsy's foot, whoever that was, he's a prince among men. I don't know what to make of it at all.

But that's what's got me thinking about Poplar, more and more lately. The idea that someone, somewhere in all the mess of that night, could have had mercy on the girl.

Gibbsy says he saw more dead Crackjaws than he could count, so it sounds like the Hectors cleaned-up the place pretty well. Someone even told him old Blankface was dead, but Gibbsy, he never saw it with his own eyes.

*

She had smooth skin. That's a dumb thing to remember because a lot of people have smooth skin. Probably a lot of people have far smoother skin than she did, too. But I remember it anyway. When we were sitting next to each other sometimes I'd think about resting my palm on her shoulder. But I never actually went through with it.

*

Dunning is usually on work detail in the laundry hall these days. He isn't hard to find. I stand nervously at the back of the room for awhile, watching him pull sheets from the mangler and loading the steam press. I'm not sure what to say to him or if he'll even listen. Last time we talked he was ready to shoot me in the face, so who knows how he'll be now. But it's worth a try.

The closer I get to him, the closer everyone else in the room gets to me. It's subtle, almost unnoticeable, but they're watching me move past the folded textiles and the drums of detergent. Their hands stop moving. They've got to be his boys, or he's theirs.

"You aren't supposed to be here," he says to me without looking up.

"I got tired of staring at the ceiling."

"Aren't you supposed to be scrubbing plates?" he says, and I'm not too surprised to know he's been keeping track of me.

I ask him if I can have a word someplace and he tells me this is as good a place as any. The machines are loud, but I guess that's a good thing and the dim lights aren't pointing any fingers either.

"Guess you're kind of a hero," I tell him. "What you did to Mycroft. I think so anyway."

He looks at me square in the eyes and says, "Kid, nobody wanted him dead. It's just nobody trusted him."

But I didn't come here to talk about Mycroft, so I get to the punch. "I wanna see what you think about if maybe our girl's alive still. She… she was playing dead in Quarantine, and that's why we started that ruckus."

"You almost shot me," he says.

"Yeah. That was Reggie, and he was just panicked. We knew you were one of the good ones."

He just laughs and folds another jumper.

"I been thinking about my pal Gibbsy. He got hurt, and a couple of Hectors came along and helped him after Mycroft hit the floor. After things settled down. I'm just wondering if it could've been the same for Poplar. If a couple of Hectors might've seen her and known she wasn't anything to worry about? Or when Reggie shot at you maybe enough of your pals chased after us that she could've crept outta there."

Dunning says, "Nobody got out of Quarantine."

"How do you know?"

"How do I know?"

"Yeah," I say, "how do you know?"

"Lots of reasons. I know because a bunch of others stayed behind even when we gave chase. The platforms were sandbagged before you even got there. Dropped the shutters. Look…if she was on the floor at Quarantine, she died on the floor at Quarantine. I'm sorry to say that. But what I really ought to say is, who cares? You and your pals and her, you ruined what was going well enough on its own. We had things under our thumb."

Part of me wants to tell him he's wrong. That he and the Herds never had any control over the situation at all. We never did either but that's not the point.

"So fine," I tell him, "but let's just say she somehow got out of there. How can we know?"

"I have no idea," he says. "Go ask your friends."

I don't know what he means at first. I squint at him in the dim light as he folds and pulls levers. The smell of detergent and starch has my eyes watering. My nose raw. "My pals don't know anything."

"No," he says, "I mean the Barkers. Out there, that's their turf, not mine. If they can't get the word out asking about your girl, I damn well can't either."

It's not what I want to hear. "They're not my pals."

Something about my tone has got the other blokes in the room on their toes. They're tilting at me.

Dunning says, "You sure seemed to be doing what they wanted you to do, if they're not your pals. Go ask the Barkers. Go ask them about your girl and leave me out of it. I'm no friend of yours."

I stare at him. So that's that. As much as I'd like to have him as a friend in here, Dunning wants nothing to do with me anymore.

"The Barkers," I say. "Fine. Yeah. Where do I find them?"

"Block 9," he says. "Don't go alone. They're not keen on talk."

"Don't go alone." That's a funny thing to say to a kid when you're not offering to go along with him. But if that's the way Dunning feels, that's the way it is. I guess I'm just glad his pals aren't putting me through the mangler right now. I've learned to count my blessings lately.

*

This part of the city has had brownouts the last couple of days, with the lights sometimes going dim for half an hour at a time. Now and then we get full-on blackouts, and the stripeys go wild. The guards shine spotlights into the commons and point guns at us until the regular power comes back.

It's probably just a problem with a few old transformers near here. Happens all the time in the older wedges.

Still, it leaves a bad taste in my mouth every time. It always reminds me of the Machinist.

*

Dunning said not to go alone, but I'm going alone anyway. The Barkers don't have any reason to knuckle me, especially after I was such a good stooge, and right now the guards should be out in droves, anyway.

But when I get to block 9 I start to realize what Dunning meant. Why he said what he said. There aren't any guards here…in fact, it doesn't look like guards are even *allowed* on this block. I know that's not the truth but the way these four stripeys are standing at the arch, I can tell they don't let just anyone stroll down the row.

It strikes me, I don't have the slightest idea what I'm going to say to these guys. I don't know what I was ever going to say to them.

"Down with Kennedy, right?"

They don't even react.

"I want to get word to some friends, and somebody told me the Barkers had a way to do it?"

"Doesn't matter if we do," says the guy nearest to me. He's leaning against the gate, and he shifts his shoulders just half an inch, enough to let me know he's got nothing against knocking me to the floor.

I'm about to say more, but I don't. It's not that I'm afraid of this guy, but a couple of familiar faces catch my eye, and suddenly I'm sick to my stomach.

Past the thugs, stacked up along three floors of dark cells, at least two dozen other stripeys are leaning against the rails. My ears start to ring. I'm on the verge of panic.

Two of them, in particular, are looking right at me. Sticks and Rake. The guys who brought us to the Machinist. I'd know them anywhere, and I don't have to wonder why they're here. Not for a second. They're here is because of me. Because I told Grovesner about them that night. It has to be, and I don't think they'd take it well if they knew. Maybe they've already guessed.

They start toward the stairs, but I don't think I want to talk to them. Not here. I tell the Barkers at the gate never mind, and I leave.

*

I'm supposed to be back at my block in fifteen minutes, but I'm skirting the commons in no hurry to be there. My mind is on other things. Not twenty feet ahead of me, this old stripey named Rosch is talking to his broom like it's his child, walking it down the ramp to the warehouse.

This is where they keep a bunch of the extra tables and chairs for when they make us watch the Bullets.

I wander down the ramp after Rosch. Already he's sweeping. Just a jumble of sharp arthritic joints, alone in the near dark, bristles scratching at the dusty wood, passing now and then through the light from the ramp. I figure he probably remembers something of the old world.

When he notices me, he leans on his broom like he was just waiting for some excuse to stop and catch his ragged breath. One eye droops dead and numb, and the other doesn't have much will left in it either.

The walls are curved and littered with rusty old fittings the size of tram wheels, like something very big had been bolted here once upon a time. The floor is scarred too, with new wood covering square patches spaced ten feet from one another up and down the middle.

"What'd this place used to be?"

The old man looks around like he doesn't understand why I'm asking. "What'd this place used to be? Used to be an engine room is what. From when the Crackjaws built it for the sea. Before we took it from 'em. Back there past all that is where the turbines were, but it's welded-up now. Plate steel about yay thick so the water won't get in."

It makes me think of Mycroft. All the work they must have done in the early days. Wringing Blankface's neck to find out how to make this place not buckle under the ice. How to anchor it to the sea cliffs where we could hide and never be found.

Rosch says, "I used to be a welder a long time back and that ain't an easy job, the job they done closing up them shafts. Was a welder in Zanzibar."

He crosses his wrists and leans against the shelves and doesn't notice the broom dropping smack to the floor.

"Zanzibar was a lie," I tell him, and I chuckle.

He squints. "Sure it was. Folks got sick no matter what we did to keep other folks out of the place. Have you heard what they been sayin'? 'Bout how they have Crackjaws here. Experimentin' on 'em. Can't understand it."

"Yeah," I tell him. "I've heard that."

The guards are calling us in now, so I hurry on my way.

*

Mocap doesn't have a post box for the prisoners. You can't use the phone. The only way to get a message out to the City is through someone who isn't on this side of the bars. And that's just not easy to do.

Some of the other stripeys have their connections. Bad folks in the rough halls always scuffling with the Bands. Money moves through here like you wouldn't believe.

I've tried using my charms on the guards. Some are decent folks, others aren't. One thing is for sure. They all go home when their shifts end. They all leave this place. But none of them ever wanted to risk helping a kid like me get in touch with any of my friends out there. They know how these things work.

So that's that. I can't go to the Barkers. The Herds won't help me. And the real criminals would rather drop me down a shaft than listen to what I have to say.

None of my fussing makes any difference. Try as I might, I can't catch a stray word about Poplar. But it doesn't matter. Pretty soon, news about Poplar finds *me*.

*

Not a lot of visitors come to Mocap. Lawyers and such, for those who can afford them, but no family. Family knows better. That's another way the City gets into your joints…they make it very clear that even *associating* with miscreants makes you pretty much a miscreant yourself. Some guy goes to Mocap for public intoxication, for instance, and his mom comes to see if he's doing okay, and they end up bringing her into Tolsten a day later saying she's a drunk too. Moms stop coming to see their boys altogether and the City's got its boot on another throat, just like they like.

I'm surprised to hear my number called this morning. "IV65536, you have a visitor, step to the rail." I don't know what to think, to be honest.

My visitor is already sitting when I get to the stall. The bars are covered in mesh steel, and the shadows distort the man's face. It's not until I'm sitting that I recognize who it is.

"Dad."

"Tommy, Jesus, we haven't slept wondering about you. Anybody hurt you?" He looks tired.

"My friends are here too. Charlie and Reggie."

"I know," he says. He gets closer to the bars, trying to get a better look at me. "I'm trying to get you all a trial. I might not be able to help them…it's just not something you do. I'm doing all I can for just you, and I still don't know…"

But before he can finish I tell him I understand. I don't expect I'll get a trial either, even with him being a lawyer and knowing the way these things work. It just won't happen. "Don't stretch yourself too far."

He doesn't know what to say. He looks at me. Just looks at me.

"Dad I need to find out about Poplar. You met her. Her dad is…"

"I can't do that," he says.

"Do what?"

"I can't go asking about her. That's City business,

not mine. You're my business, nobody else."

His hair is grayer than I remember, but that's probably the nauseous Mocap lights working against him, is all.

"Anybody mention her?" I ask.

He shakes his head. "Your mother went to ask about you at first, down on K, thinking Poplar's dad might have known where you were at. Nobody answered there. One of the windows was taped up. Sounds to me like that girl was a bad seed, Tommy, and I wish you hadn't fallen into her crowd."

And that's all he could say before he left.

He can't do anything for me. I know that. He just wants to see me is all and to be honest I'm glad to see him too. But he can't do anything for me, even if he does know the Law.

*

I never met Poplar's dad. It always seemed to me like he was never around. Poplar used to always talk about how they would go to the laundromat together, when he got off work, in the middle of the night when no one else was there. They'd sit there watching the machines, talking, and they'd bring it all home and fold it all together and then she'd go back to bed. She loved doing that.

Things hadn't always been okay between her and her dad. Poplar said her dad never seemed to care much when her mom died. He would stare at the wall now and then, but she never saw him cry. It bothered her so much for a while she stopped talking to the guy. It surprised me to hear it because she's not the type to hold a grudge against anybody, but I guess that was a long time ago.

One night she woke up to the sound of her dad coming through the front door, banging past the jamb. He'd just come back with a basketful of laundry, and he started folding the clothes in the living room. Organizing things into piles. She watched him for half an hour, from the hallway, without him knowing she was there. He was folding her mother's clothes. Still putting them into the same drawers. Hanging her shirts in the same places she had always hung them when she was alive. And that's how it started.

I hope he's okay. I'm wondering now if he still folds Poplar's clothes, there in the middle of the night, surrounded by all those crooked empty shelves. I hope he does, because she's never coming home. That's what it must mean, my dad calling her a bad seed like that. He just couldn't say the truth out loud was all. I don't want to think like that, but I can't stop.

*

I'm staring at the mess hall, at all the heads bobbing as everyone eats and chats and glares. Gibbsy has been talking to me about something, but I haven't been paying attention. The paint is peeling from the beams. The lights hanging from their long chains tremble. The walls hold us like hands protecting a flame from some devious draft.

This place is so old, so tired. It just wants to stop breathing but it can't. It has to look after us because we're all it has left, so it chirps us to sleep at night and doesn't really know any other way to make us happy.

"I'm going to tell them it was us," I say to my pals.

Reggie says, "The hell do you mean, Tommy?"

"Sticks and Rake. I'm going to tell them it was us who gave them to the Blackbands. It was us who put them here."

They both think about it for awhile, and Reggie finally says, "Coulda been it was something else that put 'em here."

"No, it was us, and I bet they know it was us. They've seen me. I don't want to sit here pretending I had nothing to do with it."

Gibbsy taps the table. "Well then okay. They might want to kill us."

"Maybe not if we're honest. But even then…well, sorry boys, that's up to them and not me."

*

The power has been dim all day, but it just started

perking up half an hour ago. The lights are still buzzing in the corridor as we approach block 9.

Gibbsy is trailing a bit. Reggie says to him, "You don't have to come along."

He says, "At least I know what I'm getting into."

We talk to the Barkers at the mouth of the block, and I tell them what I want to do. Somebody goes to fetch Sticks and Rake. We wait there awhile. When they come to the bars, I explain everything, and they just stare at us.

"I gotta family," says Rake. "You should know that. Coupla kids I ain't gonna see again."

Sticks doesn't say anything at all. They both leave back to their cells, and so do we.

*

I don't think I'll ever get used to being here, but at least I can stand it. You hear a lot about new prisoners hanging themselves a few days in. Others run afoul of the guards or the other stripeys. Some of us just shuffle along.

I'm nervous all the time but it's almost like being nervous is more of a comfort than being calm. Those first weeks, I would feel safe whenever me and Reg and Gibbsy sat together in the cafeteria. But being safe is almost worse because I know it'll end.

They've changed my work rotation. I don't wash dishes anymore. I put trash into the incinerator now. Five hours of that a few times a week and I'm exhausted all the time. I guess it keeps my mind off things.

The worst part is, I can't be around my pals as much. My shift starts a couple hours before theirs, and after that, I sit alone in the bell commons. When I'm not around, Reggie looks after Gibbsy and Gibbsy makes sure Reggie doesn't get himself into trouble, if he can help it. I just wish I could be there to keep them from getting on each other's nerves.

Anyway, maybe they're not each other's biggest problem anymore. Gibbsy always has a target on his back, since he never looks anybody in the eyes, and

Reggie keeps getting into staring matches with other stripeys. Over this or that.

I guess that's why I'm not surprised when Reggie ends up in the infirmary.

*

I'm sitting alone in the cafeteria after my rotation, trying to get the kinks out of my shoulder. The chatter from all the tables bounces up to the white-washed steel rafters and echoes a bit. I'm staring at the reflections on the glossy tile.

After awhile Gibbsy comes into the room and sits next to me, and I can tell he's upset. I ask where Reggie is.

"He got in a fight."

"Shit, where? Where is he?"

Gibbsy shrugs. "We were coming out of the commissary," he says. "Somebody pushed me, I don't know why. But Reggie hit him, and he hit back."

That's all Gibbsy says, but right away I'm

guessing "hit back" means the guy beat Reggie black and blue.

I breathe as deep as I can, and I check the clock. "Well, they won't let anybody in the infirmary until tomorrow. We'll go see him."

*

Reggie is still asleep, lying on his back. The infirmary is full of tattered cots. Three rows of them and no curtains between. Patients are scattered here and there, and cluttered carts stand at odd angles, carrying bandages and clean water.

I sit on the stool next to Reggie and Gibbsy sits on one of the empty cots. Reggie has a compress over his jaw, and his arm is in a sling. In his sleep, he winces, and pretty soon he opens his eyes and sees us.

"Tommy."

"Who hit you, Reg?"

He starts to shake his head, but it must hurt to move like that. "I don't know 'im. Some asshole. Gibbsy saw 'im. You gonna track the guy down kick out his teeth for me?"

"Nah, no use in that. You okay?"

Reggie says, "The guards just stood there watching. Didn't even give the guy hell."

"It happens."

Reggie looks at me and then at the ceiling. His eyes dilate. "Had a dream we weren't even down here anymore."

"Like they let us out?"

"No," he says. "Like, I mean, on the surface. I think something happened to the City. Everybody was living on some island instead. Not Zanzibar, but they had this town with a wall around it and these houses. Poplar was there. I saw her over this fence in some field. Going over to look at a garden. A little girl was there with her, same color hair. And the little girl, she had a puppy following her everywhere. Running circles through the grass. The wind was blowing the grass and blowing against my back, and it was weird because it kinda seemed like the way wind should feel and smell, but how should I know?"

"Sounds nice."

Reggie coughs and settles. "If it's gonna be like that," he says. "You can have it. I'll stay down here in the shade, and everybody can just leave me the hell alone. I love this place."

"Yeah, you definitely get along with people better when there aren't any of them around, Reggie."

He smiles and tries to roll onto his side, and we leave so that he can get some more rest. I have to work soon, anyway, and I need to make sure Gibbsy gets to the bell commons before then. There's a sour mood in the air today, and I don't know why.

*

The passageway to the incinerator room is narrow and low with an arched ceiling. Someone painted it white once, a long time ago, but it hasn't had much attention since and most of the rivets have rusted through the paint. Streaks like blood follow the curve of the wall and somewhere, water is dripping from a seam.

The lights don't work too well in here, and there are long stretches of pure dark. I keep catching a muffled echo, and I'm pretty sure someone is behind me, back there past the light, whispering.

The guard is sitting in his chair outside the incinerator room service door. He doesn't even look at me. I pull the latch, step into the rancid heat, and shut it behind me.

As if the furnace isn't bad enough, I've got to move fast, doing this job. A couple of lifts stand at either side. They get filled a few levels down by other stripeys driving tugs. I unload one, send it down, and start on the other. If I take more than ten minutes to unload the lifts, the bastards downstairs push the buzzer and try to hurry me along. And if the guard out there hears too much buzzing he'll come in here and wonder why I'm not keeping up with the pace.

My undershirt is soaked through. I'm breathing needles, slinging baskets into the chute.

Most of these trash baskets are bamboo. The machine-woven kind you see everywhere with a hemp latch, so they stay shut. Sometimes they leak dirty water, and the smell is terrible. Every now and then I pull a waxed canvas bag off of the pile. Carcasses from the slaughterhouses.

The lift is empty before too long, so I send it back down, holding the button until the redbell is out of sight. I cross the room, wiping my face with the clean upper part of my arm. The other lift hasn't come up yet, which is strange, but that's fine with me.

I could sit a spell.

*

Behind me, the service door opens. Its hinges let out a godawful dying-machine wail. I guess it's the guard, come to make sure I'm still moving. But it's not the guard. It's a couple of stripeys. Goddamn Sticks and Rake.

Sticks comes into the room first, shoving me back so hard I fall to the grating, hitting my elbow so hard it rings like a pipe. Rake shuts the door.

"You shouldn't go pointing fingers," says Sticks.

I don't have anything to say, so I don't say anything.

Sticks reaches down and smacks me across the cheek hard enough to turn my head.

Half a second later, Rake has a length of twine around my neck. He pulls it tight, dragging me to my hands and knees like a dog on a leash.

"We're not here to talk, and we're not here to break your bones." Which means there's only one other option.

Rake starts dragging me toward the incinerator chute. I rear back against the cord, but it doesn't make any difference. Between the two of them, they'll have no trouble lifting me over the lip and dropping me down into the cinders.

But it doesn't come to that. The lights go out. Another outage. For a second I'm too stunned by what's happening to react.

When I come to my senses, I rush forward, knocking Rake to the ground. It gives me enough slack to pull the cord loose. Behind me, Sticks is scrambling in the dark. It's not quite pitch black in here. Enough of that smoldering red haze comes up through the chute to cast a few bloody shadows, and I can see Sticks' tall figure hunched and swaying as he reaches for me.

I'm too fast. I scramble away from him, nearly tripping over a seam in the floor before reaching the door. I'm through it like a rat, and I hold it shut with the edge of my foot.

They pound on the door, inching my foot away. The guard isn't out here. No one is. The Barkers must have paid him to walk away for a while so they could get at me, but I don't know how long he'll be gone.

Another thing that strikes me as odd is that the lights are *on*, out here in the corridor. I'm thinking maybe the power came back up just as I was leaving the incinerator room but that's when I notice someone limping toward me.

Gibbsy shakes his head. "Did it go dark in there?"

"Yeah. Gibbsy…"

"I would've come in to help but I didn't think I'd be any good, so I found the breakers. Did it work?"

"It worked. Gibbsy, what happened?" I can almost guess, but my head is spinning.

He tries to help me hold the door, but with his bad foot, he's not much good at it. Sticks and Rake keep pounding. The doors open enough for one of them to fit his fingers through the crack and I can't force it back on him. They must be wedging it with their shoes, too.

"Can you find something to tie this with?"

Gibbsy says, "There's nothing to tie it to."

"They're coming out here. How'd you know I needed help?"

"Saw 'em when you left the commons," he says. "After a bit, they followed after you. I tried to hurry but…"

They hit the door hard, with both shoulders I'd guess. Sticks fits his palm through and is reaching for me, but I'm not close enough to the edge.

"Gibbsy, get out of here. Get a head start. I'll hold 'em and run when I can, but you go now. You can't run."

He nods and takes one step before stopping again. He's looking at something. At someone.

Dunning stands in the corridor, watching us.

"Get away from the door," he says.

At first, I don't. It sounds like a bad idea. I'm not much good in a fight, and neither is Gibbsy, which means it'll be just Dunning against these two. He tells me again to step back. I size him up, and I do as he asks.

The Barkers spring out of the incinerator room and all but ignore Gibbsy and me. Dunning hits Sticks hard on the side of the face. The big man jolts to the side. He falls against the wall while Dunning goes after Rake.

Rake has a knife but not for long. Dunning slaps at

it, and the knife hits the floor. Rake backs away. Dunning dips down for the knife and in the same motion brings the blade up into the underside of Rake's jaw. The wound doesn't even bleed at first. The blood doesn't come until after the blade is out again. Dunning brings it across Rake's throat, and the Barker sinks backward spurting like a fountain.

Sticks is still trying to get to his feet. I can tell he's dazed by the way he's not moving like he should. Dunning puts the knife into his chest and Sticks sinks down again.

I'm still shaking, and Gibbsy has collapsed against the wall, holding his knees, just staring. It's a good long while before I remember to draw a breath.

I ask Dunning, "What do you care?"

He says, "Help me move these guys, we need to clear out fast."

"What do you care?"

He says, "Not now. Get his legs."

I do what he tells me to do. We put Sticks and Rake down the chute. Gibbsy mops up the blood with his undershirt, and we put that into the fire as well.

"Come see me tomorrow," says Dunning, and he jogs away without another word about it.

*

They know about the murders. They've been kicking up a fuss all night. They've been asking questions. Asking if anybody saw anything. The Barkers have been stirring too. I see quite a few more of them in the commons than usual.

After Dunning and Gibbsy left, I had gone back into the incinerator room to finish my rotation, and the guard who'd been posted outside my door seemed awfully confused to find me still alive when he got back. But he didn't say anything about it, and I figure he'd be in as much trouble as me if word got out that he'd taken a walk.

When it's time to sleep, I can't. I can hear the guards walking up and down the rows, and each one of them sounds like he's coming this way.

*

Dunning is pressing sheets again when I finally get a chance to talk to him. He glances at me, and I say, "For a guy who doesn't like us much you sure have a habit of making sure we don't die."

"Turns out you earned your keep," he says. "I wanna talk to you about that."

I sit down on the edge of the table, careful of the folded stacks.

"The outages," he says. "The power going down? Do you know what that is?"

"It's been going down all week."

He says, "It's the riots. There's riots out there, happening now, been going on for a little while. People tearing up the city."

Riots. Jesus Christ. "What riots? Outside of Mocap? Why?"

"That's what I wanted to talk to you about," says Dunning. He loads another sheet onto the press and lowers the handle. Steam eases out on all sides. "Word has it, it's on account of *you*."

At first, I think he's joking. But I guess I've never known Dunning to joke, so the next thing I think is he's just plain wrong. "On account of me. Nobody knows anything about me."

I'm trying to think of some reason for him to be saying what he's saying. Dunning stops what he's doing and looks at me.

"On account of you," he says. "They saw your footage all over the city. The stuff you shot of the Crackjaws."

"No, everybody's got it wrong. My film was burned. Mycroft burned everything."

"I don't know," he says. "You're the only ones I know who got footage like that and folks keep mentioning your name. Don't ask me how. The way I see it, you did some good after all, and when those Barkers followed after you, I figured you deserved some help for it."

"We knew you were one of the good ones. Thanks."

Dunning tilts his head. "I also want you to know…I don't owe you any more favors."

I tell him, "Okay," and I let him get back to work.

It isn't until I get back to our cell block that I realize Poplar is still alive. It takes that long for it to sink in.

*

The outages come more and more often. The guards get increasingly nervous. By the time Reggie is out of the infirmary, nobody is even talking about Sticks and Rake anymore. Rumors about the riots have grown and become something more than rumors.

The first thing Reggie asks when he sees us is if Gibbsy's foot is doing okay. "A little better," says Gibbsy and Reggie reaches for him with his good hand to pat him on the back.

He laughs when I tell him what Dunning did for us. "'Bout time he stopped being a prick," says Reggie.

"Yeah, he's got his moments, Reg. So do you."

He doesn't talk much on account of his jaw, and his face is purple or black depending on where you look. But he's okay.

We sit with him, and I tell him what I think happened to Poplar. Gibbsy does his best not to interrupt me.

*

The way I see it, it wouldn't have been too hard for her to get out of Quarantine once Reggie started his commotion that night. I don't care what Dunning says. Poplar knows how to get from one place to another without being seen, and she would have taken the chance when it arose. All she would really have to do was stay low. Stay out of sight all the way to the platform. Not hard at all.

Even if they had blocked the tracks, it wouldn't have made any difference. With the locks not working, the shutters wouldn't have been much use. She could have easily propped them up half a foot gotten onto the rails.

The thing I never thought about until now was that she had two reels of film in that backpack with her. The first was from the Drowner docks and the second was all Rothschild. Everything he said and showed to us was there, and we changed reels *after* Pathology. The footage Mycroft burned was just whatever I shot later. Blankface and such.

All she had to do when she reached friendly turf was find Ron Thorn, or his pals in upper M. Thorny would have done the rest. All the developing. Distributing it to the rants.

I've been talking it over with Gibbsy, and he mostly agrees. It's a sound enough theory anyway. He's got his doubts here and there, but that's just the way Gibbsy is. Once you think about all the details, it makes sense. Especially since Poplar's involved.

God, she always knows what needs to be done.

At night when the block goes dark, I can practically see the girl. Rolling onto the tracks, in the dark, slinging the pack over her shoulders and running between the rails, not looking back, not stopping, not even slowing until she was far away from all the wonderful things Mycroft built and all the men with guns who stood to protect them. On into the deadhalls, running past the abandoned hovels, the rusty playgrounds, the swings half off their chains, the murals she painted ages ago before she started worrying too much about me to care about the beautiful things she dreamed onto the walls of Fallback. Running and running and running.

I can see her sitting in the corner of Thorny's studio with her arms around her knees while the guys ran film through the gear and stacked case after case on that half-broke table of theirs.

I can see her looking through the laundromat windows, waiting for a glimpse of her dad so that she could tell him why she never came home that night. Why she never could again.

Where she is now, I don't think I could say. I hope she's not far from here. I hope she's just outside, waiting for the gates of Mocap to fall and waiting for me to come stepping out with the crowds.

All over Fallback, the people are standing in front of the Reels and staring at the flickering lights. They're watching until they can't watch anymore, and they're spilling out into the corridors and the stations and the halls, howling in the squares, shouting in the markets, telling the City at last that this is our world too.

END

Thank you for reading! Reviews are vitally important for independent authors. If you enjoyed the book, it would mean the world to me if you would leave a quick, honest review on the book's Amazon page.

For more adventures, stories, and news, visit us at:
Dreadfulpress.com

Made in the USA
Middletown, DE
30 September 2018